Anthology: Wry Out West

Ghost Stories and Uncanny Tales

H.E. Bulstrode

Text copyright © 2020 H.E. Bulstrode

All Rights Reserved

This is a work of fiction. Names, characters, places, and incidents are either products of the author's imagination or, if real, are used fictitiously.

No part of this book may be reproduced or transmitted in any form or by any means, electronic or mechanical, without written permission from the author, except for the use of brief quotations in a review.

This is the second edition of this work, which was initially published in 2017. The text is largely unchanged, except for a significant rewriting of *The Cleft Owl*, and the correction of a small number of typographical errors.

CONTENTS

Introduction   1

Old Crotchet   2

Gwydion's Dawn   42

Agnes of Grimstone Peverell   113

3:05 am   172

The Cleft Owl   198

Further Publications   267

Introduction

Five twisted tales of the uncanny: from the acid-fried occult oddity of *Gwydion's Dawn*, to the bizarre rites of seventeenth-century Devon in *The Cleft Owl*; the psychological horror of *3:05 am*, to the vengeful fury of *Old Crotchet*, all are as distinctly odd, and unsettling, as the seemingly innocuous guide in *Agnes of Grimstone Peverell*.

The comedy is black, and the protagonists all too unawares of the sinister forces that lurk beneath the fragile veneer of the everyday world; shifting and malevolent, they are there to be seen, and sensed, if the characters should but care to look, yet more often than not, they do not. The forces of the irrational, the supernatural and the paranormal bide their time, waiting to irrupt through the divide and come crashing into the present, with a vividness as unwelcome as it is unexpected.

The horror that you will encounter between these covers is of the understated variety; it is often implied and psychological, rather than being of the type favoured by the exponents of the slasher genre, and with the exception of *The Cleft Owl*, there is as much humour as there is unease.

Unconstrained by the bounds of any single genre, amongst these tales you will find much to engage your interest should you possess a taste for mysteries, the paranormal, ghost stories, the occult, psychological horror, historical fiction and satire. Come! Old Crotchet awaits you.

Old Crotchet

Hinton St Cuthbert Manor

The blast of a blunderbuss rent the stillness of the January sky. Its shockwaves flew upwards and outwards, threatening to shatter the delicate and serene blue, framed like panes of stained glass within a trelliswork of bare boughs and twigs. Rooks screeched into flight with a startled flapping of wings, ragged and hasty, as the peppercorn shot froze in the glimpse of an eye, only for its hard and unforgiving hail to yield to gravity, and be reclaimed by the earth. The men there gathered gave out a cheer, except for one of their number – Martin Parsons – who let out a shriek as he collapsed onto his haunches, his broad hands spread by way of protection over his forward-inclined head. He gibbered and cried, his tears stinging his nipped cheeks, his mind as frozen as his ungloved fingertips. For an instant, he was back on the Somme with the Somerset Light Infantry three-and-a-half years earlier, amidst an iron rain of shrapnel. In reality, he was crouched upon the frosted ground of Mathew Sweet's orchard, beneath its oldest apple tree, and surrounded by friends observing a time-honoured annual rite.

Arthur Hinton, master of Hinton St Cuthbert Manor, and sole surviving bearer of the family name, stood holding the smouldering firearm, staring at the farmhand. It was his office to preside over the annual wassail, reinstituted only this year, now that the men were demobilised and back from the front. Hinton St Cuthbert may have been a 'thankful village', insofar as none of its number had lost their lives in the years of slaughter occasioned by 'the Hun', but some of those who had returned – such as Parsons – had lost one thing or another, not least a certain sense of rural innocence. Neither the village nor its people were as they had been, and what had been lost, could never be regained. Some men, it seemed to Hinton, just hadn't been up to soldiering, and had failed to pull themselves together after returning home – 'It's not as if he'd lost a leg, like Wheeler,' he thought. His sympathy, if it could be labelled as such, was limited.

It was Twelfth Night by the old reckoning, which is to say, 17 January; the year, 1920. Quite why this date was still reverenced so many years after the great calendar reform, nobody could recall, but then again, neither did anybody care; it remained a time of commemoration and hope for the future, as it always had been. Hitherto, it had been the custom to invite the wassailers to dine at the manor once their duties in the orchards had been discharged, but this tradition had been discontinued some years earlier, much to their umbrage, on account of the parsimonious inclinations of Gerrard Hinton, Arthur's father. Upon his succession to the estate, Arthur had sought to assuage the villagers' resentment through introducing an annual dole of cider, but this had enjoyed only partial success, being regarded as 'not proper' and 'tight-fisted'.

The elder Hinton had retained the meal, yet refashioned it in accordance with what he deemed to be in keeping with both propriety and economy, which is to say that it had become a smaller, and altogether more exclusive, occasion. The meal itself, therefore, had ceased to serve as a celebration of the common bonds of village life, and the central place of the manor within it. Whereas the Great Hall had once played host to dozens of revellers from all walks of life, with both the respectable and the dissolute each being well represented amongst their number, the annual invitees were now restricted to Hinton relations, the vicar and his wife, and a sprinkling of the more prominent, and upstanding, local landowners and their spouses.

This year though, was to be different, for Arthur's sole nephew and heir, George Simpkins, was to introduce his new wife, Celia, at the Twelfth Night dinner. Preparations were underway, but the mood of the host was more subdued than the norm, both because of the 'unmanly' display that he had witnessed that afternoon in the orchard, and what little he had been able to deduce about the character of his nephew's spouse from his sister's correspondence. In this, his eyes had alighted upon a number of comments that he had found to be unsettling, including descriptions of her as being 'flighty', 'fashionable', 'light-hearted', and 'quite averse to the pleasures of the country'. If only George's mother had found him a match with someone such as Audrey Blewstock: keen on riding to hounds, bluff and robust, she came from a family blessed with 1,800 acres and, more importantly, bereft of male heirs. Her physical appearance might be a little less than prepossessing, but her acreage, surely, ought to have more than compensated for that. The last of the Hintons let out a sigh, shook his head, and mumbled discontentedly to himself as he wandered off to inspect the hall.

At that moment, George and Celia were seated side by side in a green Talbot Tourer rattling towards their dinner, its khaki canopy providing scant protection from the cold rush of the air. It was still light enough for the occasional rustic to come out and gawp at the infrequent sight of such a vehicle as it sputtered through village after village, and if they strained hard enough, they may just have caught a snippet of the following conversation.

'Oh, really Celia! Must you be so peevish about it all?'

'Peevish? It's been five hours George. Five hours of rattling, bouncing and noise, and that's only the half of it. I'm feeling quite sick, not to mention chilled to the bone.'

'Well, I did warn you that you should wrap up warm, as it would be a long old way, but you would insist otherwise.'

'Oh? So, it's my fault is it? My fault that you would not leave Chelsea in sufficient time to allow us to take luncheon in Salisbury?'

George sighed. 'Look old gal, I'm really not going to go through all that again, for it was your decision to call upon the Colemans last night, and you are as aware as I am how long their soirées are prone to go on for.'

Celia fell into a pouting sulk, then added, 'Sometimes George, I think that you don't treat me with a high enough regard. I mean, really, why is it that you insist on bringing me down to this beastly place? It's nothing but witless yokels and the most unspeakable smells issuing from farmyards; come to think of it, I'm not so sure that these "choice" perfumes don't issue from the locals themselves.'

'For heaven's sake Celia, I'm bringing you here as I want you to meet my uncle Arthur. Is that really so unreasonable?'

'Why bring me here? Couldn't he have come up to visit us? After all, he did have an invitation to the wedding, but chose not to take it up.'

'Well, that's certainly true with regards to the wedding, but where would we put him now? You know how cramped it is at home. Moreover, unlike you my dear, he has an estate to run, and he's about as keen on the city as you are upon the countryside. Look, all that I ask is that you put on a good show for the old boy, or at the very least be civil, just for the next couple of days. All right?'

'Oh! Very well then George, if I must.'

'Now there's a good gal! See, it's not so very hard, is it?'

'Not for you, perhaps.'

'Oh, do stop being so churlish! Why not take a look at that book I gave you. There's an entry on uncle's house you know. You might find it interesting.'

'The light's fading.'

'All the more reason to read it then. Come along now, I want to hear that captivating voice of yours!'

She turned to page 27, and read the following:

Somersetshire is home to many a fine manor house, and that at Hinton St Cuthbert is no exception. There has been a manor in the village since at least the time of Domesday, but the current house is of a rather later construction, having been remodelled in the fifteenth century, with further additions to its structure, and alterations to its internal configuration, being made over the subsequent two centuries. Much of this latter work was overseen by the Hinton family, into whose hands the manor and its estate fell during the reign of Henry VIII. It is a handsome house of middling proportions, being somewhat more substantial and grander than a large farmhouse, but not possessing the ostentatious stamp of a country seat such as Montacute. Like the latter, it is faced in Hamstone, a building material much favoured in these parts, which has lent its honeyed charm to so many a south Somersetshire dwelling. Its Great Hall is remarkable for the preservation of its oak panelling, its finely plastered ceilings embossed with wyverns, and the escutcheons of families allied to the Hintons depicted in the stained glass of the south-facing windows.

She stopped.

'Is there no more?' asked George.

'No. Not a jot. Besides, I simply couldn't read any further as it would strain my eyes.'

'No need to old gal, as we're almost there. Just five minutes, or so. Bet you're excited to see the old place having read that, eh?'

'"Excited"? Hardly. It's not as if I've come all this way to stare at ceilings and panelling, but given what little you've divulged about your uncle and the company he keeps, perhaps this shall be the scintillating highlight of my entrée into rural society.'

'Steady on old gal, it's not that bad. Trust me.'

'Really?'

'Really.'

'You certainly are remarkably chipper today George. Anyone would think that you prefer the prospect of spending a few days in some draughty old dungeon to conversation with the Colemans, or afternoon cocktails with the Bickersleys.'

'Cheer up darling! Uncle will probably put us up in the tester in the guest chamber. You'll not have to worry over draughts there with those curtains, believe me.'

'No. Quite. I can picture them now: dark, heavy and mildewed, simply oozing damp and dankness. I can smell and taste the air, and already feel the spores of mould accommodating themselves in my throat and lungs.'

'Celia! You are an utterly incorrigible misery! You have the queerest and most macabre manner of expressing yourself at times.'

Her air lightened a little. 'Isn't that one of those little quirks that drew you to me George? You wouldn't be so cruel as to deny me a little fun now, would you, given this ordeal that you're putting me through?'

He smiled. 'Well . . .'

'You know I'm right, don't you? I always am. Ah! This is it, I take it?'

'It is indeed.'

With that, the car drew to a halt upon the drive, their arrival announced by the scrunch of gravel, and the fatigued sputtering of the engine. The façade of the house loomed over them as George opened the door, and proffered his hand to Celia as she alighted from the running board. She hoisted up the hem of her long dress, mindful of what she might encounter in these country parts, and looked at George, and he at her, their breath steaming in the fading crepuscular light.

'Just look at your breath!' he exclaimed.

'Ah!' She squealed with delight, took a deep breath, and then exhaled again. They laughed.

'Well old gal, we'd better get in out of the cold. Come on!'

Celia smiled and squeezed his hand as the two of them walked briskly towards the entrance. She glanced upwards at the mullioned windows, having had the impression of being watched, but glimpsed nothing other than a shadow in one of the rooms above, and to the right of, the main doorway. Whatever it was, its presence was fleeting. She shuddered, stopped, and regarded the barley twist chimneys now stood starkly silhouetted against the decaying daylight, and for a moment forgot herself, the place, and the time. A raucous cry from the rookery atop the limbs of the leafless elms brought her back to her senses.

'Are you all right Celia?'

'Um, yes George. Quite all right. It's just that . . .'

'"Just that . . ."?'

'Oh, never mind. It's nothing.'

The door opened before them to reveal a wizened old figure with a red mottled face framed by grey mutton-chop whiskers and topped with straggling grey hair.

'Good afternoon Master George; young lady.'

'Good afternoon Potter. Is my uncle at home?'

'He is that. He be expecting you. Come in sir, madam. Might I take your coats afore calling for Mr Hinton?'

'Yes, do. Your stoop looks a little worse than when I was last down Potter.'

'That it be zir, that it be. Can't be helped though, as 'tis on account of my advancing years.'

'How old is it that you are now Potter?'

'Three-and-zeventy year zir. Three-and-zeventy.'

'Quite remarkable. It's heartening to see that a man is not dissuaded from his duties by a small matter such as his age, eh Celia?'

'I'll say!'

'Well, be a good fellow and bring in our trunk would you.'

Potter's eyes smiled no more.

'Very good sir.'

'Oh, and Potter,'

'Yes sir?'

'Take care out there; it's icy.'

'Why thank you sir. I can't afford to break no bones these days, as they don't zet like they did use to.'

'Well, it's just that the trunk contains something delicate; a gift, you know.'

'Of course sir. I unnerstand. I'll be mindful o' that.'

The old man pulled the door to behind him leaving the couple alone, and picked his way across the drive, comforting himself with ill-humoured mutterings. George removed his leather driving gloves and turned as Arthur Hinton strode into the hallway.

'Ah! There you are George! Long journey, eh? And this is the new young lady of the family, Celia, I take it?'

'Hello uncle. Yes, this is Celia. She's rather chilled from the drive I'm afraid.'

She smiled, stepped forward and reached out her right hand, 'Pleased to meet you, Mr Hinton.'

'Likewise, likewise my dear. Well, we'll have to see what we can do to warm you up. Brandy?'

'That's awfully good of you. A brandy would be perfectly charming.'

'Steady uncle, she has something of a taste for cognac. You'll need to keep it under strict rations.'

'Really? I've been informed that she also has something of a taste for champagne. Am I right?'

Celia giggled, 'Champagne? I simply adore champagne! It's so very, so very . . .'

'Overpriced and overrated?'

'No! Bubbly, effervescent, enlivening!'

'Bit of a party girl, eh?'

'Rather!'

'Hmm, well, I'm afraid that I'll have to disappoint you on that score, for I don't keep it; too gassy for my tastes, and neither do I hold parties, with the exception of tonight's dinner of course.'

'Oh!'

The heavy iron latch clanked, and the door creaked open to reveal the hunched figure of Potter dragging the couple's trunk.

'Potter! What in heaven's name are you doing man?'

'Just bringing in Master George's luggage, zir.'

'Well don't go heaving it all over the floor; you could do it some damage. Go and fetch Hemmings to help you.'

'Very well zir.'

'Well, go on man! Don't dawdle!'

Potter exited to seek assistance.

'What is it with servants these days? Did you see that look of impudence in the man's eyes? He's served the family here since 1872, but since the late war I've noticed a change in his bearing; it seems to have made him, and the others, all a bit too damned uppity. Too uppity by far.'

'Well, there's been quite a bit of change uncle. Quite a bit.'

'Yes, yes! Change, change, change! We're supposed to be all for it these days, but I'm damned if I can see any merit, or advantage, in it. Anyway, let's pour a brandy for young Mrs Simpkins, and I'll give her a tour of my modest dwelling, as I know that you, George, don't have much of a head for family history.'

He led them to the library where he poured each a generous glass of cognac, and after marching them through the downstairs rooms, paying cursory attention to each, he steered them up the main staircase, and there, at its head, the three halted.

'Well, here we are, at the beginning of the family gallery. You will note, Celia, that it is laid out in such a fashion that my forebears are portrayed in an almost unbroken chain of succession, from the third in line to have dwelt in the house, up until, and including my parents.'

'You never had your own portrait painted?'

'No. An artist was commissioned to paint a portrait of myself and my wife, but before it could be executed, Esther had the misfortune to pass away.' He paused.

'I'm sorry.'

'It's quite all right young lady. It was many years ago, and I have since become inured to my life as a widower.' He smiled gently, and then resumed, 'This portrait here is of Martin Hinton, whose grandfather – Mathew – originally acquired the estate in 1540. As you can see, he is attired fashionably for the time, in ruff, plumed hat, doublet and hose, and shoes utterly impractical for country life, adorned with such fripperies as ribbons and pom-poms.'

Celia giggled. 'I rather fancy he has something of a jaunty look though, don't you think? Oh! Just who is that woman in the next painting? She looks so sombre and joyless. Quite the opposite of jaunty.'

'His wife, Lady Margaret Hinton.'

'What a queer couple. When was this painted? Do you know?'

'Sometime towards the end of her life, I would say. She looks to me as if she must have been in her fifties; she died in 1617, at the age of fifty-five, if I remember correctly. Now, moving on . . .'

The host urged his visitors past the portraits of the next two generations with little comment, before pausing before a periwigged gentlemen of a wan complexion, noting that he – Clifford Hinton – had become a cause of great concern to the family, having taken the losing side in the Monmouth Rebellion of 1685. On account of his rank, he had been spared execution during the Bloody Assizes, and although the family estate had been threatened with expropriation, it had been held in his younger brother's keeping until the restoration of his fortunes and title to the manor, following the fall of James II. There was something about the young man that Celia found alluring, other than the sheen upon his otherwise dull breastplate, and the large turquoise gemstone set in his gold ring, and turning to George, she was struck by a clear resemblance between the two.

Arthur Hinton moved briskly to the next painting. Celia's attention drifted; this brandy was very good, but the gallery had a certain chill about it that the spirit did little to ease. The unmemorable faces of the near-forgotten dead looked down upon them, as George's uncle sought to reimbue each deceased Hinton with a spark of their former being, but the anecdotes fell flat, the drone of his voice punctuated only by his solitary laugh. His quips were well rehearsed, and doubtless of some merit, but they failed to move his nephew and recently acquired niece.

'Well, that is about all there is to it. You've seen the house now, and I hope that what you have seen has afforded you some interest?'

'Why yes, thank you. It's been quite delightful,' replied Celia, forcing a smile as she experienced an involuntary shudder.

'You look quite cold my girl. I have detained you for far too long, which is most thoughtless of me. Behind this door lies your room, in which you will find both somewhere to sleep and, of more immediate importance, somewhere to warm yourselves after your journey, for a fire has been kindled to take off the chill.'

'Why, that's awfully kind of you.'

'Don't mention it. Now, George, we'll be dining at eight, so be sure to come down to the drawing room in good time my boy. Should you need refreshment before then, just ring the kitchens and ask for Potter. You know the routine.'

'That I will uncle. Thank you.'

The couple entered the room, which although warmer than the gallery, still bore a discernible coolness, despite the flames that with a leisurely lick coiled and wound about the logs in the hearth. By the light of oil lamps and candles, Celia could see the frame of the tester bed to which George had alluded, darkened with age and elaborately carved, but hung with curtains that, contrary to her expectations, bore no trace of mildew; she walked up to them, and ran her hands over their rich, dark fabric.

'How odd that your uncle has such quaint and old-fashioned lighting George. Has he never thought of laying on gas, or electricity?'

'That wouldn't be practical old gal. For the one, there are no gas mains in the village, let alone anywhere near the manor, and uncle is quite averse to lay out for the expense of installing a generator. For all of their disadvantages, it would seem that he's quite content to continue with lamps and candles.'

'Hmm. I think that I'm beginning to get a measure of the old chap. You're right: I don't think that we could get him up to London.'

'No. That really wouldn't be his thing.'

'I'm feeling quite famished. What's the time?'

'A little before five.'

'Funny. I thought it was later. Your uncle's lecture seemed to drag on for hours, yet other than what he said regarding the jaunty gentleman and his miserable wife, as well as the Clifford fellow, I don't remember a thing, other than changes in hairstyles and hats.'

'I'm surprised that you even remember that. You looked as if you were sleeping on your feet. It's a wonder that uncle didn't notice.'

'That's a bit rich George, considering that you didn't say a word, and spent the whole time trying, and failing, to stifle your yawning. Still, at least your poor conduct put me in a good light.'

'Oh, really Celia!'

'Don't you "oh really" me George. It's true. Now, what about that tea?'

'Very well then. I'll call for Potter,' he said with an irritable note in his voice, before duly tugging the bell pull. Tea was not long in coming, and once the two of them had taken their fill, they divested themselves of the greater part of their garments, and made themselves comfortable. For the remainder of their leisure, they luxuriated in snoozing, before rising and dressing in good time for dinner.

Old Twelfth Night

As Celia and George passed beneath the eyes of Lady Margaret Hinton, Celia paused to glance at her afresh, and seemed to discern some change in her expression. Quite what it was, she could not fathom, leading her to conclude that her memory had been playing tricks on her. She looked away from the painting and straight ahead, and to the left of the top of the main staircase, noticed a door into another room at the end of the gallery, a room that must look out over the main entrance to the house. It struck her as odd that George's uncle had not shown it to them.

'Oh look – another room! I wonder why your uncle didn't show us into it. Any idea why, George?'

'No. Why do you ask?'

'Just idle curiosity. You know what I'm like. Have you seen inside?'

'No, I haven't. Now come along! I'm utterly famished.'

With that, he put his arm around her waist, and walked her down the stairs and into the drawing room, where they encountered a number of well but unfashionably attired folk, mostly of middling years and generous girths. An elderly couple, judging by the presence of a dog collar and their state of apparent isolation, were clearly the vicar and his wife. Otherwise, the room was warm and the scene animated. The majority of the guests appeared to have arrived, and were enjoying the manor's hospitality in the form of port and cider. Although George knew one or two of them by sight, their names remained unknown to him. It was a milieu in which neither he nor Celia felt much at ease, owing to its alien nature, so it came as a relief when his uncle entered the room looking slightly flushed, possibly from drink, embarrassment, or a combination of the two. He waved an arm in the air to draw everyone's attention.

'Ladies and gentlemen! Forgive me for interrupting, but I would just like to say that we are still waiting upon Richard Wainman of Creech Langley, and the Buttermans of Newton Gifford. Once they have arrived, we will retire to the Great Hall for our Twelfth Night dinner. If they should not be here by a quarter past eight, then we shall start without them. Thank you!'

He then caught George's eye, and with courteous nods and smiles to the other guests, made his way over to introduce the Simpkins to the older couple.

'George and Celia, might I introduce you to the Reverend Bantham and his wife, Constance.'

'Pleased to meet you reverend,' said George. 'I'm surprised that we've not met previously.'

'Pleased to meet you too young man, and your good lady wife. Yes, it is something of a surprise that we have not met before today,' intoned the vicar in a somewhat scornful tone, 'for your uncle has made mention that you have visited on many occasions for the weekend. If you should do so again, you would be more than welcome to grace our church with your presence.' He stared over the rims of his glasses with an expression of censorious piety, as his wife looked Celia up and down, before blinking dismissively, and promptly raising a teacup to her lips.

'I shall bear your invitation in mind, vicar,' replied George, with a rather forced smile, interrupted by a nudge in the ribs from Celia.

'Darling, might I have a word?'

'Of course dear. If you might excuse us reverend, madam.'

George smiled, and was led out into the passageway whilst the Banthams exchanged knowing glances, ignored by the other guests, who kept a good distance from them. The reverend whispered something into his wife's ear, a *bon mot* it would seem, judging from their matching smirks.

'I don't know if I'm going to be able to stand this George. Why in heaven's name did your uncle introduce us to those perfectly awful people? He knows that we're not church types, doesn't he?'

'Well, yes, he does, but I think that he meant well in doing so.'

'"Meant well"?' she snapped.

'Yes. Well, I'm thinking that it's his opinion that we should be introduced to the most respectable figures in village society, and down here they don't come much more respected than the residents of the vicarage. That's why we're to sit next to them for dinner.'

'Sit next to them! Really George, I'd sooner be sat next to some uncouth yokel than to that Bantham couple. Have a word with your uncle would you, and make it clear that he needs to rearrange his seating plan.'

George looked awkward.

'George!'

'Yes, my sweet, I shall speak to him; don't you worry about that.'

'Good. Well, go on then!'

George diligently obliged, and informed his uncle of Celia's wishes.

'Oh, what a pity! I had really hoped that you'd both enjoy their company. Still, there's room for manoeuvre; I shall seat them elsewhere, but should neither Wainman nor the Buttermans turn up, there could be a problem.'

'Thank you uncle. You really don't know how relieved Celia will be.'

'Don't mention it George. I know that they're not everyone's cup of tea, but I was struggling to think of who to seat them opposite. The Nowells can't abide them.' He glanced at his watch. 'A quarter past eight! You take Celia through to the Great Hall while I go and gather up the others.'

Whilst the guests made their way to be seated, Potter took the hats and coats from the Buttermans who apologised for their late arrival, before being escorted directly to dine.

As host, Arthur Hinton was seated at the head of the table, with George and Celia to his right, facing Joseph and Ruth Fear; the pattern repeated along the length of the table: the Banthams opposite the Buttermans, and the Nowells the Banks. Of Richard Wainman, there was no sign, leaving the seat opposite Hinton empty. The master beckoned to Potter, who walked over and inclined his head to receive instruction.

'This is a bad show Potter – thirteen of us at table. Go and find Hemmings to help you fetch down the Lady of Cartagena.'

'Of course, zir.'

Celia placed a hand upon George's thigh, closed with his right ear, and from her lips breathed a question, warm and damp, 'Who is "the Lady of Cartagena"?'

He sensed as much as heard her question, turned his head towards her, slowly, and said, 'I haven't the foggiest. Why do you ask?'

'She is being "fetched down".'

'"Fetched down"?'

'Yes.'

'What a peculiar thing to say about a guest; particularly of a woman. She must be a rum gal if she's happy to be bundled about like some kind of parcel.'

'Quite! Perhaps she's wrapped up in string and brown paper.'

Arthur Hinton, having overheard the young couple, looked on with an amused expression.

'So, you're wondering as to the identity of the Lady, eh?'

'Oh! Why, yes,' said Celia.

'You'll see her soon enough, but I can guarantee that you'll never have seen another like her.'

Irritated exclamations from Potter and Hemmings interrupted the jovial chatter of the expectant diners, as their dim forms entered the room bearing what appeared to be a small figure akin to a mummy case, their straining shadows flickering across the oak panelling, like a magic lantern show magnified by the glow of the candlelight. They deposited their burden upon the vacant chair; it was no mummy. Hinton rose from his seat.

'Ladies and gentlemen! With the arrival of the Lady of Cartagena, our number is now complete. Let us raise a toast to the fruitfulness of this coming year's apple harvest. Wassail!'

'Wassail!' came the massed reply, followed by a downing of mulled cider, then the resumption of chatter from a host of flushed faces. Potter and Hemmings scuttled about refilling glasses, and the maid was instructed to make ready the first course for serving.

Celia felt bemused. She stared at the mannequin in its honoured position at the far end of the table, and instantly experienced a slight shortness of breath; she was beset with a high-pitched ringing in her ears; she grew cold, yet sensed the prickle of sweat upon her scalp. Her vision started to flash and speckle. She clutched her husband's arm.

'Darling, look!'

'At what?'

'The dummy. It's repulsive. That expression; that gaze. It's almost as if it's sneering in disdain.'

'Are you all right old gal? You look quite ashen.'

'I don't know George. I'm feeling a little faint.'

'Would you like to go and lie down? You had that funny turn earlier too. You're probably suffering from a lack of sleep and the chill of the journey.'

She paused. 'No. I'll be all right. Just pass me the wine would you.'

The effigy seemed familiar, yet she had never seen it before, indeed, never seen anything of its type. It appeared to be fashioned from leather, measuring between two to three feet in height, and attired in a costume characteristic of that of a lady of the early part of the seventeenth century, clearly a woman of the middling to upper orders, who lived a life far removed from daily toil. Her figure was rather plump, and bore the stamp of having borne many children, which is to say that she was generously proportioned about the girth; her large hips emphasised by a farthingale. Her low-cut long-sleeved gown was of a faded purple, or mauve, over which was draped a brown mantle. To the rear of her neck was a stiff ruff, her reddish-brown hair possessing a sculptural quality that lent the face a slightly owlish look. The accreted filth of three centuries enveloped the figure in a dull tawny patina, which seemed fitting, given the infrequent bathing habits of people at that time.

'You seem a little out of sorts Celia. Rather pale. Are you feeling quite well?' enquired Arthur.

'I'm just feeling a little faint, that's all. Tell me, who, or what, is the "Lady of Cartagena"?'

'Oh, the Lady! I hope that she's not been the cause of this upset?'

'Well, I really don't know what to say; it's silly really, but I do seem to recognise her.'

'Recognise her?'

'Yes.'

'From where?'

'I don't know.'

'Hmm. Well George, you told me that your new lady wife was 24, not 324!' Arthur Hinton guffawed to himself. 'I'm sorry Celia. Please excuse an old man's humour.'

'That's quite all right.'

'Well, I suppose that you'd like an answer to your question?'

'If you wouldn't mind. Oh, and why is it that you brought her down to table this evening? Am I the only one who finds this odd?'

'Ah, now my dear, your second question has a very straightforward answer, for look around you and tally up how many of us living, breathing souls are sat around this table. Tell me: how many of us are there?'

She paused to count, 'Thirteen.'

'Precisely! Now, we couldn't be having thirteen to dine at such an occasion, could we?'

'I suppose not.'

'No. So, this is why this evening, as at all other mealtimes when we find ourselves of this number, the Lady was brought to table. We wouldn't wish to tempt ill fortune, and she is our insurance against it.'

'How did you come by her?'

'Steady on Celia, you'll be boring uncle to death with your constant questioning. She really is a most regular inquisitor at times uncle.'

'No, no, quite the contrary George. It makes such a charming change to be able to speak to a young lady about family matters, especially when considering that someday, she too will need to follow certain protocols and traditions.'

'"Protocols and traditions"? How interesting!' exclaimed Celia.

'Oh yes my dear, there are many such observances that the family has kept down the centuries. They may seem a little peculiar to modern eyes, but they are of the utmost importance. Now, where was I? Ah, yes! The Lady of Cartagena has been in the family for many generations, and has been present at table when required ever since she was introduced to the house when it was in the ownership of Martin Hinton, which is to say, sometime during the initial part of the reign of the first King James. She was purchased from a Dutch merchant who had taken her as part of his booty whilst engaged in privateering off the Spanish Main, hence her title.'

'It's such an awfully long time ago that I really can't imagine. How odd that someone must have taken such pains to fashion a mannequin that is so disagreeable to the eye. Looking at her face, she looks to be a cantankerous old bird; a real old crotchet if ever I saw one.'

'Do you think so?'

'I struggle to see how anyone could think otherwise. What's your opinion George?'

'Well, to be frank, I haven't really taken much notice. Now, let's see. Hmm. Not much of a looker I suppose, but who is after 300 years or so? I can't say that I can see much of an expression at all, if truth be told.'

'Really? Can't you see that perfectly distasteful air of disdain?'

'No. Look, perhaps you need some rest old gal? We simply didn't get much sleep last night, and plainly the cold of the journey has left you chilled and feeling a little feverish.'

'Don't you presume to know how I feel, George! It's not my fault that you are so poor at reading a woman's emotions. I, after all, should know '

The Fears had been watching these exchanges with interest, but discerning the barbed comments of the young lady, had decided to keep out of the conversation, seeking refuge in exchanging some stilted chit-chat with the Banthams. Celia's attitude and demeanour had confirmed Hinton's apprehensions about his nephew's match, with no amount of cider or wine proving adequate to lubricate conversation between them throughout the three courses that ensued. It was thus with considerable relief for all parties that when the meal came to an end, Celia announced that she was tired and needed to retire for the night. George had wished to stay up to speak with his uncle, but mindful of Celia's mood, realised that he should take his leave and accompany her to their room.

Reaching the top of the stairs, Celia halted, and holding up her candlestick, once more scrutinised the portrait of Lady Margaret Hinton.

'How peculiar!'

'You really do have a thing about that picture, don't you? I never knew that you were so interested in art.'

'George, George, look at her!'

He blinked, leant forward and peered at the image. 'I'm looking Celia. What's so odd about it? She looks just as she did when uncle showed it to us earlier.'

'Don't you see the resemblance?'

He turned to look Celia square in the face, and with an air of mock gravity said, 'Now, don't worry darling. You don't look a bit like her, and that's God's own truth.'

'Stop playing the fool George! I know that it comes naturally to you, but I'm starting to find it tiresome.'

'Celia!'

'Shh! Isn't she just the spitting image of Old Crotchet?'

'Old Crotchet? Who in the devil's name is "Old Crotchet"?'

'The Lady of Cartagena!'

'Oh! Why, yes, perhaps there is a little of a semblance between the two: they're both women; both dead, appear to have been of a similar age and are dressed in very much the same fashion.'

'I say that they're meant to be the same woman.'

'Well what makes you draw that conclusion? You've heard uncle Arthur's tale regarding the provenance of the mannequin, and I recall that our distant forbear merely purchased the object from a Dutchman. I don't remember him mentioning that he also procured his wife from the self-same source.'

'There's something queer about this George, and I don't like it. I would swear that she's wearing the same mocking, disdainful expression as Old Crotchet.'

'Let's get to bed old gal. You need a rest.'

'I shall ask him about it tomorrow.'

'You do that, but come on – let's get to bed.'

He gave her a playful pinch.

'Ouch! What was that for?' She had slapped him.

'I'm not in the mood.'

The fire had done its work insofar as the bedroom was now of a comfortable temperature, and whereas George fell asleep quickly, his slumber accompanied by a light wheezing and the occasional snore, Celia lay awake, trying to make sense of her feelings regarding the painting and the mannequin. The elaborate carvings of the bed caught her eye, at last distracting her from obsessing about the long-departed mistress of the house. Its headboard bore an ornate scene depicting mermaids, Indians and pairs of turtle doves flanking a Tudor rose; the rest of its oak frame being covered with an intricate foliate design, of leaves and stems intertwined.

The shadows cast by the candlelight heightened the relief of the carvings, making them appear more substantial, imbuing them with a certain sense of life and, at times, movement. She closed her eyes, and yawned. Her back complained to her that the mattress was lumpy, whereas her nose informed her that her breath was sour. Her head began to ache, and she felt herself falling.

Celia awoke to feel her fringe matted to her forehead, her nightgown clammy and cold with sweat, as was her pillow. The air had grown thick and stale, and as she tossed and turned beneath the heavy quilt, sleep eluded her. Time ticked by, and she reached across to embrace George. Upon doing so, she started, for instead of pyjama silk, her fingers met bare flesh, a nakedness that was cold to the touch. Something else was different; his habitual wheezing and snoring had ceased. She rolled over, fumbled for the box on her bedside table, struck a match, and lit the candle. The room seemed to have changed in some way.

Her eyes, sore and bleary, demanded to be rubbed. She obliged them. In the far corner of the room, she espied something large, curly and dark. It did not move, and was resting on an object next to a dressing table, surmounted by a mirror in a tortoiseshell frame. She fixed her gaze upon it, but although she recognised it, she initially dismissed it for what it was: a long periwig, of the sort worn by a gentleman of fashion during the latter part of the seventeenth century, resting upon its wooden stand. She inhaled sharply, then looked to George to wake him, but gasped as she saw that his head was now shaven. She reached down to turn his face towards her. The eyes flashed open, green and raging. She screamed, and fell into a faint.

'Celia! Celia!'

'George?'

'Of course it's me! Who else would it be? What's going on?'

'I don't know. What time is it?'

He picked up his watch from the bedside. 'A quarter to seven.'

'You're in your pyjamas!'

'Well, yes. What else would you expect to find me in? Spats?'

'The dressing table is gone, and the wig!'

'Really Celia, just how much did you drink last night? What have you been dreaming about?'

'I wasn't keeping count George.'

'You never do, and that's half the problem. Now look, I thought that bringing you to bed at a reasonable hour would help to dissipate those queer impressions that you seemed to get into your head yesterday, but it's clearly not done the trick. Perhaps a good brisk walk down to the village after breakfast might clear away that wooliness, eh?'

'It all seemed so real.'

'Just a nightmare old gal. We all get them from time to time.'

'It was the man from the painting!'

'Oh, it's back to paintings again now is it? Which fellow was it? The "jaunty" one with the pom-poms? Wearing those in bed doesn't seem awfully practical if you don't mind me saying.'

'No. The one who looked like you: the rebel; the young man in the long wig.'

'Ah! Now old gal, don't you see something of a flaw in your reasoning?'

'A *flaw*?'

'You said that he looked like me, so given that I am me, how could you have told the difference? Don't you think, given that he's dead and I'm alive, and that you and I climbed into this bed last night and out of it this morning, that it was actually me that you saw?'

'He had green eyes. His hair was shaven.'

George paused and sighed. Celia's persistence regarding these delusions was beginning to concern him.

'You need a good breakfast. I'll ring for Potter to make some tea. Now, come along and get dressed!'

Questions at Breakfast

They took breakfast in the drawing room. There they found Arthur Hinton already enthusiastically tackling a plate of bacon, sausages and eggs, a fleck of yolk stuck to the bristles of his moustache, seemingly as happy as a pig that has just snuffled a truffle, and equally as noisy.

'Ah, good morning! Did you two newlyweds sleep well?'

'The sleep of the dead, uncle.'

'Well, I'm glad to see you back from Hades young fellow. And you, my dear?'

'For the first half, yes; for the second, not so much so. I—'

She faltered, overcome by reservations regarding disclosing her nocturnal impressions.

'Strange. It's the most comfortable bed in the house, so if it wasn't young George keeping you awake, I don't know what was. Still, I'm glad that the old tradition has been kept up.'

'"The old tradition"?'

'Have you not told her George?'

'Oh, I quite forgot to uncle.'

'Sometimes my boy, I wonder just how much attention you've paid to what you've been told over the years. These matters are important you know. Now look, before I explain, sit down and help yourselves to breakfast.'

Celia skewered a sausage and cut it into thin slices, pecking at them with an evident lack of enthusiasm, sluicing away the grease with numerous cups of Assam. George ate all that was placed before him, oblivious to his spouse's absence of appetite, whilst Arthur relaxed with a copy of The Times, and upon hearing his nephew discard his knife and fork, commented, 'I see that the Reds have taken Kolchak. Russia's done for now.'

Neither George nor Celia responded. Who was Kolchak? What did it matter?

'Perhaps you would be more interested in an explanation of the family tradition to which I alluded earlier?'

Celia nodded, mustering a weak smile.

'It goes back a long way, to the time when the bed came into the house, which is a somewhat misleading way of putting it, for it was fashioned in the very room where it stands today. This was the marital bed, constructed for the arrival of Lady Margaret Hinton, on the instruction of her husband-to-be. It cost a great sum, and consumed the efforts of Elijah Reynolds – one of the finest woodcarvers in Bristol – for many months; he was brought down to the estate especially to work on the task, absorbing himself in his labours to the detriment of his health, for want of any other distraction in this isolated setting. It was said, that he did not survive its making by more than a month, and rumoured that he had put so much of his soul into it, that nothing of the latter remained at the time of his death. Ever since, it has served as the marital bed for each of the Hinton heirs, and George, given that I have no son, is but the latest of those to have slept in it, with you, his new wife.'

His enunciation was clear and even until he made mention of his lack of a direct heir, at which point a distinct quaver could be heard in his voice, which was on the point of breaking. Celia remained silent, for her sense of discomfiture had grown still further whilst the tale had unfolded; she now realised that she had lain the night in Old Crotchet's bed, and would have to do so again until the end of her stay. Arthur had anticipated a reply, so was struck by Celia's silence. The two men perceived how her vivacity, which had been so apparent the preceding afternoon, had deserted her. She poured herself another cup of tea, almost mechanically, so stiff and unthinking were her movements.

'Do you think you might be coming down with something Celia? You look so awfully pale.'

'I'm tired George; just tired. But, if you don't mind me asking, uncle,' she swallowed after enunciating 'uncle', as it was the first time that she had addressed him this way, 'have there ever been any unusual occurrences in the bedroom in which we slept?'

'"Unusual occurrences"?'

'Yes. It's just that . . . oh, I feel so silly saying it,' she paused, her eyes moistening, 'it's just that, something strange happened last night.'

'Really?'

'Yes, but, if you don't mind, I'd rather not go into it. It's just that I wondered if the room has any . . . peculiar associations.'

Arthur scratched his neck and rubbed his nose. 'No. No, I've never heard anything unusual about it.' His feet moved uneasily; he scratched his cheek.

'I was also wondering about the room overlooking the main entrance.'

'Which room?'

'The one above, up on the right.'

'Ah, yes! What about it?'

'Well, when you showed us around yesterday, we didn't get to see inside.'

'We use it for storage, so it's rather dusty I'm afraid, which is why I didn't show you into it. I didn't want you to get your clothes dirty.'

'What do you keep in there?'

'Just bits and pieces, as well as the Lady of Cartagena, when she's not on duty, that is.' He smiled broadly.

'Do any of the servants use it?'

'No. Why do you ask? It's just a storeroom.'

'Well, when we arrived yesterday, I fancy that I saw someone staring at me from the room. I looked up, and saw a shadow move across its windows.'

'It's not possible my dear. Until I sent Potter and Hemmings up there just before dinner yesterday, nobody had had cause to set foot in there this past year.'

'How about getting wrapped up and going out for that walk Celia?'

'Yes, yes! Why not take up young George's suggestion my dear? A bit of fresh air should do you good. Down to the village is it George?'

'Yes uncle. I'm thinking that later we might drop in at the White Hart for a spot of lunchtime refreshment.'

'What a splendid idea! Well, you'll have to pardon me for not joining you, as I'm afraid that I've business to attend to about the estate.'

The young couple crunched across the gravel of the driveway, Celia pausing to turn and glance up at the windows of the upper storey. There was nothing to be seen other than a reflection of the grey January sky. Little conversation passed between the two of them as they strolled along the drive, then out along the bridleway flanked by bare hedges, studded here and there with the bright red of rosehips. From time to time, the silence was broken by the cawing of the crows, and the soughing of the boughs that rubbed and creaked in the strengthening wind. Nothing more of note happened that day, or during the remainder of their stay.

Farewell to Chelsea

It was not long before Mr and Mrs Simpkins had returned to their busy life in Chelsea: cocktail parties, balls, and excursions in the Talbot; cigarettes, champagne and hampers from Fortnum and Mason. Life had returned pretty much to its old course. Pretty much. There were some differences. It took some time for Celia's habitual humour and acerbity to return, but once it was back, George realised how much he had enjoyed its absence. They became expectant parents, and as Celia's belly grew, so did her appetite, and to such an extent that their friends and acquaintances became quite convinced that she must be expecting twins. If truth be told, she was going a little to seed. Behaviour that not so long ago, when she was a bright, svelte young slip of a thing, had been taken for playful flirtatiousness, was now perceived, in the plumper version of herself, that now oft glowered out from increasingly sunken and darkened orbits, to be ill-tempered sniping. Mrs Simpkins, it seemed, was becoming a nag, and a bully.

On 17 October, Celia gave birth to a baby boy. For the child, she held but little regard. He was demanding and cried a great deal, and when she looked at him in a state of fatigued irritation with his puling and whining, her stare was returned with a flash from a pair of brilliant green eyes, imbued with an intense wilfulness. His hair proved reluctant to grow. Rumours began to spread amongst their friends, for George's eyes were hazel, and Celia's grey, but others dismissed them as 'nonsense', for the infant strongly resembled George, but, strangely, not Celia. There seemed to be a third element at play in the child's makeup, but nobody could fathom what it was, or where it came from. The couple struggled to come up with a suitable name, but eventually settled upon Clifford, which he was duly christened on Saturday 30 October. Both were aware that the name had some link with George's family, but they were unable to recall what it was, or how they'd come to hear of it.

It was on the late afternoon of Thursday 18 November that George received a telegram notifying him that his uncle – Arthur Hinton – had been involved in a terrible accident. That preceding Saturday his blunderbuss had unexpectedly discharged its shot into his face. Potter, hearing its report, swiftly followed by a thud and an animalistic screeching, had rushed to find his master lying disfigured, and bleeding profusely upon the floor. It seems that he had ventured into the storeroom to search for something. The doctor was sent for, the domestic staff doing what they could in the interim to staunch the flow of blood, which proved to be only partially effectual. Upon seeing the bloody pulp that had once been Hinton's face, the maid fell into a faint. The doctor could do little other than inject the patient with morphine, which afforded scant relief to his pain. How the accident had occurred could not be ascertained, as part of Hinton's jaw was now absent, and only the stub of his tongue remained; moreover, his hands had become so palsied that he was unable to write. Infection set in, and sepsis took a rapid hold. By the early hours of Thursday morning, Arthur Hinton lay dead. George Simpkins was thus, pending the payment of extensive death duties, now in possession of Hinton St Cuthbert Manor. He broke the news to Celia, who shook her head and stated that she was 'in no mood for moving to the country'. No mood or otherwise, that was where she was going.

The funeral took place the following Thursday, the service being attended by the deceased's Chelsea relations, who also included his sister, Marjorie. A large number of mourners from the village shuffled into the church to pay their respects, and the familiar faces of the Fears, the Buttermans and the other Twelfth Night dinner guests nodded their condolences to George and Celia, as they walked past to take their place in the family pew. The ceremony was presided over by the Reverend Bantham, who conducted himself as if he were addressing God alone, rather than the relations of the departed. As the service ended, the last of the Hintons was laid to rest in the family vault. The locals eyed the newcomers with a combination of curiosity, suspicion and mistrust: George may have been Arthur's nephew, but he was a creature of the city, who could know nothing of running a country estate. Almost four centuries of continuity had today come to a close.

A wake was held back at the manor, and after the guests had departed, George and Marjorie Simpkins withdrew to the living room, whilst Celia retired to bed complaining of a headache, Clifford being entrusted to Hattie, his nanny.

'So George, now that you are to be master of the manor, have you made arrangements?'

'Arrangements, mother?'

'Yes. I'm assuming that you will wish to settle your affairs in London as soon as is practicable, and then move your family to Hinton St Cuthbert?'

'Well, yes, I suppose so. It's just that I really hadn't expected this, at least not so soon. Such a beastly way for uncle Arthur to go. So unexpected.'

'Yes, it was. One can never foresee such things. It's been three years since we lost your father.' She looked down, unconsciously stroking her ring finger.

'Yes.' He paused to draw on his cigarette. 'I've not really done anything as yet. As for Celia, you can guess what her thoughts on the matter might be.'

'Yes, well, we are all aware of Celia's opinions on a whole range of matters, this one not being the least of them.'

'True.'

'So, when will you leave Chelsea?'

'I'm not sure. She won't like it.'

'That's a given George. There's not a great deal that she does seem to like, other than socialising, and flirting with your friends.'

'She's not done much of either lately.'

'Really? That seems hard to believe; most out of character.'

'It is. Then again, she's hardly been at her best these past few months, has she? Childers used to be rather keen on her, but he's gone uncommon cold on her of late, and he's not the only one.'

'Then that, surely, should make it all the easier to leave London?'

'Perhaps. We'll see.' He stubbed out his cigarette, ran a hand through his hair and then turned to stare out of the window, contemplating the distant view of Ham Hill, blurred and dimmed by the fine drizzle bleeding from the low cloud.

* * *

George notified Celia that the Chelsea flat was to be sold, and that their belongings were to be packed and moved to Somerset in time to set up home at the manor just after Christmas. She had not taken the news well, with it precipitating a number of fierce rows that formed the subject matter of much gossip in their social circle. This, combined with Celia's emergent reputation as a frumpish shrew, resulted in the withdrawal of invitations to a number of social engagements. With the couple finding themselves increasingly frozen out of fashionable society, Celia reluctantly acquiesced to her husband's plans. When they left London on Monday 3 January 1921, neither of them knew that it would be the last that they would see of the capital.

Life began afresh at the manor. As during any handover between the generations, there were changes, with provision being made for the installation of both a generator and a telephone line, whereas the annual wassail in the orchards was discontinued. On the other hand, there was continuity, so the staff at the house were retained, as was the 17 January dinner, which George perceived as useful in cementing his place in local society. There would, however, be no wassail toast. Potter was consulted as to who should attend the meal, and invitations were duly despatched.

The evening of the dinner was soon in coming, and the faces familiar from the preceding year filed through the door into the Great Hall, this time to the gramophone accompaniment of Al Jolson's Swanee. Richard Wainman was there too, having made a special effort to attend, keen to make the acquaintance of the new master. The guests were greeted and shown to their places, and once the last of them had arrived, Potter totted up the tally: as last year, thirteen in all. He gave Hemmings the nod, and the two men absented themselves for a few minutes to fetch down the Lady of Cartagena, whom they placed in the seat opposite the head of the table.

The smile that Celia had managed to muster faded the instant she caught sight of the mannequin, smirking at her in that supercilious manner that she had divined the last time that she had set eyes upon it.

'George, why did you ask them to bring *that* down?'

'Oh, but I didn't old gal.'

'Then tell them to take it away. You know how I can't abide it.' She took a sip of champagne, placed her glass upon the table, and then sat, arms folded and legs crossed, avoiding eye contact with the expectant diners. George beckoned to Potter.

'Now look Potter, I know that on occasion the old Lady over there has been brought down for dinner, but my wife really doesn't care for her, so be so good as to take it back upstairs, and leave it there. She won't be required in future.'

'Are you sure, zir?'

'I am.'

'But there be thirteen of you at table.'

'That's by the by. I'm not one for superstition, so, be a good man and get Hemmings to help you up with her.'

'Very well, zir.'

Up she went. The other guests were a little surprised, the Fears passing comment upon their now unlucky number, but the dinner passed off without incident. Celia retired to bed early, with a headache, but without her husband. Superstition belonged with wassailing and Celia's good humour: in the past.

The next day was as drizzly and dank as the one before, and the one that would follow, and the mood seemed scarcely brighter. George and Celia were taking breakfast in the drawing room.

'Why must you eat those things?'

'What's wrong with them?'

'They stink to high heaven. You know how much I dislike them George.'

He paused, a piece of kipper impaled upon his fork midway between plate and mouth.

'Well, I knew that you didn't eat them, but I didn't realise that this meant that I couldn't eat kippers either.'

'You should eat something less offensive. Given that I've given up so much to follow your whim in coming down here to live, surely you could give up such a trifle as kippers on my behalf?'

'I happen to find them very agreeable,' he replied, underscoring this fact by shoving the piece of fish into his mouth.

'Well, I don't.'

George sighed.

'There's nothing for me to do here George. It's so dull.'

'Why don't you go and drop in on young Clifford and nanny?'

'You know that I don't like children George, and Clifford is such a little beast; always screaming and throwing tantrums. He's a veritable bundle of venom and vomit.'

'I can't think where he gets it from. Now look, why don't you go and see what you can get the servants to do about the house?'

'Is that all you can suggest?'

She put down her napkin, rose to her feet, and flounced out of the room, her hair bobbing with annoyance. George poured another cup of tea, and returned to savouring his kippers.

Celia strode to the servants' quarters, and took the key to the room at the end of gallery; the room used for storage – Old Crotchet's room. There was a slight stiffness to the lock, but the key turned readily enough, and as she stepped in, she looked about her. Her curiosity was further piqued by what she saw. What it contained wasn't clear, for everything was hidden, draped in dust sheets, dimly defined in the weak morning light. The air was fusty, and possessed an unpleasant metallic tang that made her want to gag. She glanced at the floor, and there saw a large stain of a rusty hue, a port wine blemish upon the oak floorboards. She sensed a prickling in her follicles, and the incipient, involuntary sweat of fear. Her breathing grew shallow, and quickened in pace.

There was a noise, faint but close. A scratching. It stopped. Celia turned, her eyes alighting upon one of the many objects that stood there neglected and, seemingly, forgotten. Although it was covered, something in its height and dimensions drew her towards it. She sensed its familiarity, crept forward, and pulled back the sheet. Before her was a mirror in a tortoiseshell frame, placed upon an aged dressing table. She recognised them in an instant as being the same items that she had seen the first night that she had slept in the house. Its glass invited her gaze, but she dared not look into it, and took a step back.

To its left, she saw something out of keeping with the rest of the objects in the room, for it was concealed not beneath a dust sheet, but a richly embroidered cloth of red and green; it was smaller too. She reached out a hand, and ran it over the fabric, sensing the contrast between the coarseness of the linen, and the smoothness of the silk tracery. It was old. Very old. Celia took a hold of it with both hands, and with care, drew it upwards, and placed it on the dressing table. She reached out again, and touched the head and the face, the leather dry and brittle from three centuries of being. It exuded a warmth; a fleshly warmth.

Celia regarded the figure – dumpy, dowdy, disdainfully smirking at the younger woman.

'I've had enough of your smirking, you old crotchet. I'll be rid of you before the day is out.'

She heaved it upwards, toppled over backwards, and screamed as the mannequin fell onto her. There was a thud. Silence.

Hemmings was the first to arrive in the room, having been alarmed by the sound of a shriek as he was clearing away breakfast. He found the Lady of Cartagena lying face down on the floor, so bent over to stand her up, and was about to place the cloth over the figure when the master of the manor rushed into the room.

'I say Hemmings, what the devil has been going on? What's all the shrieking about?'

'I don't know sir. It seemed to come from this room, but as you can see, there's nobody here.'

'It sounded like a woman.'

'Yes sir. That's what I thought I heard.'

'Peculiar. Damned peculiar. And besides, what's this place doing opened up anyway? Did you unlock it?'

'No sir. Mrs Simpkins took the key when she came down to the servants' quarters a little earlier.'

'*Mrs Simpkins* took it?'

'Yes sir.'

'Where is she?'

'We thought that she was here.'

'Well, plainly she isn't. Have you seen nanny or cook?'

'Oh yes sir, they're both downstairs.'

'I see, I see. In that case, given that Celia has been in a most frightful mood this morning, I'll warrant that she was the source of the screaming. She's probably gone back to bed. Oh, and why are you standing there with a cloth in your hand next to that thing?' he said, gesturing at the effigy.

'It had toppled over sir. I'd only just righted her when you came in. I was just about to cover her up.'

'How odd. Still, knowing how much Celia dislikes it, I daresay she probably came in here and pushed the old gal over. Well, let's take a look at her and see if she's been damaged.'

George bent down to inspect the figure. It seemed to be unharmed, but there was something different about it.

'Hemmings, my imagination appears to be running riot this morning, but tell me, in all honesty, when you look at the face of the Lady here, what do you see?'

Hemmings scrutinised its visage, his eyes widening with surprise.

'It's very strange sir, for it seems to have changed.'

'In what way?'

'Well, the expression is the same, but the face itself is different in some way.'

'Yes. That's what I thought. How long have you worked here Hemmings?'

'Twelve years sir.'

'And how many times have you seen this mannequin?'
'Quite a few, although I can't say exactly how many.'
'Has it ever changed before?'
'No. Never.'

George stared at the antique once again, his eyebrows knitting themselves into a state of disbelieving perplexity, before he turned to address his servant, a knowing twinkle in his eyes.

'You know Hemmings, I've never noticed this before, but the face bears the most remarkable resemblance to Celia. I suspect that's why she's never liked it.'

Gwydion's Dawn

Introducing Mr Turner

'I have a *surprise* for the boys.'

Just what this might be, Gwydion Turner refused to say; it was characteristic of the man, for it was in his marrow to cultivate an enigmatic air, and in this he was well practised, for he had devoted his life to it. Quite what he did and who he was remained largely a point of conjecture for the people of his adopted home, but their speculations only ran so far, for he was but one of many 'characters' who had taken up residence amongst them. Glastonbury – Avalon, the omphalos – a small Somerset town which, somehow, had become a cosmic attractor for seekers of something or the other that they could but dimly define, or describe. The locals, on the other hand, knew both what they were and what to call them: hippies; the stoned and the deluded; cider-drinking crusties, self-professed psychics, spiritual healers, con artists and tricksters, wafting about the high street in a haze of patchouli and dope smoke. They did not realise that they were in *reality* graced by the presence of those who were adepts in arcane knowledge and esoterica many years in the acquiring: geomancers and channellers of chakras; seers and grail seekers; mediums and tarot readers. Still, they could be thankful that in between the head shop and an establishment selling crystals and New Age knick-knackery, glowed a dull beacon of normality: an estate agents.

Gwydion Turner not only had 'a *surprise* for the boys', but also for their mother – Catherine. He was, apparently, single; she was divorced. Each entertained hopes regarding the other, but when their eyes met as he regarded Ms Thornton as she rose from excavating some piece of sodden timber long buried in the peat, the desires that were unearthed were as primal, and ancient, as any discarded and forgotten fragment fashioned from the tree of life. They both, in their own ways, saw the other as a means of restoring their vitality; their youth. He was childless, whereas she had two sons, but for some reason Gwydion appeared as keen to meet the latter as he did Catherine. Thus it was that their meeting was arranged, and the prospect of a 'surprise' was dangled before her sons by way of an inducement for them to accompany her on that still September evening.

As the car choked its way through the Levels, past trees and hedgerows wearing the tired greens of early autumn, the blackthorns heavy with sloes, and the boughs in the orchards weighed down with apples ripe for the plucking, Catherine's mood rose as the sun set. Her excitement was building at the prospect of peeling back the layers that enveloped the mysterious Mr Turner.

The outline of the hills darkened against the fading light of the empurpling sky, as the warmth of day yielded to the chill of the coming night. The moorland air was still and aflutter with an insect host through which flitted the occasional bat; it breathed no secrets. It held its peace, as it always had done, as the Thorntons arrived on the outskirts of South Pennard.

Before them stood the Royal Oak, a pub of some antiquity that had fallen into a state of neglect, if not quite yet, into the mire upon which its infirm foundations rested. This lack of solidity showed itself in the deep fissure that staggered up through its whitewashed walls from the ground to its eaves, and the skewed porch that was coming adrift from the main body of the building. Its inn sign was chipped and fading, the leaves of the painted oak flaking off in seeming sympathy with the season, doing little to entice them inside; yet there was the promise of 'a *surprise* for the boys', so in they went.

As they entered the lounge bar, the handful of regulars paused to regard them with stares hard and long, whilst two stuffed owls peered blindly from their glass mausoleum upon the windowsill. Of Gwydion, there was no sign. Still, his absence would at least make for a cheaper round. For herself, Catherine bought a glass of Liebfraumilch (she was, you see, something of a sophisticate in matters of the vine) and a couple of pints of Lamot for her sons – Hugh and Morgan. They seated themselves at the table next to the inglenook, where they waited for some minutes, the young Thorntons complaining of their hunger. They would have to be patient. Gwydion's absence served only to compound Catherine's anxieties, which she sought to assuage through retreating to the ladies' to check her hair – an elaborately coiffed mass of blonde curls that required frequent attention and lacquering. The Thornton brothers meanwhile supped their beer, absorbed in a discussion of such weighty musical matters as the relative merits of the use of overdrive, feedback and surf-inflected reverb, whilst making irritated comment about the jukebox from which boomed the voice of Bonnie Tyler – 'Turn around, bright eyes.'

The bar door creaked open, announcing the entry of a figure, tall and slight of stature, bearded with shoulder-length brown hair flecked with grey; a man dressed in a suit of purple crushed velvet, with a matching cravat billowing extravagantly over his white shirt, his eyes shielded by aviator shades. Behind him was a young woman, many years his junior, petite and exceptionally pretty, with long black hair. There was something vulpine about him, but as for his companion, her character seemed to be of a different cast. There was a suppleness in her movements, and yet her eyes betrayed a certain awkwardness and vulnerability; they flitted about the pub, resting nowhere, least of all upon the purple relic of the sixties that was ordering a drink for her at the bar. When he looked at her, there was a distance in her eyes which betrayed no trace of affection.

'It's got to be him,' whispered Hugh to his brother.

'Who?'

'Gwydion, with, I presume, our "surprise".'

'Hah! I think you might be right.'

'Interesting. Things could be looking up, but I suspect, judging by his dress, that his conversation may not be overly riveting. It looks as if we could be in for an evening of chit-chat about *energies* and astrology. As for her though, well, I'd not wish to hazard a guess.'

'She looks fit enough, but what's her brain like?'

'Addled, probably, given that she's hanging around with him. Still, it's not her brain that interests me; at least, not for the moment.'

Morgan laughed. 'If her brain's addled, then what does it say about mum's seeing as she's so taken with *him*?'

'Just goes to prove my point; she's away with the fairies, as well you know. If I'm not mistaken, Gwydion will shortly be in the ascendant and making a conjunction with her in the first house before you can say that his aspects are favourably aligned with her midheaven.'

Convulsed with laughter, a froth of lager spurted through Morgan's nose, drenching the ashtray and surrounding table, prompting Gwydion and his young companion to turn their disapproving gazes in their direction. A frown flashed across the old hippy's forehead, but swiftly melted as Catherine barged back into the bar.

'I wonder what the old boy's going to make of you,' said Hugh, 'the lager snorting beast of Lamot.' Morgan laughed.

'Gwydion, it's you!'

'Naturally.'

'And who's this? Aren't you going to introduce me?'

'Oh, why of course – this is Dawn. Dawn – Catherine.'

'Pleased to meet you Dawn. So, tell me: why are you hanging around with this old fossil then?' Catherine smiled, but received no reply from the young woman other than a mumbled 'Pleased to meet you,' followed by silence and a wry grin.

'And where are the boys? Am I to take it that they happen to be the two young men seated over there?' asked Gwydion, with a nod in the direction of the inglenook.

'That's them. How did you guess?'

'They're the only two young men in the bar, so I had my suspicions, but as you weren't here I couldn't be sure.'

Morgan attempted to mop up his nasally discharged lager with a couple of torn-up beer mats, but with little success. He deposited their sodden remains in the ashtray as Gwydion and Dawn were introduced. Catherine was the first to speak.

'This is Gwydion, one of the assistants on our Community Programme dig, and Dawn, his . . .'

'Friend.'

'His friend, Dawn.'

'Hello, I'm Hugh.'

'And I'm Morgan,' said the younger brother with a diffident wobble in his voice. Dawn did not speak, her reply consisting of nothing more than a dismissive smile. She appeared to be more interested in the melting of the ice in her drink, and the pattern of the grain in the darkly stained wooden table, than in the two young men who regarded her with a mixture of curiosity, lust and bewilderment.

The normal stilted pleasantries attendant upon introductions being out of the way, they scanned the limited menu and made their choices. More drinks were ordered, and after a little lubrication four of the five found themselves engaged in a conversation that could, in some respects, be described as 'meaningful'. Dawn, however, remained disengaged, aloof, or possibly simply bored, staring intensely at pieces of irregular stonework in the fireplace, and tracing the lineaments of an old pikestaff mounted upon one of the walls. She took her time over her food, slicing the potatoes into fine slivers, which were then subdivided before being coated in gravy and delicately deposited in her perfectly proportioned mouth. The beef met the same slow, drawn-out fate, growing cold and leathery in the process.

Catherine had surmised that the main object of the evening – from Gwydion's perspective – had been to become more acquainted with her in a romantic sense. It had therefore struck her as odd both that he had invited her to bring her two sons, and that he had been accompanied by a young woman; a young woman who appeared to possess no interest in any of them. Moreover, she sensed that his conversation became animated only when he spoke to Hugh, with both parties enjoying a discussion of the former's musical past.

'San Francisco in '66 to '68 was home to just the coolest vibe, but for me, it had grown stale by '69. Sonic Kaleidoscope were on the brink of breaking big in '67, but it never quite happened.'

'Cool name!' said Hugh.

'Yes. We thought so too. You know, some of the dudes we used to hang out with back then were the sweetest people, but man, would they rip you off! I could not believe it when I first heard Jefferson Airplane perform 'White Rabbit', with my riff.'

'Your riff?'

'Yes, from 'Slow Draw'. It was our signature piece; eleven minutes thirty seconds of blissed-outness – live. Polydor wanted us to cut it to three thirty, which was just way too short for our taste. We managed to get it down to eight twenty, but the breadheads wouldn't have it, so we told them where to go.'

'You wouldn't sell out?'

'No way! There was just something about that vibe – that vibe of playing live, at a happening – that can't be replicated on a '45.'

'Right.'

'I was through with it all after three summers of Haight, and I got out before Altamont. When I returned to England in spring '69, I found myself hanging out in Ladbroke Grove. That's when Bolan got to hear of me. He'd just fired Steve Peregrine Took, and was looking for a new percussionist to cover a gig at the Star Inn in Guildford.'

'You're having us on Gwydion; you never played with Marc Bolan!' said an astonished Catherine.

'I did. We hit a rare groove that night; 'Tyrannosaurus Rex' truly roared. Blissful!'

'How is it that you never told me?'

'How long have we known each other?'

'Four weeks.'

'You've answered your own question.'

'Was it packed?'

'Believe me; those eight in the audience witnessed a spectacle that was truly unique.'

'Eight? Is that all? It wasn't exactly what you'd call a popular gig, was it?'

'There was some mix-up with the payment for the fliers, so they never got distributed.'

'Really?'

'Yes, really.'

'So, if it went so well, why didn't you stay with him?'

'Two words: Mickey Finn.'

'I didn't know that you were a gin drinker. Jesus Gwydion, just how much did you drink to piss him off so much that he ditched you?'

'No, no Catherine; you misunderstand. He chose Mickey Finn to play the bongos because he thought that his looks complemented his own. He thought that I looked a bit . . .'

'A bit, what?'

'Old.'

'How old were you?'

'Twenty-seven.'

'And him?'

'Twenty-two.'

'Strange,' said Hugh, interrupting, 'given the quality of his lyrics.'

'He was a poet. Unique. A genius.'

'A "genius"? I suppose that he could be described as such, if mimicking the lyrical complexity of a nine-year-old girl obsessed with unicorns, stars and all things a-glitter defines "a genius".'

'You are, perhaps, too young to understand the content of his words, and the way that they related to the times. It was different back then.'

'Evidently. "Get it on, bang a gong". Deep stuff.'

'Hugh! Don't be so rude!'

'Oh come off it mother, I'm just having a little joke with Gwydion here.'

'Perhaps he might find that your lyrics aren't quite as brilliant as you think?'

'If Bolan was a "genius", then surely what I write must be up there with Shakespeare, only better?'

'Oh, stop it! He's full of himself at times Gwydion. I don't know where he gets it from. University I suppose.'

'No, no, I don't mind. Really. It's interesting to hear the young man's views. What's the name of your band Hugh?'

'Woland.'

Gwydion smiled, 'A reference to Bulgakov. I approve. Does this signify an interest in the occult mysteries and the dark arts?'

'An interest in satire and symbolism, nothing more.'

'I think, on the contrary, that it shows a subconscious interest in these darker matters of the spirit seeping through into your conscious mind. You should not try to rationalise such things, but rather to feel your way through them; to let your instinct take control. What do you say, Morgan?'

'I think that what Hugh says is what Hugh thinks.'

'But what of your own opinion?'

'I thought it was a good name. I've not read the book that the character comes from, but it's got a good ring to it.'

'Anyway, Gwydion,' interrupted Catherine, 'I've been meaning to ask you: how did you end up on the dig? Have you been unemployed for a long time?'

'"Unemployed"? That's how the DHSS would have it, I suppose,' he said in a nettled tone, 'but I've been engaged in the most fascinating and exacting work for a number of years. It's just that it's unpaid, and as such, not classed as *work*. However, if you must press with respect to technicalities . . .'

'Well, yes, how long has it been?'

'Nine years, give or take a few months.'

'Nine years! How on earth have you managed to get by?'

'I don't need much to live on. I have found a means of subsisting.'

'Well, what did you do after Bolan dismissed you and before you signed on?'

'I returned to Somerset, but nothing of real consequence or interest happened during that period. It would be dull for all of us if I were to recount it.'

This reticence on his part to account for these missing years prompted a sense of unease in Catherine. What had he been doing? The unsavoury consideration that he might have spent time behind bars flashed through her thoughts. If so, what had he done to merit such a lengthy period of incarceration? Her attraction to him was cooling with some rapidity. Hugh, on the other hand, harboured suspicions of a different nature.

Bored with listening to Gwydion's recollections, Morgan had twice sought to engage Dawn's attention, having noted her shared disinterest in the topics under discussion, but to no avail. It had taken some effort for him to speak to her, shy as he was, with the double rebuttal serving only to send him back to the bar for more lager. Gwydion, by way of contrast, felt at ease, and relaxed into his narrative.

'In the summer of '76, I came to live in Glastonbury, which is when I fully got into the scene, and started to devote myself to the Great Work. I was, and remain, a seeker. I'd given up on music by this time, as I'd taken things as far as I'd wanted to. The tinder of my imagination had been set alight in Weston-Super-Mare that spring, when I attended a séance led by Isis Price, daughter of Aubrey Price, one of the founding members of the Hermetic Order of the Golden Dawn. For a number of years I had felt a connection with the Order, and what she said served only to confirm and explain this sense of a bond, and close familiarity. Her explanations helped me to realise who I was; to discover my true self.

'When I came here, I was surrounded by so many teachers, and from them I learned things of which most people remain forever ignorant; such wisdom as is only imparted to a few, and which cannot be found in the books that line the shelves of public and university libraries; knowledge that, wrongly, is deemed to be false. Yet, I still found that I was little more than a dabbler, and for a number of years dipped into Wicca, kabbalah, and the writings of Crowley. For some reason, I couldn't find a sense of fulfilment in any of these; there was something in each system, each set of beliefs, that was lacking, but when Isis passed away in 1978, she bequeathed to me a set of papers in her will, accompanied by a letter.'

Here he stopped to take a sip of wine, thick and red, as if by way of a sacrament in memory of the old woman. He hesitated, closed his eyes and drew a number of slow, deep breaths. Dawn was now staring at him with rapt attention and a look of expectation, fully re-engaged with the conversation. He resumed.

'The papers in question had belonged to her father, and dealt with a wide range of matters relating to the administration of the Osiris Temple in Weston, as well as the rites and beliefs of the Order; there were also a number of Aubrey's diaries and notebooks. Initially, my attention had been drawn to some of the more standard publications that had been printed in small editions and circulated to the group's senior members, but once I had familiarised myself with these, I noted that they contained frequent annotations in their margins which, clearly, had been made in Aubrey's own hand. These all referred to his notebooks, looking into which proved to be truly revelatory, for they detailed his own work and researches, that sought to extend the Order's knowledge with a view to realising its ultimate aims. This in itself excited me greatly, but what thrilled me still further was what Isis had written in her letter. Upon our meeting she stated that she had at once recognised me to be the reincarnation of her father, and that she believed it to be my destiny to continue his work from where he had broken off.'

Hugh's suspicions, it seemed, were coming to be realised. Despite the wine, Catherine's face had come to display a sweaty pallor, her cheeks now devoid of their earlier rosy hue, with all trace of her previous good humour having vanished. Hugh sat in a state of wide-eyed fascination, scarcely able to believe that this man was able to sit there and deliver up such palpable rot whilst keeping a straight face. Morgan was puzzled, but the change in his mother's mood and appearance prompted a sense of disquiet. Yet the reason for Dawn's accompanying Gwydion this evening now seemed a little clearer, for her expression betrayed a sense of complete belief in what her companion was saying; she was, reasoned Hugh, a devotee of some sort, who had fallen under the older man's spell.

'In the instant that I read those words, I felt a charge run through me,' continued Gwydion. 'Memories flooded back; memories of a much earlier time, in my previous life. It is difficult to explain to someone who has not experienced anything of this nature, but the sensation was overwhelming. From that day onwards, I have known myself to be Aubrey Price, albeit clothed in a different fleshly raiment.'

Hugh drained his pint glass in an attempt to suppress a fit of laughter. His body quaked a little, but disguise his mirth he did. Just.

'Now, although I realised that my mission would henceforth be to pursue and further the work of the Order, matters had changed greatly since Aubrey's time, for the Osiris Temple had closed many decades earlier, and there had been a schism within the organisation itself shortly before the First World War. The Hermes Temple in Bristol had closed in 1970, before I had a chance to visit it, or to make contact with its few remaining members. It thus fell to me to seek to revive and restore those structures essential to the realisation of the Great Work. With this in mind, I sought out other like-minded individuals here in Glastonbury to reconvene the Order, but this time in line with Aubrey's refinements, and stipulation that membership should extend no further than to four Elementals and one Node representing the Eternal Feminine.

'The Order was refounded on 20 April 1981, when I, together with the three other Elementals, came together with Dawn, to remake that which had been lost. From that day on, I have been able to build upon and advance Aubrey's works. We are on the verge of achieving what has been sought for so long, but the Order needs to be made whole once again before this can be done.'

'I thought that you had just stated that it had been recreated in line with Price's instructions for four Elementals and a *Node*?' remarked Hugh.

'What you say is true, and I am glad to note that you have been listening attentively. However, the Order has not been whole since one of our number transitioned from Minor to Major Adept on 21 June this year. It was his birthday – a highly propitious date, which is why he was accepted as an Elemental – and it marked the fulfilment of his thirty-third year, thirty-three being the age at which such a transition should take place. Although there was some hesitancy on his part to transition, we reassured him of its importance, and he placed the pentacle in the most propitious spot before following the rite of departure.'

Catherine here knocked over her wine glass, its content spilling over the table and onto her dress.

'Oh!'

'Are you all right? Here, allow me to help you mop it up,' said Gwydion.

'No, no, it's all right. I'll do it.' Catherine took out a tissue and did what she could to clear up the mess. 'You'll have to excuse me, but I need to clean myself up and get some fresh air.'

She drew herself unsteadily to her feet and walked out of the bar insisting that she needed no company. Dawn was now staring intensely at the table, her body held rigid. Hugh examined her face, and thought that he could divine traces of fear, as well as a considerable sadness in her expression. Morgan sat awkwardly knowing not what to do, before resolving to buy another pint for himself and his brother.

'I am sorry to see that your mother seems to be unwell,' remarked Gwydion.

'She's sensitive. It'll pass.'

Gwydion nodded slowly. 'Hmm. Good, for I wish to ask her something.'

'I think you'll find that she'll not be in the mood for discussing that sort of thing this evening.'

'No, no, it isn't what you're thinking, I can assure you.'

'Then what?'

'You are curious. Good. For as you have learned tonight, so am I.'

'True, but it would seem that our curiosities relate to different matters.'

'You may think so now, but that will change. Tell me Hugh, how old are you?'

'Nineteen.'

'And what date is your birthday?'

'Why do you ask?'

'As you may know, I attach considerable importance to such matters.'

'Very well then, I'll leave you to fathom it out: it falls upon the spring equinox.'

'A fortunate moment in time; the date, however, varies.'

'It does, so given that you know my age, you will, surely, be able to work it out for yourself.'

Gwydion grinned, before adding, 'I can see that you have a mind and a will of your own.'

'Obviously. Who doesn't?'

'You would be surprised at how many are willing to be led, particularly if they are persuaded that in doing so they are pursuing their own desires.'

'I'll grant that there's a truth in what you say.'

'And what of your brother's date of birth?'

'The fifteenth of May.'

Gwydion paused. Not only would Hugh be the more serviceable of the two, but also his birthday made him an ideal replacement for Hunter.

'Although we have only met this evening, I should be glad if you would do me the honour of sharing my company within the next week. There is something that I would like to discuss with you.'

'I return to university on Saturday. I should have gone back already, but I've been late getting things together.'

'Where are you studying?'

'At Bristol.'

'That is to the good, for it makes what I am to propose workable. You do, I take it, visit your mother during term-time as well as during the holidays?'

'Sometimes, but university life holds somewhat greater attractions.'

'Do you drive?'

'Sort of. I've not passed my test.'

Here their conversation was brought to an abrupt halt by the booming of the landlord's voice: 'Ladies and gentlemen – your attention please! A lady has been found lying passed out in front of the pub. Does anyone know who this might be? Is anyone missing?'

There was a brief pause, broken by Gwydion: 'One of our party left the table some time ago landlord. I'll go and see.'

'Right you are sir,' replied the publican.

'Jesus! I wonder if it's mum.'

'Don't worry Hugh. I'll deal with it,' said Gwydion.

'I'll come too,' said Morgan.

'Dawn, why don't you and Hugh take a short walk together.'

A knowing smile lit up her features which now seemed to take on a feline aspect. 'Come!' she said, taking hold of Hugh's hand, 'Let's walk.' He did not object, and meekly did as instructed. After all, never is it easier for people to be led, than when they believe themselves to be acting in pursuit of their own desires. This principle, it seemed, he had already forgotten. Beer and lust: a heady combination that has led many astray. He was now conscious of little other than her touch, the breathy cadence of her voice, and his desire to lie with her. She, on the other hand, was sober, and acutely aware of the power that she exerted over him; he would do her bidding, whatever it might be. Did she wish to lie with him, or to him? He could not be sure.

The two of them ventured no further afield than the pub carpark, where they sauntered about its perimeter, for it had grown too dark to take a stroll along the lane, hemmed in by hedgerows and flanked by deep ditches. She said nothing, moving with a sinuous ease, as lithe and sensuous as her smile and looks were knowing and calculated. She glanced at Hugh now and again, just enough to pique his interest, and keep him in her thrall. She stopped.

'Close your eyes.'

He closed them.

'Hold out your hand.'

He proffered his right hand.

'Take this and read it, but on no account read it before tomorrow, and when you open it, be sure to be alone.'

''What is it?' he asked. She said nothing.

Morgan appeared. 'Mum's come to. She says she wants to leave.' Hugh's heart sank.

'Surely we ought to stay a little longer? She's not fit to drive. She needs time to recover.'

'She wants to leave now.'

'Shit! All right, I'm coming!'

Morgan was taken aback by his brother's ill-tempered reaction.

'What's wrong?'

'Nothing. Nothing's wrong.' There was a certain lack of conviction in his words. They walked back to the porch to find Gwydion steadying Catherine on a bench.

'Hugh?' she asked uncertainly.

'What happened mum? Are you all right?'

'I don't know. I'm not feeling well. We need to go.'

'Right, but you can't drive; you're in no state to.'

'I know. You'll have to.'

'But I've had four pints!'

'Morgan's drunk more than that.'

Hugh paused to regard his mother. Her face was even more ashen than earlier, the lines around her eyes grown more distinct and deeper; she looked old. He felt himself suddenly sober.

'Okay, I'll drive.'

Gwydion helped Catherine to her feet, and opened the car door allowing her to slump into the passenger seat.

'We shall speak again,' he said. She assented with a weak nod.

'Let's go Hugh.'

Blackmore Cross

The car lurched into the night with a grinding of gears and a puff of black smoke. Hugh hadn't driven for weeks, but after a couple of minutes of bumping over the uneven tarmac, warped and deformed by the shifting of the peat below, he regained a certain confidence in his ability to keep the car from swerving into the rhynes that flanked the carriageway.

Unhurried wraiths of mist drifted across the road, exhaled by the dark waters into the cooling night, as moths fluttered awkwardly towards the headlights, disorientated by the twin moons of the oncoming car, their beams as deceitful and fatal as wreckers' lights on a Cornish clifftop. Bile stirred and welled up from the driver's stomach. He choked it back, his sense of nausea exacerbated by the fact that the car heater was jammed on full. There was nothing that could be done other than to wind down the window to admit the heavy air of the moors, here and there scented with slurry spread over the low-lying pastures. Bulrushes waved from the ditches in the light breeze, a puffball seemingly skewered upon one, spreading its powdery spores into the midge and mosquito-filled darkness.

'How are you feeling mum?' asked Hugh.

'Hmm?'

'How are you feeling?'

'Not well.'

'What happened?'

'I had to get out. I felt so sick. I couldn't breathe. It was Gwydion's aura. There's something dark about the man; there's a presence about him. I remember going outside, then the next thing I know is that there's some stranger standing over me asking if I'm all right.'

'How did you fall?'

'I don't know.'

'Did you hurt yourself?'

'My left arm. It hurts when I flex my elbow. *Ah!*' She flinched.

'Jesus!'

Hugh swerved to the left to avoid a battered old Land Rover spattered with muck, the face of its driver – an elderly farmer – fixed in a sozzled smile as he asserted his ownership of the road. The wheels of the car bumped along the verge, mowing down and flattening the stands of cow parsley, narrowly missing the edge of the ditch.

'Hugh! Watch it for fuck's sake!' yelled Morgan.

'Shit! Shit! Shit! You try driving with a skinful, it's not easy!'

'Quiet the two of you! Be careful Hugh, and for God's sake slow down!'

'Okay, okay! What about your arm? It's got me worried.'

Catherine flinched and let out a groan. 'I feel sick. Take me to Dr Harris's in Blackmore Cross.'

'It's almost ten.'

'He won't mind. We go back a long way.'

With that, Catherine closed her eyes and fell into a light sleep. Hugh too was struggling to keep his lids from drooping. He slowed the car to a dawdle, irritating the handful of other drivers who proceeded to tailgate and dazzle him, until they overtook in a furious dash on those stretches of road that didn't wend and wind as much as a staggering English drunkard on his desultory way home. Half an hour later, they arrived at their destination on the outskirts of Blackmore Cross. Before them stood Dr Harris's home, a handsome dwelling fashioned from the local limestone and dating from the initial years of the eighteenth century. From one of its tall and graceful windows shone a lone light. The doctor, it would seem, had yet to take to his bed.

As Hugh turned into the driveway, he misjudged the width of the gateway, scraping the passenger-side of the car along one of the stone gateposts.

'Bugger!'

Catherine woke with a start.

'What happened?' she asked drowsily.

'Nothing. We've arrived. How are you feeling?'
'Worse.'
'Let me help you out.'
'Careful with my arm.'
'Don't worry. Here – take my hand.'

Catherine did as instructed. He pulled her up and eased her out of the car. Her legs felt weak, and although she had drunk only a little, she struggled to keep her balance, and was kept from falling only by her sons' efforts to steady her; they walked with her arms draped over their shoulders.

'You need to lose some weight,' said Hugh.

'You cheeky devil!'

Dr Harris, who had been dozing after a heavy dinner, was disturbed from his slumbers by the noise of feet scuffing up the gravel of the driveway. Burglars? It certainly didn't sound like badgers ambling to and from their sett on the opposite side of the lawn. He peeked through his curtains, but it was too dark to see a thing.

He made his way to the door, switched on the porch light, and peered out into the darkness. Three figures emerged from the gloom, resembling two soldiers supporting a wounded comrade. As they drew closer to the light, he was able to make out their faces, and was relieved to see that he was not about to be robbed. He was, however, somewhat alarmed by the condition of his old friend.

'Catherine! What on earth has happened to you? Come in, come in! Quick now, before the insects fly in with you.'

She raised her head, but it promptly slumped back down, her eyes still closed.

'I hope that you don't mind, doctor,' said Hugh, 'but you can see the condition that she's in. She blacked out earlier, and after she came round, she asked to be brought to see you. She's hurt her arm. It was the fall.'

'Oh good Lord! No, no of course I don't mind. Come now, why don't you two bring her into the lounge, and I'll take a look at her. How are you feeling Catherine?'

She looked up at him, and just managing to open her eyes replied, 'Queasy.'

'Take her over to the sofa. Try to make her comfortable whilst I go and ask Denise to fetch some pillows.'

'Thank you doctor.'

'Heavens Hugh, have you been drinking?'

'Just a little.'

'You shouldn't be driving in such a condition.'

'I know, but there was no option – look at her.'

'Hmm. Yes, yes, I suppose so. But that in itself does not make you fit to sit behind a wheel young man. You have been somewhat reckless in having done so, but the main thing is that you have all arrived here in one piece. So, to ensure that you all remain in that state, I would rather that you, your mother, and your brother spent the night here. Agreed?'

The doctor's chastisement left Hugh feeling mildly embarrassed and guilty, but he was relieved at the offer of a bed for the night.

'That's very kind of you. Thank you.'

'Don't mention it. It would be negligent of me to allow you to leave the house under the influence of the hop. Now, the pillows. I'll be back shortly.'

Hugh and Morgan laid their mother down on the sofa, her hair now bedraggled and unkempt. Something caught Morgan's eye: a piece of twig lodged in the curls above her left ear. He bent over and pulled it out.

'Must've been uncomfortable,' he commented.

'No doubt,' agreed Morgan.

Their mother yawned and opened her eyes.

'Where am I?'

'On Dr Harris's sofa. At least you're not on his *couch*, as you know why patients get laid out on that,' remarked Hugh.

'You never stop, do you?' she remarked in a weary voice.

'No, not really.' He grinned, as the door opened to reveal their host returning with two pillows.

'Catherine my dear woman, what in heaven's name has happened to you? No, don't answer, not just yet. Now, lift your head. That's a good girl. Excellent! So, let's take a look at you. Which arm was it that you hurt?'

'My right.'

'Excuse me rolling up your sleeve my dear, but I need to check for any damage. Now, if it hurts, be sure to tell me.'

She nodded and the palpation began, eliciting an occasional wince and groan from the patient.

'Hmm, you're lucky it seems. Nothing more than a bad graze and some bruising. No breaks or fractures, but it's bound to feel tender for a few days, so take care not to knock it.'

She sighed weakly, nodded and closed her eyes.

'Just relax now; I'm going to take your pulse.'

He took hold of her left wrist, held it, and counted. The pulse was rapid but weak, and her skin felt clammy to the touch. Her breathing was shallow and intermittent. He turned to Hugh.

'She's in shock.'

'Shock?'

'Yes. She needs to rest. She can sleep in one of the guest rooms. Did you hear that Catherine?'

'Hmm?'

'We're going to put you up in one of the guest rooms tonight. You need to rest, and I need to keep an eye on you. Is that all right?'

'But, . . .'

'No buts my dear. We can speak in the morning. You must sleep.'

Her head slumped back onto the pillow.

'Be so good as to lift her up would you Hugh, Morgan. Thank you. Follow me gentlemen. I'll sort out sleeping arrangements for you both shortly, once we've had a quick word.'

* * *

Once Catherine was in bed, they returned to the lounge by way of the kitchen where they collected a pot of tea that Denise had made for them.

'She really is in a bad way. I knew that she was of rather a sensitive disposition, but I've never known her to be like this. What happened?'

Hugh took the lead, his brother too diffident to speak.

'We were out. We went for a meal and a few drinks at the Royal Oak in South Pennard, at the invitation of one of her acquaintances. We'd not met him before, but mum had struck up something of a friendship with him a few weeks back on an archaeological dig that she's been managing for the Community Programme. He was one of the assistant excavators,' he paused.

'So far all so unexceptional. Go on.'

'She was keen that we go out with her this evening, as this friend had said that he had some kind of surprise for us.'

'A "surprise"? How intriguing. Was it this that caused the shock? People can react in the most unpredictable ways when confronted with the unexpected.'

'I don't know. To be honest, I don't even know what the surprise was, as he didn't say. At a guess though, I'd say that it was the young woman he brought with him.'

'A young woman? What was she like?'

'Slim. Quiet. Attractive. A bit nuts perhaps. She'd have to be to hang around with him.'

'What makes you say that?'

'If you'd seen him and heard what he said, you'd understand soon enough. He was some kind of sixties throwback . . .'

'Ah! Just your mother's type then?'

'Hah! Well, you could say that, yes. That's what we thought, at least just after we arrived, but she seemed to become more withdrawn as the evening went on, and he spoke about the importance of his "Great Work" and how he'd recreated some occult order to help him realise its ultimate objectives. It was bonkers, and his manner was so, so . . . pretentious.'

'Would he be from Glastonbury, by any chance?'

'Where else would he be from? I don't know what it is about the place, but it's a complete nutter magnet.'

The doctor smiled.

'A great many of the people who have set up home there do appear to hold the most unorthodox beliefs. But tell me, what was it that caused your mother to black out?'

'This Gwydion' – upon mention of the name the doctor's eyes flickered with unease – 'had just been telling her about how he believed himself to be the reincarnation of someone mixed up in the occult whom I'd never heard of, and then mentioned that a member of his order had recently "transitioned". He didn't explain what this meant, but it involved some kind of departure. No sooner had he mentioned this, and she spilt her drink. She left the table to clean herself up. About ten minutes later the barman announced that an unconscious woman had been found near the pub entrance. It was her. She can't remember blacking out, and can't provide any explanation for what happened other than that she found Gwydion's aura to be very dark, and that this had somehow made her feel sick and short of breath.'

'"Aura"?'

'Yes, I know. I don't know what it means either. It's codswallop so far as I'm concerned, but she believes in all of this New Age rot.'

'Yes, it's not the sort of thing to which I give any credence. I'm glad to hear that you give such short shrift to this popular nonsense. Now Hugh, you mentioned that this fellow's name was Gwydion; did you happen to catch his surname?'

'Turner.'

'Turner. *Gwydion Turner*. I suspected as much. Most unfortunate.'

'Why? What do you mean? Do you know him?'

'Yes, I'm afraid that I do.'

'How? Was he a patient?'

'Now, look my boy, this really isn't easy; ordinarily I would not breathe a word of what I am about to tell you. You must realise that this puts me in a very difficult position, ethically speaking, for it breaches the confidentiality of the doctor-patient relationship, but knowing his character and his past, it would be negligent of me not to warn you, given your mother's apparent regard for this man.'

'Warn me?'

'Yes, warn you.'

'What of?'

'Look, why not pour yourself another cup of tea before I explain. I need to put this as succinctly as I can, without divulging information that could be damaging to the reputation of others, so you must not, under any circumstances, repeat what I say about this man to anyone else. Do you understand?'

Hugh felt himself grow sober, and suddenly became acutely aware of the cold alcoholic sweat that soaked the back of his shirt. He shuddered. 'I understand.'

'Good. But what about you Morgan? Do I have your word that you will not repeat this to anyone?'

There was no reply.

'Morgan? Morgan?'

His brother gave him a nudge, but he was out cold.

'He's asleep, and once he is, there's little that will wake him.'

'How I wish I could say the same of myself! Age is a thief of sleep my dear boy, as you yourself will one day learn. Very well, we shall, in that case, have to assume that he will not be privy to what we are about to discuss.'

'So, tell me: what is there to warn me of? I'm hardly the type to fall for the sort of charlatanism that he peddles.'

'I can see that, but your mother, as we both know, is a different matter. She is – how can I put it? Rather more susceptible to such beliefs. You should seek to ensure that she drops all contact with him outside of work.' Hugh nodded, and the doctor resumed. 'Gwydion Turner is not to be trusted. He has not always been known by that name, for he was christened Alan Richards in late March 1940. He grew up in Banwell, and after a string of short-term jobs, his family lost touch with him for a number of years, receiving nothing other than the occasional letter from America. He returned to Somerset in late October 1969 after a short period in London.'

'This seems to fit with what he said. How did you come to know him? You don't strike me as someone who was into the psychedelic scene.'

'You've guessed correctly with respect to that scene my boy: I must definitely was not *into it*. He was on my caseload from November 1969 to April 1976. For most of that time, he was in institutional care. I'm not sure if you know this, but my speciality was in psychiatric disorders.'

Hugh gulped. 'No, I didn't. I was aware that you had some interest in such matters, but not that you had any formal specialism in that sphere.'

'Well, that's how it was, although my conventional medical training meant that I was also able to practise as a GP at other points in my career.'

'Right.'

'I first became acquainted with Alan Richards upon his admission to the local mental hospital. He had been sectioned after behaving erratically, and threatening his family and neighbours for refusing to recognise him as an emanation of the Godhead. Richards had insisted that he had been a founding member of the Hermetic Order of the Golden Dawn, and would frequently sit in a bedroom at his parental home repeating some jumbled and nonsensical formulae at the centre of a pentacle that he had chalked onto the floor. Not only were they distressed by this behaviour, but also by the fact that he tore up a new carpet to gain access to the floorboards so that he might draw. When I was to interview him later, I asked him to repeat the verses that he had concocted. Although they included elements of Latin, they were, by and large, gibberish.

'The specific incident that led to him being sectioned occurred towards the middle of November 1969, when he hit his father with a blunt instrument for daring to interrupt his ritual. Upon later questioning, he said that he had no recollection of having struck him, stating that he had instead sought to disable a demon that had lurched into the room at that point. He had been relieved that the demon was so easy to immobilise, and after striking it, he had fallen into an ecstatic trance during which he had traced a verse in the demon's blood. His mother had stumbled into this scene after returning from shopping. Her son did not recognise her, so she ran out to a neighbours' house to call for an ambulance and the police. The latter discovered a quantity of dried mushrooms in the room, which were later identified as fly agaric. Richards had used these as a means to enter his ecstatic states, explaining that he had gathered them owing to his lack of access to the LSD that he had hitherto used for this purpose whilst living in San Francisco. His father, thankfully, recovered.'

'Shit!'

'Hugh, I realise that what I am saying may be a cause of shock and some concern to you, and that it seems to be the vogue to readily deploy expletives these days, but to my ears the use of such language is deeply unpleasant. So, if you wouldn't mind?'

'Sorry doctor.'

'Thank you. Now, let's see, with respect to Mr Richards it became clear that his routine abuse of psychedelic substances had had a permanent impact upon his psychological state during those periods when he was not using the drugs; they had tipped him over into a form of paranoid schizophrenia. As with all such patients, the persecutory delusions from which he suffered were unique, but shared a general pattern. However, the nature of these is not something that should concern you, and it would be giving away too much to go into further specifics.'

'I'm . . . stunned. It seemed clear enough that there was something unusual about him and that his beliefs were odd and irrational, but I wouldn't have guessed that the man was capable of violence.'

'It always comes as a shock for those who have no direct experience of these cases. Contrary to the fashionable idiocies of Thomas Szasz and R.D. Laing, schizophrenia is not some mere 'social construct', but an often terrifying and debilitating condition.'

'So, how did he come to be released?'

'After more than six years of therapy and anti-psychotic medication, his behaviour appeared to be under control. There had been no violent episodes for three years, and although his beliefs were still unorthodox, he was no longer held to be a threat. As part of our efforts to reintegrate him into society, and to place the stigma of his mental illness behind him, we encouraged him to choose a new name, and that name, as you are now aware, was Gwydion Turner.'

'Do you think that he's cured?'

'Nobody, to my knowledge, has ever been cured of schizophrenia. It's a condition that can only be managed, albeit, imperfectly.'

'Could he still be violent?'

'It's quite possible, and from what you say, I would venture to state that this would be more likely than not. Your mother must keep well away from him.'

Hugh nodded. 'I agree, but knowing what she's like, she probably won't listen.'

'I shall apprise her of Mr Turner's history in the morning, and underscore how important it is that she drops all contact with the man. Keep an eye on her, and call me if she appears not to take this warning seriously.'

'I will.'

'Good.'

'However, . . .'

'"However", Hugh? However, what?'

'What was also odd about this evening was that Gwydion seemed more interested in me than my mother. He asked me to meet him again within the week, before I go back to university.'

'Don't. Don't so much as call him.'

'Okay.'

'Does he have your mother's number?'

'Yes, unfortunately.'

'What about her address?'

'I don't think he knows it, but I'm pretty sure that she'll have said which village she lives in.'

'Is she ex-directory?'

'Yes.'

'Good. She mustn't give him her address under any circumstances. I'll tell her as much before she leaves tomorrow.'

'There's a snag though.'

'A "snag"?'

'He works on a Community Programme project. She's his manager.'

'I know. You told me earlier. Although that potentially makes things a little more awkward, there should be a way around it. Is she ever alone with him whilst working?'

'No. She's in charge of a team excavating a Neolithic trackway, so there are always a few others around.'

'In that case, there should be no cause for undue concern, providing that she takes the necessary precautions, and ensures that she is never alone with him.'

'Are you sure?'

'Quite sure.'

'But there's one other thing.'

'Go on.'

'I was given this whilst Gwydion and Morgan were with my mum this evening.' Hugh drew a crumpled envelope from his jacket pocket.

'By whom?'

'By Gwydion's companion – Dawn.'

'What's her surname?'

'I don't know. Nobody mentioned it.'

'It's all right; I don't know anyone of that name. Did she give any reason for asking you not to open it until tomorrow?'

'No.'

'Well, open it then.'

'Should I?'

'Unless you think that it contains a curse, or such like.' The doctor grinned. 'Besides, it's already past midnight, so you have fulfilled your obligation.'

Hugh hesitated.

'Do you think that it might contain something personal? Would you prefer to open it in my absence?'

'No. No, of course not. I don't know the woman. She didn't exactly say a great deal. I've no idea what could be inside.'

Hugh carefully opened the envelope and pulled out a single sheet of folded A4 paper. He unfolded and read the following message:

Meet me at 8pm this Thursday evening in Penniless Porch, Wells. There is something I must tell you. Tell nobody, least of all Gwydion.

'Curious.'

'What do you make of it doctor?'

'There's not a great deal to go on, is there?'

'Not really.'

'Well, what can I say? How did you find her conversation this evening?'

'"Conversation"?'

'Yes. Her conversation. How did she relate to you? Was she lively? Flirtatious? Did you expect that she might offer you an invitation?

'She scarcely said anything. In fact, she was silent throughout the whole meal and the drinks that followed.'

'But you took a walk with her, didn't you say?'

'Around the car park. It hardly merits being called a *walk*.'

'What did she say?'

'She said nothing, other than telling me to close my eyes and hold out my hand, which is when she gave me this envelope. She also told me to – ah, I had forgotten this! – "to be sure to be alone" when I opened it.'

'She wanted to keep your meeting a secret.'

'So it would seem.'

'Will you do as she asks?'

'I don't know.'

'Remember what I've told you about Gwydion Hugh. If she's as mixed up with him as I suspect she may be, it would be best to keep away from her.'

'Yes, yes, you're right.'

Dr Harris readily perceived that Hugh was unsettled as well as exhausted, and showed him to his room, leaving Morgan asleep on the sofa. When morning came, Catherine was told of the doctor's misgivings regarding Gwydion, which, fortunately, she seemed to treat with some seriousness. She was insistent that Mr Turner had possessed 'a powerful dark aura' that had overcome her, and made it clear in no uncertain terms that she would not be having any further contact with him other than in a strictly professional capacity. Of Dawn's note, the doctor made no mention. The Thorntons returned home.

Kicking Kerouac

The atmosphere in the Thorntons' cottage was subdued. Catherine proved reluctant to speak about the preceding evening, and in line with Dr Harris's advice, retired to bed for the day, leaving Hugh and Morgan to nurse their hangovers. The elder brother went upstairs to identify what he needed to pack before returning to university, whilst the younger fried up some eggs before sandwiching them between two crudely hewn chunks of bread, wolfing them down greedily and almost choking in the process. The yolk oozed out and dribbled over his fingers, staining his jeans.

By the time that Hugh came down to the kitchen, Morgan had headed out for a walk to clear his head. He left behind a grease-smeared plate and a frying pan containing an ocean of liquid lard, congealing and whitening as it cooled, like pack ice forming at the start of an Arctic winter. A fragment of egg white stuck to the pan's long-vanished non-stick surface. A hint of vomit bubbled into Hugh's throat. He needed to eat. Opening the fridge, he surveyed its contents: neither eggs nor bacon, just half a pint of milk. He took it out and clicked on the kettle, grabbed a packet of cornflakes from the shelf, and cajoled the last of its contents into his bowl; there must have been about eight flakes in all. He swore, and then opened the breadbin. Inside he discovered a curled crust of stale sliced white, resembling a piece of moist cardboard in both its texture and its flavour. It would do; it would *have to* do.

As he sat drinking his tea and nibbling at his margarine smeared slice of toast, he unfolded the note that Dawn had handed him, and pondered over its request, or, more accurately, instruction, to meet her at Penniless Porch that Thursday at 8pm. He knew where it was, for he was familiar with Wells, but why did she wish to see him? He had assumed – given Gwydion's promise of 'a surprise' – that it had been his intention for him to become acquainted with Dawn, and yet she was making it clear that Gwydion should not know of their meeting. Moreover, she hadn't shown any interest in either him or his brother the evening before, so her issuing him with an invitation seemed all the more perplexing; it didn't make any sense, at least not from his perspective. Then again, neither she nor Gwydion struck him as logical, so why should it.

He cradled his mug of tea, mulling over what to do. By the time that he took his next sip, it had grown cold; undrinkable. Whereas his rational mind told him to ignore the note, his emotions told him otherwise; the message, and Dawn herself, had kindled a curiosity in him that he was unable to extinguish. He had preparatory work to do, but found himself unable to focus; much as he enjoyed Smollett, he was not in the mood for reflecting upon the merits of the eighteenth-century epistolary novel whilst his head and stomach were in their current condition.

He lay down on the sofa and picked up a book that his girlfriend had lent to him – Jack Kerouac's *On the Road*. She had been raving on about this for months, as had a number of her friends: 'You've got to read it. You'll love it. I know you will!' 'Of course I will. Just as much as I enjoyed the *Female* fucking *Eunach*,' he reflected. He was as suspicious of popular books as he was of popular people. Still, she'd be wanting it back next week, so he'd better read it.

Hugh prised apart the leaves of the paperback and struggled to keep his eyes moving beyond its opening lines. By the end of the first page his hackles were already rising; after three or four more, he was convinced that he had Kerouac's measure, and was by now finding his prose style insufferable. For the next hour, he lay there, forcing himself to read on. By lunchtime, it was all he could do to prevent himself from physically ripping it apart. For the first time in his life, a book had defeated him.

'What an utter fucking *wanker*!' Hugh pitched Kerouac across the room, vowing never again to waste precious minutes upon the worthless words spewed out by that 'speed-fuelled, jive-talking, bebopping, pretentious tosser of an egocentric Yank'. It was in that moment that he realised that he was finished with Lisa. He felt a sense of catharsis rapidly succeeded by hunger; he was desperately tired and needed something to eat. For better or for worse, he resolved that he would meet Dawn that Thursday.

Rushing past the Good Earth

The bus juddered towards Wells, its windows running wet with condensation; breath and sweat returned to the state of pure water. Hugh found most of the faces familiar, even though he couldn't affix names to them; some of the passengers may even have recognised him, but if they did, they didn't let on. A child, bored with the journey, lifted his finger to trace in the moisture – a cat, a tree, a house – whilst his mother held up a hand mirror to regard her hair, distressed at the sight of the heavily lacquered mass that the rain had collapsed onto her head. She sat there all a-fidget, primping and plumping it to little effect, her thick mascara smudged panda-like beneath her tired eyes. Towards the front sat an old man, his days of concern for such tonsorial matters long since passed, his pate shining pink and, apparently, still wet. Whenever the vehicle paused at the many village stops, his whimpering mongrel would jump up, pawing excitedly at whoever walked past.

'Get down Vobster! Get down! Don't mind him missus, he's just being friendly.'

The 'missus' or the 'mister' usually did mind, and the threatening growls released by the snapping cur suggested that it wasn't as affectionate as its owner averred. A pungent concoction of wet dog, cigarette smoke, body odour and beery farts prompted Hugh to move further back; the smell followed him. He should have passed his driving test.

His mother and brother had been led to believe that he was meeting up with old friends for a drink before returning to university. It was, he reasoned, safer to lie than to reveal his intent, although he felt the occasional pang of conscience for having done so; it reflected poorly upon him. He was not one for deceit, but deceive on this occasion he must. Little did they suspect that he was on his way to meet Dawn, and little did he know why he was going to meet her, other than to sate his curiosity in, he hoped, something of an agreeably base fashion. His face flushed at the thought, a clammy sweat beading on his skin in the humid air of the bus. His senses felt heightened and his head was abuzz.

It was dark as he alighted from the bus and dashed past the drizzle-soaked queue outside the Regal, his thoughts coursing ahead, trying to predict what the evening might bring. Unlike the young woman whom he rushed to meet, he had consulted no astrological ephemeris to prognosticate the evening's outcome. He hurried up Priory Street past the Good Earth, along Broad Street and up and along the High Street, noting the pubs as he passed: the King's Head, the Star Hotel and then, finally, the Crown in the Market Place itself. It was ten minutes to eight when he stepped into the darkness of Penniless Porch and sat down on its stone bench, a seat that had provided a cold comfort for beggars over the centuries. He looked across the Market Place, eager to catch sight of Dawn, but for the next quarter of an hour or so saw nobody other than the occasional customer walking into, or staggering out of, the Crown. By ten past eight, he was beginning to grow anxious. He closed his eyes and breathed deeply in an effort to calm himself. His pulse began to slacken, and his vital warmth ebbed away into the cool dampness of the evening air. He shivered and rose to his feet in an attempt to warm himself. It was then that he espied a petite female figure dressed in black heading towards him. Dawn had come.

There was a lightness in her step, and a certain seductive grace to her movements. A knowing smile spread across her face as she drew close to him, and without saying a word, she put her arms around the small of his back, pressed her body close to his, and stared into his eyes. He moved to kiss her, but she pulled her lips away and whispered into his ear.

'Come!'

He almost did. The warmth of her breath singed him with desire. He felt weak, and said nothing as she pulled him out of the porch and led him by the hand across the empty expanse of the Market Place.

'Why did you ask me here?'

'Shh!'

He thought that he knew the answer, or at least, he hoped he did; she too knew what he thought he knew. She led him on into the darkness.

Hugh followed Dawn up the stairs and into her flat. It was shabby and smelt of joss sticks, the walls a nicotine-stained former cream, the colour of flypaper. The lounge was small and uninviting, its walls unadorned but for a colourful chakra chart curling up at the corners. 'What the hell is a chakra?' he mused to himself. She sat herself down on a black vinyl sofa partly covered by a patterned cotton throw and a couple of ethnically embroidered cushions; a tear slashed into one of its arms revealing the orange yellow foam of its interior. Dawn beckoned to him to sit beside her. He did so, and placed an arm around her shoulders; she removed it, placing it upon his leg.

'Why have you brought me here?'

'Because I like you.'

'You have a strange way of showing it.'

'You don't understand.'

'Now that, I grant you, is true: no, I don't understand.'

She was silent. What was she playing at? Although he could not be sure, his gut instinct was that she must be 'simple'. Why else, after all, would she be hanging around with Gwydion?

'You don't say much, do you?'

For a brief moment, she looked hurt, but then a sly smile spread across her face as she lifted her head to regard the young man.

'Why are you looking at me like that?' he asked, feeling unsettled.

She furrowed her forehead then said, 'I don't want to hurt you.' She reached out and brushed his fringe, sparking a frisson of desire that jolted his hairs from their follicles as if they had been caught in some charge of static. She snatched away her hand, her mood abruptly changed. 'I'll make you a drink.'

'Thanks.'

Hugh's heart raced, his sense of lust tempered by confusion. Whilst she busied herself in the kitchen, he found himself staring at the shelf in one of the recesses next to the boarded-up fireplace. On it sat an incense burner, some tattered blue exercise books, and a handful of dried teasels in a chipped white pot.

'It's time to speak now,' she said as she entered the room carrying a teapot and two mugs on a tray. Her expression was now blank. 'Milk? Sugar?'

'Two sugars but no milk.'

'That's odd,' she commented. 'So are you,' thought he, before adding, 'I like it that way, although it's no good for my teeth of course. I have a mouth full of fillings. Look!'

He opened his mouth wide, and pointed to his amalgam packed molars. She ignored them.

'I'm not interested in your teeth,' she said in a dismissive tone. 'You must understand that what I am about to tell you is difficult for me to speak of; it's not something that I'm supposed to talk about.' She paused. 'I'm scared.' A note of genuine fear had suddenly entered her voice.

'Scared?'

'Yes.'

She clammed up and slumped down onto the sofa next to him, her gaze locked onto the floor, her body frozen. Her mood swings and erratic behaviour had Hugh on the brink of panic.

'Look, Dawn, please don't worry; you can speak to me. I'll listen. Whatever it is, you can trust me. What is all of this about?'

'It's difficult. I don't know where to start. I don't know whether I should be doing this, but I've no-one to speak to.' Her eyes moistened.

'Go on – speak. I don't mind what you say.'

'It's Gwydion.'

'Gwydion?'

'Yes.'

'What about him?'

She made as if to speak, but halted; her eyes flicked downwards and her head followed. Hugh put his arm around her. She flinched. He pulled it away.

'I'm sorry. I didn't mean to . . .'

'It's all right.'

'Here, have some of this,' he said, picking up her mug and offering it to her.

'Thanks.'

She cradled it in her hands, her fingers fine, white and slender, topped with nails as glossy and black as anthracite.

'I don't trust him any longer.'

'Why not?'

She sighed and fixed Hugh with a steady gaze.

'I can't tell you everything, at least not now; it's too difficult. It takes time to get your head around this stuff. You probably wouldn't believe me anyway. I think that I'm only just beginning to wake up. I can't believe that I've been so stupid; so naïve. It all seemed so much fun at first, but now . . . now it, now it . . .' she broke down and sobbed. Hugh was overcome by the urge to comfort her, but dared not put his arm around her, for fear of how she might react.

'I'm sorry.'

'It's all right.'

'It's been so hard since Jeff, since Jeff . . . *transitioned*.'

'Who is Jeff?'

'Jeff was the fourth elemental within our group; he *transitioned* from Minor to Major Adept on Midsummer's Day. Since then, our circle has been incomplete, and Gwydion has been seeking a replacement.'

'I don't understand.'

'Why would you? I knew you would find it difficult.'

'What do you mean by *transitioned*?' There was no answer. 'Don't you want to talk?'

'I do, but . . .'

'Look, you can tell me whatever you wish. I won't be shocked.'

A feeble smile made a momentary appearance upon Dawn's face. 'I believe that you speak sincerely, but I find it too hard to talk about; you'd just find it too incredible. That is why I have written something for you to read. It's easier to write rather than speak about these things. It explains everything, or at least as much as you need to know, but first, I want to know if I can trust you.' She stared hard into his face, a look of doubt in her eyes.

'You can trust me.'

'How do I know?'

'You can't know for sure; not until you've placed that trust in me.'

'Very well, in that case, I have a favour to ask of you – an important favour.'

'What is it?'

'Take what I have written, read it in private, and then do with it what you think best. It may seem outlandish to you; in fact, I'm certain that it will, but I swear that it is true; every last word of it.'

Hugh hesitated.

'Please! I need your help,' she implored.

'Okay. I'll do as you ask.'

She lifted herself up from the sofa, took a few steps across the room, and picked up one of the exercise books lying on the shelf in the alcove.

'Here!'

She handed it to Hugh. He looked at the childlike drawings of the sun and the zodiac inked onto its cover.

'No! Don't open it. Not now. Read it tomorrow, when you're alone. Promise me.'

'I promise.'

She looked down at the floor, then into his eyes.

'Thank you.'

The last bus home had gone, so she brought him an old quilt and a pillow and he made himself as comfortable as he could on a musty old sheepskin rug which stank of stale incense and dope smoke. He slept poorly that night, itching to acquaint himself with what she had written, his fitful slumber punctuated by frequent vivid and disturbing dreams. When she came through to the living room the next morning, they exchanged few words other than a handful of awkward pleasantries. Having dropped her guard for him, she had once again clammed up. He could sense her vulnerability, and felt guilty about leaving her, but with neither food nor milk in the flat, she released him into the fresh morning air to seek out breakfast, and make his way home.

The bus was almost empty, but Hugh secluded himself in a seat towards the rear of the vehicle, and with a head befuddled from lack of sleep, he opened the book, rubbed the grit from his eyes, and began to read.

The Testimony of Dawn Willis

I, Dawn Willis, of Flat 3b Chamberlain Close, Wells, Somerset, declare the following to be a true account of my involvement with the Hermetic Order of the Golden Dawn (the Order), revived and led by Gwydion Turner.

The Order was reconvened under the leadership of Gwydion Turner on 20th April 1981; it was my sixteenth birthday. He, Jeff Hunter, Jonathan Apsley, Miles Carver and myself met on Ham Hill at 11pm to enact the founding rite: the bonding of the four Elementals about the Node in the presence of the Convenor, himself also an Elemental. The rite was completed, and the power of the four Elementals energised by their linking with the Eternal Feminine. Thus was the first step taken towards the perfection of the Great Work begun by Aubrey Price before his death in 1918. Gwydion Turner was formally acknowledged as Convenor: Price's successor and reincarnation. Our circle was declared complete, all members vowing that they would not leave it, other than through transition from Minor to Major Adept, or through unexpected death.

Henceforth, we were to meet upon each solstice and equinox to re-enact the rite of the bonding of the Sun and the Earth, of the Masculine Principle and the Eternal Feminine, maintaining the flow of energy within the circle of the Order. Brean Down, Brent Knoll, Maesbury and Ham Hill – high places long ago held sacred – these were to be the theatres of our rite and our veneration.

The Convenor could ask the group to meet at other times he deemed either necessary or propitious, and it was his task to hold and further the secrets of the Order and its power. It was the duty of each member to support the Convenor, the three other Elementals providing money, and myself the congress with the Eternal Feminine necessary for his pursuit of the Great Work. This work and its tasks came to us from Price through his notebooks, and for the first two years, Gwydion was pleased with our progress. In late January 1984, he called a special meeting of the Order, and told us that he had made a discovery in Price's writings which led him to believe that they could go no further without obtaining something that had been interred with Price in his tomb. He did not say what it was, but he stated that it was essential that we break into the tomb to obtain it. This surprised the rest of us, and Jeff Hunter made it clear that he wished to have no involvement in the scheme. He was sternly reminded of his vows, and told that all members of the Order had to act as one under the direction of the Convenor; if they did not, all of their efforts would have been for nothing. With reluctance, he agreed to take part.

It was difficult to plan, so it wasn't until a night in late November that we crept into Arno's Vale Cemetery in Bristol under cover of darkness. Gwydion had already identified the site of Price's burial, so it was easy to find. Apsley and Carver set to with crowbars, and after much effort, prised away one of the slabs that made up its upper casing. Gwydion shone a torch inside, and drew out an ebony box which he did not open in our presence. This is what he had been looking for. He seemed pleased, but this satisfaction was not to last.

Early this year he stated that we had not taken everything that was needed during the first visit, and so a decision was taken to return to the cemetery. This time, he was accompanied only by Apsley and Carver. They got what they were after, but were almost caught as they fled from Arno's Vale carrying what they had sought in a sack. Shortly afterwards, Gwydion called Jeff and asked him to his flat, voicing his concerns that Jeff seemed to be waning in his dedication to the work of the Order, and noted that he and I had been growing too close. Such intimacy, he said, 'would threaten to unbalance the energy of the circle', so Jeff was warned that he should 'back off'. Gwydion left the room for some minutes, during which Jeff noticed the ebony box that he had seen taken from Price's tomb. It had been placed on its side in a bookcase. He opened it, and inside found three copies of a handwritten manuscript. He picked up one of them, and quickly scanned it. In this, he discovered that Price had written that for the Convenor to realise the Great Work, the three other Elementals and the Node must first transition from Minor to Major Adept, with the Convenor transitioning immediately after having taken final congress with the Node.

This was all he was able to read before Gwydion returned to the room, and snatched the papers back from him, stating that only the Convenor had the right to read what they contained. They came close to blows, and relations between the two of them grew worse still thereafter. At the spring equinox, Gwydion declared to the Order that Jeff must transition on Midsummer's Day, explaining to us that this was necessary because of his waning enthusiasm for the activities of the group. A replacement would be found as soon as practicable. Jeff looked worried, and later confided in me that he wished to leave, and that he had no intent to transition. I was therefore shocked to find that he was not with us when we met on the summer solstice. Gwydion announced that Jeff had made a successful transition that morning, and that his departure to the next plane was a cause for celebration. The work of the Order would thus stand in abeyance until a replacement Elemental could be identified and inaugurated.

Jeff's body was found by his landlord when he came to collect the rent at the beginning of July. It was hanging from the light flex in the lounge ceiling. His death was reported in the local papers as a suicide. It is my belief that he did not transition of his own free will, and that he did not die by his own hand.

Gwydion Turner recently announced that he had identified a possible replacement for Jeff, this being the son of the woman who oversees the Community Programme on which he is working. She had told him, unsuspectingly, of the young man's date of birth, so he engineered a meeting with him under the pretext of a 'date' with the woman – a Catherine Thornton who lives on Blackmore Heath. This went ahead, and I was entrusted with the task of seducing the young man in question: Hugh Thornton. I found myself unable to do this, upset as I was by the loss of Jeff, and my disillusionment with the activity of the Order.

Having laid out these facts before you, I wish to make it clear that I believe Gwydion Turner to be complicit in the death of Jeff Hunter, and suspect him of murder. Gwydion Turner can be found living at 7d Magdalene Court, Glastonbury.

Galpin, Chard and Reade

Hugh's hands were covered in a film of sweat that rendered the page damp and tacky to the touch. There was a distinct smell to it: slightly sweet, and stale. His digits were so moist that he felt he could almost taste the paper through their pores; the distinct flavour of wood pulp. Here and there he had smudged a word, the blue ink staining and marbling his fingers, lending them the appearance of having been worked upon by the most inexpert of tattooists. Sunlight flashed across the page, momentarily bleaching out the text. He glanced up and turned his head to stare through the grime of the window at the landscape around him, his thoughts paralysed by what he had read. The hills rose like giant molehills from the stillness of the Levels, their slopes bathed in the September sun, standing proud of the wisps of fog that dissolved in its strengthening rays, like ghosts that cannot survive the coming of day. His eyes closed, and he savoured the warmth upon his face as thoughts began to whirl and coalesce, returning him to the present and to the unsavoury implications of what he had just read. Could it really be true? Dawn had warned him that he would find it difficult to believe what she had written, and now he understood why. Was any of it true? Could it be that she was just a fantasist? A mentally unstable and impressionable young woman, whose word could not be taken at face value? Was he being excessively harsh on her, his judgement clouded by his impressions of Gwydion, and her association with him? If, on the other hand, what she had asserted were true, then it would be upon his head, upon his conscience, that responsibility for any ensuing harm to her would fall. He could not risk ignoring the content of her testimony, and its unpalatable implications.

It seemed a pity to spend such a fine autumn day in onerous and unbidden deliberations such as these. When Hugh had taken the decision to meet Dawn, he had not anticipated becoming entangled in anything of so serious and dark a nature, and had he had done so, he would have kept well away from her, and never responded to her invitation. Now though, it was too late; she had taken him into her confidence, and he held in his keeping a testimony which contained an allegation of murder. He would have to do something, but what? The idea of going straight to the police scared him, for surely they would dismiss such an outlandish story and the assertion that this exercise book, covered in childish zodiacal scrawls, constituted valid evidence in support of a murder allegation. They might as readily charge him for wasting police time as look into the matter. No. He couldn't just pitch up at a police station. He'd need help, but from whom? Only one name suggested itself: Dr Harris. Instead of going home, Hugh would leave the bus at Blackmore Cross and seek his help.

* * *

Walking into Dr Harris's driveway, Hugh noted a flash of red on one of the gateposts scraped from the car by his clumsy manoeuvring on the Monday night. His mother had not, as yet, noticed the damage, courtesy of the coating of cow muck acquired the following morning on the drive home, and should it stay dry, she wouldn't notice until he had gone back to university. Then again, it seemed that events might conspire to hinder his timely return to Bristol. *What was he thinking?* Here he was, fretting over scratched paintwork, when he was about to appeal to someone to look into an allegation of murder.

Lost in his thoughts, he paid little attention to where he was placing his feet, and thereby came to acquaint his left boot with a substantial deposit of badger scat, sweet and musky, that found secure lodging in its tread. He flushed with irritation and swore beneath his breath.

It was a little past eight as Denise, the doctor's wife, answered the door. The hour being relatively early, she assumed that it might be the postman, or the milkman, so was surprised to find an unkempt looking red-eyed student on her doorstep, his five o'clock shadow on the brink of maturing into a fully-fledged beard. She was a bright and spritely woman, always well turned out, albeit somewhat starchily, so regarded the spiky-haired young man with a little sniffiness, that was accentuated still further by the olfactory unpleasantness emanating from his boot which she mistook for body odour. Tramps were becoming younger these days, so it would seem. She hadn't met him when he had called earlier in the week, so didn't recognise him, and upon being told that he needed to speak to her husband urgently, she informed him that he had walked into the village for a copy of the *Telegraph*. Once he had explained who he was, her attitude softened a little, but as she was busy the young man could, if he wished, come back in half an hour or so and speak to Dr Harris then. He thanked her, and asked her to be sure to tell her husband that he had called.

Hugh wandered off to saunter about the village, pausing at the bridge to regard the water below. Luxuriant tendrils of lime green weed waved languidly in the flow of the river, the surface of its cool, clear waters sparkling with sunlit diamonds, disturbed by the nip of the occasional trout in pursuit of flies. His ears felt cleansed by its burbling song, and as he drank deep of the clean country air, he sensed all the more the contrast of this freshness with the staleness of his breath, unbrushed as his teeth had been since the preceding morning; he craved a drink, and to freshen up. First, however, he needed to remove the badger scat, a feat that he accomplished through the careful deployment of a twig to ease the excrement from his treads, some dock leaves, and a gentle rinsing of his sole in the river.

From there, he made his way to the churchyard, where he spent half an hour or so contemplating the worn inscriptions on the lichen-spattered tombstones, and reflecting upon what he was to say to Dr Harris. When the church clock struck the hour at nine, he gathered his thoughts and retraced his steps along the lane past cottages of rough-hewn stone and red-pantile roofs, their gardens alive with the busy buzzing of bees bumbling through their final work of the season. His earlier sense of unease lessened as he approached the doctor's house, confident as he was of receiving a sympathetic hearing, for he had been impressed by Dr Harris's character. He found Dr Harris seated on a deckchair, reading the *Telegraph* and enjoying the morning sunshine with a pot of tea. Hugh's return was announced by the scrunch of boots upon gravel, which prompted the doctor to look up from his paper. He folded it, and lay it on the grass, greeting the young man with a broad smile.

'Hugh! What brings you here this morning my boy? How is your mother? Is she quite recovered?'

'Good morning doctor. She's fine, thanks. Much better. She stayed at home on Tuesday, and as she was a bit wobbly on Wednesday, didn't go back to work until yesterday.'

'Good! Good! I'm glad to hear it.'

'But, to be honest, I'm not feeling too good myself today.'

'Really?'

'No. It's not anything physical though. I've come to ask for your help.'

'My *help*?'

'Yes, your help.'

Dr Harris peered at Hugh over the tops of his wire-rimmed glasses, before carefully removing and folding them. 'So, what is it that seems to be the problem?' he asked in a concerned tone.

'This,' he replied, proffering the exercise book to the retired GP. 'If you read the piece that starts on page eighteen, you'll understand what the problem is. I'm hoping that you can help me. It's not long.'

The doctor reached out his hand and looked at its tatty cover, his eyebrows raised disapprovingly at the symbols scrawled upon it.

'I take it from these drawings,' he said with a note of scorn as he pointed to a crudely executed depiction of a ram, 'that this is not yours, Hugh?'

'No doctor, it's not mine. It was given to me.'

'By whom? A *child*?'

'No. The title will tell you who gave it to me.'

'Hmm, I see. As you've not been very forthcoming Hugh, I suppose I had better read it. Judging from its cover, its contents would not ordinarily be the sort of thing that would hold any interest for me, but I'll read as you have asked. I'll not be giving up the *Telegraph* for this in future though.' He gave a wry smile, then put on his glasses and read, his eyes moving swiftly over the uncertain handwriting, whilst Hugh stood and looked about the garden, regarding the neatly trimmed lawn and hedges, his thoughts drifting back to the grubbiness of Dawn's flat, and to Dawn herself. His reverie was interrupted by Dr Harris.

'Hugh my dear boy, this is disturbing; very disturbing. I am glad that you brought this to me.'

'Thank you doctor.'

'Now, did I not warn you that you should keep a safe distance from Gwydion and his associates?'

'You did.'

'Still, what is done is done. If what is written here proves to be true, this is a serious matter; a very *serious* matter indeed.'

Hugh nodded. 'I know. That's why I came to you.'

'What is your opinion as to the veracity of what this young woman has written? Can she be held to be a reliable witness?'

Hugh paused, and then said 'I've no reason to believe that she's lying. She swore that what she had written was true. Although her way of thinking is odd, it seems to me that what she has written here is factual. I brought it to you because I thought that if I went straight to the police with this they wouldn't believe me. As you are familiar with Gwydion and his background, and your word is respected, I thought that they might take this allegation seriously if they heard this story from you, rather than from me.'

'I understand. I must thank you for having such confidence in me Hugh. Now, we must decide what to do. Before we go any further, do you think that anyone is imminently at risk from Gwydion? Did Dawn express any concern about anything that might be about to happen?'

'No. From what she's said and what she's written, I don't think that anyone's in any immediate danger. As for what to do, Dawn didn't even tell me to contact the police. She simply asked me to read this alone, and then do what I thought best, which is what I have done.'

'I see. Clearly, we cannot simply sit upon this matter. The police must ascertain whether or not there is any substance to this young woman's allegations, but as there is no prospect of any further crime being committed in the immediate future, I think it wise that you should take some tea and breakfast before we visit the station, if you've not already done so, that is. Have you eaten?'

'No.'

'Very well, in that case, I shall ask Denise to rustle up something for you. There's nothing like a hungry stomach to discompose one's thoughts, which really wouldn't do if we are to speak to the police.'

* * *

Once breakfast was finished, Dr Harris made a call to check that someone would be at the village police station, before he and Hugh took a brisk stroll to speak to Constable Galpin. The sceptical constable took some persuading that this was a credible allegation rather than an outlandish hoax, but Dr Harris's conviction prompted him to act. He called his colleagues at Glastonbury Police Station, and asked for two constables to be despatched to the dig just off of Withywell Drove with a view to taking Gwydion Turner in for questioning. Constables Chard and Reade found themselves charged with the task, but upon arriving at the dig they were informed by Catherine that Gwydion had not appeared at work that morning; neither had he been onsite the previous day. They thanked her, and set off for Gwydion's flat.

Chard parked the patrol car in Benedict Street, and the two policemen made their way to Magdalene Court. He was in one of his sardonic moods.

'Description: middle-aged man, slim build with long brown hair and beard, slightly greying. Mode of dress: hippy. Now, have you ever seen anyone looking like that round here Reade?'

'What, like him over there? Or him, just a bit further up the street opposite the Mitre?'

'Precisely. Not exactly very useful as far as a description goes now, is it? It's about as useful as looking for a lost cat, and being told that it has four legs, a head, and fur. Just as well we have the bugger's address, otherwise we'd be rounding up scores of these long-haired loons for questioning.'

'Can't we stop off for a pint. I'm gasping!'

'Tempting as it may be Reade, I must say no. I'm up for promotion shortly, so I don't want any blots against my name, and if we do step inside the Mitre this lunchtime you can be sure that Abraham Cooper will be blabbing about it all around town. He's got a looser tongue than Valerie Phelps, and she's got a mouth on her mind.'

'True enough. Maybe go for one later?'

'I wouldn't say no, but I b'aint be going in the Mitre. How about the George and Pilgrim's?'

'A good choice Constable Chard. A good choice.'

'Right, let's get this business out of the way then. The sooner we do it, the sooner we can have a pint.'

The two men approached Madgalene Court, a small block of flats, squat and grey, thrown up in the sixties like a misplaced and mistimed tribute to the Atlantic Wall. Chard pressed the bell to 7d. There was no answer.

'Well, he don't seem to be at home. May as well go then, eh?'

'Don't be stupid Reade. It's an allegation of murder we're dealing with here, not non-payment of a parking ticket.'

Reade grinned and Chard pressed the bell again. Nothing.

'Damn!'

Reade turned to see an elderly lady making her way towards the block.

'Here, this old dear might know something.'

'That she might. Let's see then.' Chard greeted her as she took out her keys.

'Good afternoon madam.'

'Good afternoon constable. What brings you here? No trouble I hope?'

'No, no, my love. We're just looking for a neighbour of yours. A Mr Gwydion Turner. Do you know him?'

She crinkled her nose in distaste. 'Yes. That I do constable, but not well. Why's that then? Has he been up to something?'

'What do you know about him?'

'Well, not much to tell the truth. He's a bit of an odd sort if you don't mind me saying. Comings and goings at strange times, and such like.'

'Really now?'

'Yes,' here she also looked at Reade, and bent her head forward so as to take the two men into her confidence, and in a whisper said, 'He has a young lady friend. Much too young to be with him. And strange men here too.'

'Strange men?'

'Yes. Like him. You know – hippy types. I don't know what they get up to, although I have my *suspicions*.' She nodded knowingly, a note of menace in her voice.

'Interesting madam. Very interesting, but before we go any further, would you mind giving us your name?' asked Chard.

'No, of course not constable: Paterson. Mrs Sylvia Paterson.'

'Do you live here with your husband Mrs Paterson?'

'No. He's dead, God rest his soul. Passed on three year back.'

'I'm sorry to hear that madam,' added Reade.

'That's all right young man. It's nice to be single again,' she said with a playful gleam in her eye.

'When did you last see Mr Turner, Mrs Paterson?' asked Chard.

'About ten minutes ago at the post office on the High Street. He had a bag of shopping with him, so I would have thought he'll be home soon. I'd make a good detective wouldn't I?' she smiled as she looked Constable Chard in the eye, to whom, it seemed, she had taken something of a shine.

Chard chuckled, before replying, 'Now, that you might Mrs Paterson, but please, don't let us detain you any longer, as I can see that you're in need of a cup of tea. Would you be able to let us into the foyer to wait for Mr Turner?'

'Of course constable!'

'Why thank you very much my dear.'

'Don't mention it. His flat's up the stairs, then first on the left.'

Mrs Paterson went into her flat leaving the two policemen to await Gwydion's return. It wasn't long until they heard a key rattle in the communal door. Reade lumbered to the top of the stairs. Gwydion looked up, his eyes hidden behind his aviator shades.

'Is that Mr Turner?' enquired Reade, calling down.

Gwydion started, dropped his shopping, slammed the door shut and locked it behind him before Reade could even get down the stairs.

'Bloody hell Reade! Why did you have to go and startle him you silly sod? Go and ask Mrs Paterson to unlock the door for us! Quick now!'

'All right, all right, keep your hair on.'

By the time that the two men had got out of the block, Gwydion was nowhere to be seen. They radioed an alert calling for backup, and within the hour, colleagues from Wells had joined them in their manhunt about Glastonbury. No sign, however, was to be found of Gwydion, who had last been sighted at 4.15pm in a call box. A decision was taken to search his flat, and by 8pm that evening, men were poring through his belongings searching for clues. In his wardrobe, they found a sack containing the disaggregated bones of a human skeleton, which they were later to identify as belonging to Aubrey Price. It was not until gone nine that evening that someone realised they had not yet questioned Dawn Willis. When a member of the team suggested that she could be at risk from Gwydion, officers were sent to her flat as soon as they could be mustered, but when they arrived, they found it locked. After forcing the door, it was discovered to be empty.

Carver's Farm

Miles Carver stood gazing out of his farmhouse window, telephone in hand, waiting for a reply. Dusk had fallen over the orchard, through which pipistrelles flitted from his crumbling barn, chasing midges and mosquitoes. 'Every living thing,' he reflected, 'seems to be chasing after some other living thing.' Unlike the bats, he was not in pursuit of winged insects this evening, but he had marked his quarry all the same.

'Come on, come on and answer why don't you.'

He was getting impatient, and was about to hang up when there was a voice at the other end of the line.

'Hello?'

'Hello Dawn. It's Miles here. How be on?'

There was a pause. 'Fine. Why are you calling?'

'Well, can't you guess?'

'No.'

'I've got something here I thought you might like to try, knowing how keen you are on it.'

'Really?'

'Yes.'

'What's that then?'

'You'll never believe it, but I just bumped into Steve Bishop today, fresh back from St Paul's with a load of gear to shift. I scored a quarter of pot. Only twenty quid. Thought you might like to come round for a smoke. What do you reckon? Are you up for it? I'll come out and drive you down if you like; you can stop over.'

Silence.

'You still there Dawn?'

'Yes.'

'Well, do you want to come down or not? I'm not interrupting anything am I?'

'No.'

'Well come on then, give me an answer girl!'
'Okay.'
'Right then, I'll see you in half an hour.'

He put down the receiver and grinned.

'Told you she'd come. She can't resist that stuff, even though it do muck her head up good and proper. So, are you going to get Jonathan over while I fetch her?'

'Yes, I shall call Apsley, and start the preparations in your absence. You were right with respect to Dawn. I'm impressed by your resourcefulness. I was concerned that she may have taken fright, and thus might not wish to venture abroad tonight, but your powers of persuasion have proven my apprehensions to be misplaced. Once we have convened, we shall put into action that which I have deferred for too long. Tonight will see the culmination of our Great Work.'

'It will be a glory to behold Gwydion. I thought that it would not be for many a year more until we saw this. It is a privilege to have been chosen. The girl will do our bidding; I'll make sure of it. Trust me. The portal will open. The power shall be ours.'

'It shall. Take care to avoid any police; take a detour, if necessary. Now, leave! I need to prepare.'

Carver fired up his rusty Escort and bumped off down the track. He had inherited the farm from his parents, but had failed to keep it in good order, keeping to a minimum what he spent on the upkeep of the buildings and livestock. What had been a perfectly good labourer's cottage had already lost its roof and become uninhabitable through neglect, but then again, it wasn't easy to rent out such properties down here in the moors, places with neither a bathroom nor an inside toilet. It struck many as strange that Carver, a farmer's son rooted in the soil of his family's county, should have fallen for some of the more way-out beliefs and practices of the New Agers who had flocked to nearby Glastonbury; a farmer's son ought to have more sense than to get mixed up in all of that, but get mixed up in it he had.

* * *

It was a little before a quarter to nine when Gwydion heard the scrunching of stones beneath the tyres of Carver's car as it entered the farmyard. Dawn was with him, as planned. She had been less conversational than usual during the drive back, and struck Carver as being agitated. Her eyes had roved restlessly about the car, and she kept teasing the cracked skin about her thumbnails, and plucking at her eyebrows. He had asked her whether anything was wrong, but she replied that there was nothing the matter. The dope, he said, would calm her, to which she had replied, 'Perhaps.'

The door snagged as it was pushed open to reveal an empty kitchen, the remains of Carver's lunch – a roast chicken – strewn about the table, bluebottles feasting upon the broken fragments of carcass. Daddy-long-legs danced their drunken way into the house, rushing in upon the air behind Carver as he ushered in his guest.

'What a stink! Don't you ever wash up?'

'I've not finished eating yet,' he replied. Wouldn't you fancy a bite?'

'Hardly.'

'Well, let's go into the lounge then.'

The two entered to find Gwydion and Apsley standing in silence with their eyes closed. Dawn gasped. Gwydion's eyes opened.

'Welcome, Dawn!'

'Gwydion! I didn't expect to . . .'

'You look startled Dawn. Why? Do you have something that you wish to tell me?

'I just, I just didn't expect you to be here.'

'No. I shouldn't imagine that you did. But here I am.'

'Yes.'

'It is a shame that you failed to entice the young Thornton to join us. Why could you not persuade him?'

Dawn remained silent.

'Your lack of a reply shows that the strength of the circle is waning Dawn. I cannot let it wane any further. It is my fault for not having found a replacement sooner, yet incomplete as the Order may be, Hunter's departure is not so distant as to have broken its resonance; his presence lingers still. Our situation is such that we must make an attempt at realising the Great Work tonight, inauspicious as the timing and circumstances may be. There will be no other opportunity, for those who would stop our activities are closing in. We will prepare for the rite as upon any of our quarter days, the difference being that we shall not enact it in some high place, but here in the orchard, amidst the ripened fruit. The harvest of our labours is at hand. As the new day breaks, the power shall be ours.'

The Call of Anubis

Sergeant Helm was not in the best of moods. Constables Chard and Reade had already bungled what should have been a straightforward operation, leading to a hurried and expensive deployment of police resources, but what compounded his sense of irritation was the fact that he was spending his Friday night overseeing the search of a stale-smelling flat, instead of attending his daughter's piano recital in Bath. As for his wife's opinion on the matter, he could make a reasonable conjecture as to what it might be.

'Constable Reade!'

'Yes, sergeant.'

'Take some care man; I asked you to search the place, not to wreck it.'

'Certainly sergeant. Right you are.'

Reade returned to rummaging through a chest of drawers. 'Jesus! This do reek to high heaven. It don't seem like he do wash his clothes much,' he reflected.

'Still no trace of anything out of the ordinary in his bookshelf, Constable Chard?' enquired Helm.

'No sir. Well, not unless you do count the subjects of the books themselves mind, for you could hardly call them "ordinary". Not much to my taste, I must say.'

'No, I shouldn't suppose that there is.'

'I mean, I do prefer—'

'Get on with your work constable. You can save your refined literary criticism for the pub.'

Chard looked somewhat crestfallen, his expectations regarding promotion now firmly on the ebb.

Helm's personal radio gave a hiss of static and crackled into life. His colleague's speech inaudible against the din of the search, he absented himself to the communal landing where he could hear and speak more clearly. It was Constable Lawson, radioing from Dawn's flat. He had some important news, which was not unexpected. Helm paused to compose himself, then returned to his team who were still busy poring through Gwydion's belongings. He called for silence.

'Gentlemen, I have an announcement to make. Apparently, Dawn Willis is not at home. This, naturally, as I am sure you will all be aware, constitutes a matter of some concern, for if Mr Turner has got wind that she has anything to do with our investigations, he may be tempted to act rashly. The young woman could be in significant danger. The problem is that we do not know where she currently is, nor who, if anyone, she is with.

Now, as Mr Turner has taken to his heels, it would not be unreasonable to assume that he may be seeking refuge with one of his confederates, the most likely being Jonathan Apsley, or Miles Carver. I would ask you all to redouble your efforts to locate the addresses of these two men. I want this place turned upside down, and no scrap of paper ignored. Search through his books, and empty any receptacle that may conceivably harbour an address book or diary. Time is of the essence gentlemen, lest we have a much more serious case on our hands. Thank you.'

Carpets were lifted, the chairs and the sofa probed, and the mattress turned over. Nothing. It was then, shortly before 10pm, that Constable Chard let out a triumphant cry, having found Gwydion's address book hidden inside a mauve jar of dried flowers. He opened it to find it filled with impenetrable crabbed handwriting, plainly intended for the writer's eyes alone. It was thus with some difficulty, and thanks to the aid of Constable Hooper who had an eye for untangling such things, that the addresses of Apsley and Carver were deciphered.

Apsley's house, it transpired, was also in Glastonbury, so Helm was in an instant back on the radio to redirect Constable Lawson's squad car to investigate. Nestling beneath the foot of the Tor, the address turned out to be a substantial Victorian residence of brick, its façade clad in a mature Virginia creeper picked out by the torches of the approaching officers. No chink of light could be discerned emanating from any of its windows, and upon trying it they found the front door to be securely fastened. With there being no reply to their knocking, the combined efforts of two men ensured their entry.

The only living being that they encountered proved to be a grey-blue Persian cat, that was set shrieking about the place by the intrusion of the law into its otherwise undisturbed abode. Apsley was, if one discounted a rather vulgar and prominently displayed fantastical sketch by

Félicien Rops, evidently a man of some wealth and taste, his home being filled with antiques, its walls adorned with watercolours and an early sixteenth-century Flemish tapestry depicting the Fall from Eden. There were also a number of photographs from the turn of the century, showing men and women attired in costumes inspired by Ancient Egypt. It was clear, however, that they did not depict some group of amateurs involved in a production of Aida. Their expressions and props suggested something of an altogether more earnest, and disturbing, nature. Lawson paused, and picked up a framed picture that stood next to them.

'Evidently taken more recently. Look – same costumes, but different people; in colour. Now, I wonder if one of them might be Apsley?'

His attention was now drawn to an ornate pair of candlesticks, their stems fashioned to depict nymphs and dryads, standing on the drawing room mantelpiece. His eyes lingered a short while, before turning to an array of bookshelves upon which stood an extensive collection of esoteric texts, both new and ancient, the latter rendered brittle by the passing of the centuries. Lawson radioed back to Sergeant Helm:

'No trace of anyone at Apsley's address sir, just a cat. There's nothing that would seem to directly incriminate him in any sort of illicit activity, although some of the artwork, particularly a large piece in the hallway, could be said to be pornographic. He is evidently a man with some money behind him, judging by the amount of paintings and antiques that fill the house.'

'Very good Lawson. Return to Turner's flat to await further instructions. We are approaching Carver's Farm, so you may have to wait some time. I'll radio later. Over.'

* * *

Whilst the police were immersed in searching his flat and regarding Apsley's artworks through eyes that could hardly be said to belong to appreciative connoisseurs, Gwydion had acted quickly to direct the remaining members of the Order in enacting their rite one last time. This occasion, however, was to be different, for it was the final chance that he would have to realise his ambitions. With Price's instructions firmly memorised, and the police sure to be closing in, there was a hurried air to proceedings, which if conducted faultlessly could be concluded, he reasoned, before the arrival of the forces of the law.

Dawn was led out to the orchard with a sullen resignation, so at variance with the attitude that she had hitherto displayed when she had freely given herself over to the rite. A fire was soon kindled in a gap left by the death of one of the trees, and once the flames had taken hold and the four had taken up their positions at the cardinal points, their faces illuminated by the orange glow, Gwydion uncrossed his arms and outstretched them in a cradling arc, his palms turned inwards to the blaze. His face grew stern, his features picked out by the deep shadows cast by the uneven light. He closed his eyes, drew in his breath, and bowed his head. There was a pause of some seconds. It was then that his lids reopened, and he spoke in a tone familiar to those gathered – loud, clear and sonorous:

'I, the murdered Osiris, made whole again by my wife and sister; I, the Convenor, the fourth Elemental and embodiment of the active principle, of the Dionysian, the Promethean, the re-embodied recreated Christ by the grace of Lucifer reborn, convene our circle this night in sacred rite. In this place, the undying spirit of heaven's ever-rekindled fire, by its jealous genius guarded, do call upon the unfleshed shade of Aubrey Price to join in congress, to complete our oneness with the Node, to re-establish harmony and order within the cosmos. By Thoth, by Ra and by Anubis, I command you manifest yourself and partake of the joys of Isis, of Sulis Minerva and of Venus, of each and every avatar, of the divine manifestation of the feminine principle. By Hecate's clear light, shall our true path be shown. By Ishtar's winged grace, I scatter this blood in the knowledge of life eternal in this fleshly realm.'

With a wooden ladle, he scooped a quantity of pig's blood from a bucket, and poured it over a stick around the end of which was bound a rag torn from the clothing of the hanged Elemental. With this, he daubed each of the three, repeating the formula, 'By the blood of the boar shall you know earthly strength.' He then returned to his place, fixed his gaze upon Dawn, and uttered the instruction with which she always complied: 'Upon this night, the Node, the Great Axle about which we and all living beings revolve, gives herself over, willingly, in pleasurable complaisance, to the renewal of our Order, and of the greater order beyond. This is our will.'

The ritual proceeded, and that which was commanded, was done.

* * *

It was just after 11pm that the two cars arrived at the farm, the first containing an impatient Sergeant Helm along with Constables Chard, Reade and Hooper, the other two further officers and an Alsatian with its handler. They were surprised to find that no lights shone from any of its windows, and that it appeared to be deserted. What was equally unexpected was that when they tried the door they found it to be unlocked. Upon entering and turning on the light, an ill-tempered fury of flies had flung themselves angrily about the kitchen, their plump bodies glistening and gorged on chicken fat. The men had then thundered through the remaining rooms, desperate to locate Gwydion and his associates, but they found no one.

'We'd best break into two parties and search the adjoining outbuildings,' commented Helm.

''Scuse me for interrupting, sir.'

'What is it Hooper?'

'There appears to be a glow coming from behind the barn over there. Look – sparks!' he said, pointing.

'Well I'm damned! Right, scrap what I've said. Reade, Chard and Hooper – come with me. Nicholson, Ellis and Pierce, you take the dog and scout around the far side of the building. We'll take the other. Let's get to it!'

They spilled out of the house beneath the light of the waxing Moon, fanning out into two lines as they entered the orchard behind the decaying barn. It was then that they caught sight of the bonfire and its votaries, standing around it in ritual formation, picked out in relief by the light of the flames. The Alsatian got a sniff of them, started to tug, winding itself into a frenzy of snarling and barking, gobbets of slaver flying from its unmuzzled jaws as it strained at its leash.

'The call of Anubis!' exclaimed Gwydion, still lost in his ecstatic state.

'No, Gwydion! Wake up!' yelled Carver. 'It's the police!'

The latter took to his heels and fled, relying upon his knowledge of the orchard's layout to keep his footing in the unlit obscurity beyond the reach of the firelight. The police called out for him to stop, but their order being unheeded, they unleashed Sasha, who baying with a vicious enthusiasm, hurtled off to hunt down his quarry. The farmer, however, lacked the fleetness of a hare, and thus his attempt to outrun the Alsatian, whose speed was more than a match for the best of runners, was but an act of doomed and instinctive folly born of fearful desperation. The dog was soon upon him. He shrieked as it brought him to earth by his left hand, drawing blood and tearing his tendons into a ragged mess.

Apsley too had dashed into the darkness, but failing to see a low-hanging bough struck his head upon it, causing him to crumple to the ground, pummelled by a shower of ripened fruit. Subsequent revelations as to the workings of the physical world were not, on this occasion, to be forthcoming.

Gwydion's composure cracked. He launched himself in pursuit of Carver, stumbling blindly into the night, his long robes flapping and hindering his stride. The dog rushed past him, but his relief was to be short-lived, for he was soon upon the limits of the orchard, which he discovered were marked by a ditch, into which he tripped and plunged with an unanticipated celerity. He let out a scream as he fell headfirst into the peaty blackness, through the weed and the slime into the silty still domain of the chub, the perch and the pike, his thoughts as sinuous as an eel, struggling in this Stygian stream, this barrier between the worlds of the living and the dead. His mouth gaped to admit the stinking, foetid and muddied fluid, his lungs aburst with a chilled and filthy pain, as his jaw struck the bottom, showering a gritty suspension into the water that lodged in his open yet unseeing eyes. No ferryman to save him; no welcome at the other side; no flash of recollection; no lingering reflections over what had been, only the end: transition.

Dawn, the Node, the Great Axle, around which the cosmic order revolved, stood amidst the chaos, dazed by the scene that was unfolding about her. Her slender frame atremble from fright and the cold, she did not speak as Sergeant Helm placed his jacket around her shoulders, offered some words of comfort, and led her back to the warmth of the house, whilst Carver and Apsley were administered first aid before being taken in for questioning. The two officers who had run off to retrieve Gwydion were to find themselves thwarted in their efforts. To their great puzzlement, they were unable to find him amidst the bent and broken bulrushes that pierced the meniscus of the stagnant waters. They could see clearly enough where he had entered the rhyne, but there was no indication as to where he may have climbed out. They urged the dog to follow his scent, but the creature would not budge, and just stood there, staring at the black surface, whimpering.

'Can't think where the bugger could have got to. I heard him fall in, clear enough, but I didn't hear no swimming,' commented Ellis.

'Me neither. Strange,' replied Pierce.

'You can say that again. S'pose we ought to try setting Sasha loose in the neighbouring fields, as he might have crawled out into one of them.'

'May as well give it a try. We'll not do much good standing here now, will we?'

They searched for the next hour or so, but finding nothing, returned to the farm and wrapped up operations until the next morning. A police diving team was called in to trawl the ditch, its members bobbing around like disorientated seals, their heads peeking into the early mist, but nothing was found amidst the ooze other than some old hubcaps, as well as the well-rotted remains of a mink. Of Gwydion Turner there was no trace. He had dissolved into the tenebrous murk of the rhyne.

Coda: Arno's Vale

Trials are tedious, and it would be an ordeal to pick through the minutiae of what occurred at the trial of Apsley, Carver and Willis, which took place early the following year. The judge's summing up will thus have to suffice in providing an overview of what occurred, but before turning to his words, it is worth further considering the fate of Gwydion Turner.

The police had intended, quite naturally, for him to have stood in the dock alongside the three other surviving members of the Order, but this intention was not to be realised, for despite extensive efforts to locate and apprehend him, the elusive magus seemed to have disappeared without trace. There were a number of theories as to what had happened to him, one of the most favoured being that he had somehow managed to swim some distance out into one of the larger drainage channels, and had subsequently drowned. It was then supposed that his body had either sunk and been absorbed into the mud, or had eventually been discharged into the Bristol Channel, where borne upon the tides it was swept far out to sea. The three remaining members of the Order, however, held to a rather less orthodox explanation, the details of which they did not care to volunteer to their questioners. After all, they had followed Gwydion's instructions which they were told, and believed, marked the culmination of his 'Great Work'. His physical disappearance seemed only to bolster them in their belief that he had been successful.

Such esoteric matters were, however, beyond the consideration of the court, which limited itself to the examination of evidence of a more prosaic and tangible nature. The judge thus summed up as follows:

'In the light of the evidence placed before this court and jury, the time has come to pass sentence upon the three accused. It must be said that this case is most peculiar, the like of which I have not had the displeasure to have presided over hitherto. Given that the primary defendant, the instigator of the deeds here considered, still remains without the reach of the law, the verdict can be nothing other than imperfect, and the truth of the matter surrounding the death of Jeff Hunter cannot, as yet, be satisfactorily ascertained.

'With respect to Miss Dawn Willis, and her role in these affairs, it is thanks to her that this trial took place. Without her testimony, no action would have been taken, and the crimes that we here in this court have considered would have gone both unexamined, and unpunished. Since the time of her arrest, she has shown herself to be a willing and helpful witness, and it is for this reason, that she will receive a non-custodial sentence for her involvement in one instance of grave robbery, and her initial failure to report a second. The court therefore imposes a fine of £50 upon the defendant.

'Turning to the two other defendants, both Jonathan Apsley and Miles Carver are found guilty of two counts of grave robbery, in which they were willing and eager participants. The law does not look kindly upon the despoliation of the resting places of the dead, and thus demands that such a lack of respect should be punished with an appropriate degree of severity. For this reason, each of the two aforenamed defendants will receive a custodial sentence of eighteen months. As for the charge of aiding and abetting the suicide of Jeff Hunter, the jury was unable to find conclusive evidence with respect to their involvement, and thus returns an open verdict on the said Hunter's death.'

* * *

Here came to an end the experiment to realise Aubrey Price's vision in a revived Hermetic Order of the Golden Dawn. Of its three members who stood before a jury in early 1986, the following can be said. Subsequent to his release from prison, Miles Carver fell into heavier drug use, sold the family farm, and by the early nineties had become destitute. He was reduced to begging on the streets of Glastonbury, and was found dead in his bedsit in August 1993, having apparently overdosed on heroin. Jonathan Apsley returned, with some success, to art dealing and portfolio investment. He cut all ties with Carver, whom he had never viewed as his social equal, and henceforth held himself aloof from the Glastonbury alternative scene, although rumours circulated regarding his ongoing esoteric activities involving visitors from London. To all intents and purposes, he remained on the right side of the law. As to what happened to Dawn Willis, little is known other than that she returned to live with her parents in Wells for a time, and then left to set up home on her own.

As for the mortal remains of Aubrey Price, these were placed in the care of his closest living relation – his great grandniece Amelia – upon whose decision their reinterment took place at a private ceremony in Arno's Vale Cemetery in February 1986. This second 'funeral' was a quiet affair, lacking the emotional charge normally attendant upon such occasions, for the deceased was unknown to those few distant relatives who cared to play the part of mourners.

Upon the resealing of the tomb, a few flakes of snow drifted upon the air, and alighted upon the heads of a small group of people who held themselves at a distance, surveying the scene with an unsmiling regard. One of them caught Amelia's eye, and held it for a time. There was no warmth; no acknowledgement, just an intense gaze that seemed to signify that he felt an integral bond with Price, and that he belonged to them, rather than to the family enacting their sham ritual of mourning. It was a puzzle for Amelia as to who these individuals were, or how they had found out that the ceremony was taking place, for there had been no publicity. Not only was their presence unexplained, but it was also unwelcome. Moreover, although they appeared youthful, there was something distinctly old fashioned about their dress and their deportment; they spoke little, and then only amongst themselves.

As the party walked away from the tomb, Amelia glanced in the direction of the huddle of strangers, once more arresting the attention of the young man whom had stared at her so intensely. His mouth creased into a wry smile, and she could not help but look at him again, as something stirred in her memory, something unsettling. The cast of his facial features was somehow familiar, yet it did not put her in mind of anyone that she knew. She must, she reasoned, have seen his likeness in a photograph, although she was possessed of the conviction that the face she had in mind was considerably older.

'Are you all right, Amelia?' asked her husband, placing his hand upon her arm, thinking that the emotional strain was beginning to tell.

'Yes, I'm fine. Let's go. I'm chilled to the bone,' she replied, whilst casting one final glance over her shoulder, only to catch a knowing look in the young man's eyes. He removed his hat, and with a melodramatic flourish made an exaggerated bow, before straightening himself up to bid her farewell with, at last, a smile; as sardonic a smile as she had ever seen. As the mourners left, he, and his companions, closed in upon the tomb.

Agnes of Grimstone Peverell

The Critic Awakes

Jack Frost has done his work, etching upon the glass his coruscating signature – a creation of the most intricate delicacy, its unique fronds and fractals of crystal waiting for the weak light of the solstice sun to bring forth its glint, to celebrate its fleeting life; in its beholding, we capture its transience, and with that, our own. No critic's eye could look upon it unmoved; no human hand could match its peerless craft, for not even the genius of the finest artisan, made manifest in glass stained incarnadine or lapis blue, might match the luminosity of frost's window work. Yet for now, all this goes unseen; the curtains are drawn, and dawn is yet to break.

* * *

Lionel Smallwood awoke to the sound of a ringing in his ears and an itch in his left auditory canal that begged to be scratched; it was not the start to the day that he had wished for, but then again, it seldom was. Contrary to a lifetime's advice, as well as to all known rules of etiquette, he inserted the little finger of his right hand into the offending passage in an effort to ease his discomfort. He sensed the yielding of the hairs that had sprouted unbidden from his auricular orifice at some indeterminate point in early middle age as the tip of his finger eased past them in its ingress towards the rich and flaking waxy deposits that lined its sides. A quantity embedded itself beneath his fingernail, whilst the rest retreated further into the warm darkness of his head, adding yet more bulk to the compacted mass that pressed upon his tympanum. The ringing intensified, as did his annoyance, both physical and mental; the hearing in his left ear was now all but extinguished, the sounds of the outside world transformed into a muffled indistinctness.

His wife, Frances, slumbered on oblivious to her husband's cares and ineffectual efforts to alleviate his predicament. Although still dark, he sensed that the time to rise was not far off; there would be no need for an alarm today, awake as he was, with a pronounced ringing in his ears that could neither be turned on, nor switched off. He might as well, he reasoned, take advantage of his wife's unconsciousness and treat himself to an Irish coffee, which he did, whilst he fired up the laptop – *just in case*. It was just as well that he did, although it cannot be said that he was pleased that he had. As he squinted at the glare emanating from the screen through the greasy smudged lenses of his half-moon glasses, his eyes watered in an effort to wash away the soreness, but the irritation remained, soon to be supplanted by an irritation of an altogether different nature.

Frances stirred, rolled into the hollow left by Lionel's now absent form, and let out a groan. There was no particular reason for the issuance of this sound, which made it seem as if she was undergoing some minor agony; it was simply the noise that accompanied her reacquainting herself with consciousness, signifying no more than 'I'm awake Lionel.' He though, interpreted its meaning as 'drink up quickly Lionel, before I catch you.' He darted a furtive glance at the moving surface of the duvet that betrayed the stirring of his wife beneath, and gulped down the last of his coffee. Frances prised her lids apart, her lashes snagging together like the teeth of a Venus flytrap, sticky with last night's forgotten mascara. She smudged a finger over them, releasing them from their half-opened state, and peered into the wan blue glow issuing from the computer screen, that cast chill shadows upon the walls of her sister's guestroom. Lionel's nose appeared in prominent, crooked silhouette; alert, and hawk-like.

'What are you doing?'

'Checking my emails.'

'Emails? At this time? We're on holiday for heaven's sake.'

'*Were* on holiday you mean: we're going to have to cut things short.'

'What? Why?'

'Work.'

'How can that be? It's only four days until Christmas, and you've nothing lined up until after New Year.'

'I know, but try telling that to my old *friend*, redbrick Radley.'

'Radley? Claire Radley?'

'Why yes, of course – what other Radleys do I know?'

'You could have a whole raft of Radleys secreted away in that address book of yours for all I know, but as for Claire Radley, what is this thing you have about her? You really don't like her, do you?'

'What's there to like about the woman? She's out of her depth, and she knows it, even if it is only on a subconscious level.'

'Aren't you being just a little harsh on her for having gone to a redbrick? Which one was it, by the way? You've never said.'

'"Harsh"? Not really. She's a bloody irritant; a loudmouthed and opinionated irritant. Now, as for which redbrick she went to, what does it matter whether she studied at Leeds, Liverpool or some other grimy post-industrial second-rate institution? She couldn't even get into Durham for heaven's sake.'

'But aren't you forgetting something?'

'Me? Forget something? I wouldn't have thought so.'

'Our daughter – she didn't get into Oxbridge either.'

'Well, that's an altogether different kettle of fish; she went to the Courtauld.'

'And how does that differ from going to a *redbrick*?'

'Obvious, isn't it?'

'Is it?'

'Well, of course it is woman! The Courtauld may not be a college either of our alma mater or of Oxford, but it is widely reputed to be amongst the finest institutions in the world when it comes to the study of the history of art.'

'There's no need to get so aggressive Lionel, especially at this hour. You know what the doctor has advised with respect to your blood pressure: you need to *keep it down*, at all costs. You getting yourself into a state over this non-issue of where Claire Radley studied is not going to help things, and neither, judging by the aroma of whisky that I can detect, is an Irish coffee.'

'Damn it Frances, I'd swear upon my life that you were half bloodhound unless I knew otherwise.'

'Well, I wonder what other *compliments* you may pay me today. Being a critic, a renowned wordsmith, I would expect a greater linguistic repertoire on your part. Where's the poetry, Lionel? Have you forgotten how to weave the language of love?'

'You're starting to sound like a Mills and Boon novel Frances.'

'So, you've read one of them, have you?'

'Don't be ridiculous; of course I haven't.'

'Then how do you know that I'm starting to sound like one?'

'One need look no further than the blurb of such creations as to be fully conversant with the nature of their content.'

'Do you treat all of your critical assignments with such a cavalier disregard for the content of works that it's your job to review?'

Lionel scowled.

'I'm only teasing, darling,' she continued. 'Of course, they're no better, nor worse, than any of the grand opus produced by the late Barbara Cartland, and neither of us did care for what she wrote.'

'The late, great Barbara Cartland: the only individual to have provided plausible evidence for the existence of automatic writing, judging by the utter absence of thought which went into any of her novels. Still, it's a relief to hear that you've not fallen into reading such pulp; you had me worried for a moment. Now, I'm afraid that I have a rather delicate favour to beg of you.'

'A "delicate favour"? Really Lionel, one moment you're chastising me for coming over all Mills and Boon, and then you start using phraseology befitting the chaste heroine of some long-forgotten Edwardian novel. Anyway, what is it – this "delicate favour" that you would wish to ask of me?'

'Hmm, perhaps I was being a little flowery, but that doesn't alter the nature of the task that needs to be done: I would be much obliged if you were tell Monica that we'll be leaving today. As she already has arrangements for this morning, we'll be venturing into Grimstone Peverell without her.'

'*I'll* have to? But, why not you?'

'You're her sister; she'll take it better from you.'

She paused, and gave him a knowing look, then with reluctance conceded: 'Very well then – I'll tell her.'

'Good woman!'

'But why do we have to leave Lionel? That, my dear husband, you have yet to explain.'

'Oh yes – so I have; quite remiss of me. The long and the short of it is that Radley wants me to review a new production that's being premiered this Thursday evening.'

'A production premiering two days before Christmas? You seem an odd choice to review a panto, if you don't mind me saying.'

'It's not a panto my dear. Far from it in fact. Now, as you are well aware I would normally quail at the prospect of enduring such a tasteless and plebeian entertainment as pantomime, but on this one occasion, I rather wish that it were.'

'Why, for heaven's sake? I've not noticed you take any recent interest in the acting abilities of the soap opera set?'

Lionel vented a snort of which a warthog would exhibit considerable pride, his glasses momentarily lifting from the bridge of his nose, as his head made an involuntary jerk upwards.

'Soap stars? Pah! The dregs of the acting profession, which by reason of their mass appeal, rise to the very top – like scum.'

'Good God, Lionel! If this production you have been tasked with reviewing is even worse than some celebrity-larded pantomime, the mind fair boggles as to what manner of ordeal Claire Radley has managed to devise for you.'

'In the normal course of affairs she would never have assigned me this task, being as aware as anybody of the vehement antipathy that I possess towards the avant-garde drivel of which she is such a vocal proponent. Yet, thanks to her young darling, that lover of anything and everything that is "transgressive" and un-English – Jonathan Howlett – crying off, ostensibly upon the pretext of some malady that the layabout has lately picked up, the honour has fallen to *me*.'

'Sometimes, Lionel, you manage to speak a great deal whilst actually saying rather little; what is it that she has asked you to review?'

'*The Scurrillion* by Rosie Clemens; the venue – the Hoxton Observatory. Have you heard of this Clemens woman?'

'Should I have?'

'Hmm, no; I don't suppose that you should have. Now, let me fill you in: thirty-five years of age, performance artiste, peace protestor and environmental activist; a writer of blank verse that elicits equally blank emotions in the minds of reader and listener alike. Born and bred in rural Devon, her mother, now in her late sixties, lives but a stone's throw from here in Cerne Abbas, and has been a lifelong do-gooder and busybody of the most interfering and irritating sort. Get the picture?'

'I rather think that I do.'

'And thus, my dear, you will not be surprised to learn that *Ms* Rosie Clemens relishes wallowing in the cesspit that is the fundamentally alien cultural milieu of contemporary urban England. Not only does she wallow in it, but she also "celebrates" it. As for *The Scurrillion*, it is an avant-garde piece set in 2309, in which a scientific séance led by Joanna Dee, a genetic alchemical magus, calls to account the spirits of dead politicians resurrected in their full physicality through the use of preserved DNA samples. They are then cross-examined by members of the audience, who are invited to question them for their actual, and alleged, crimes. Its focus is upon the Iraq War and climate change. At the end of the performance, the audience will be invited to pass and enact judgement.'

'And that's the sort of thing that *The London Courier* wishes to promote these days, is it?'

'It is. Such a far cry from when I started out with them. Can you remember when that was?'

'I was expecting Ruth at the time, I seem to recall.'

'You were, and had that bloody inexplicable craving for Vesta Curry.'

'Yes, that was *odd*. So, that would make it some 33 years or so since you became the much-fêted young reviewer acquired by *The Courier*? How times have changed.'

'That's right: 33 years in all. It was Teddy Beaumont who took me under his wing; one bottle of port too many, poor chap. He'd weep if he saw what *The Courier* had become today.'

'From what you've said about him over the years, I don't doubt it; you always were close. You never much took to his successor, let alone to Radley. Still, it's no use harbouring regrets regarding Beaumont luring you away from *The Telegraph*.'

'No. No use – no use at all. Do you remember what my first assignment was for *The Courier*?'

'My recollection is, unsurprisingly, a little dusty, but, oh - hang on! Was it Michael Frayn's *Donkey's Years*?'

'It was! It seems that the dust lies not too thick upon your memory my dear; it was a masterful piece of farce. Dear old Penny Keith's performance was a joy to behold; she, quite deservedly, won the Olivier Award for the Best Comedy Performance that year. It was such a privilege to be a guest at the cast's celebration dinner, and such a relief to get away from those blasted Vesta curries of yours.'

'You never did stop complaining about them.'

'Would there be any reason not to? Haute cuisine they most certainly were not; they even failed to rival your shepherd's pie, which in itself always was insipid at best.'

'I'd agree that those curries were not devised with the delicacies of the gourmet palate in mind, but I don't seem to recall you complaining about my shepherd's pie at the time.'

'I didn't want to dissuade you from the joys of culinary experimentation, and neither did I wish to incur your disapproval, my sweet.'

'Has it ever struck you Lionel that we're rather like a Chinese meal?'

'"A Chinese meal"? What in God's name do you mean woman?'

'Sweet and *sour*.'

'Very droll my dear, but I would venture to say that even the sweet may be sour on occasion.'

'A natural transformation in response to provocation, wouldn't you say? Then again, I think that it might be more accurate in such circumstances to describe our pairing as sour and sour, although, admittedly, it doesn't quite sound right.'

'Agreed. Not right at all; just like your shepherd's pie and Radley's taste for avant-garde *vibrancy*.'

'"Vibrancy" – the very word makes me shudder.'

'That makes two of us, and doubtless a few million more.'

'Have you replied to her yet?'

'No. I'll fire off a quick email just to let her know that I'll be covering the play as requested. I may drop into the office first thing on Wednesday.'

'It's a shame that we have to dash off. Monica was so keen to show us around the Christmas market and the Minster.'

'Well, all I ask is that you break it to her gently; I don't want to be on the receiving end of that temper of hers. Tell her we'll be back to visit at Easter.'

Welcome to Grimstone Peverell

Monica fell into a sulk upon being informed that Frances and Lionel were to cut their visit short. She thought being called back to London to review a new piece at the Hoxton Observatory rather a poor excuse, and asked whether not Lionel might be willing to leave on his own, and return to collect Frances on Christmas Eve. His answer that such a suggestion would be 'far from convenient, to put it mildly,' failed to endear him to his sister-in-law, not that there was much scope for him endearing himself to her anyway.

The electric gates slowly opened onto the lane leading to the main road into Grimstone Peverell; it was iced over and lined with a light covering of snow, the thoroughfare being of insufficient consequence to merit the attentions of a gritter, even if it had been wide enough to accommodate the passage of such a vehicle, which it was not. It was on occasions such as this that the couple felt smugly justified in having purchased themselves a Range Rover, despite its limited utility in negotiating the streets of Kensington. A quarter of an hour later they found themselves in the town centre car park, witnesses to the damage unleashed by a bald-tired rust bucket which skidded into the stationary car behind, before swerving its way past a panicked family of onlookers weighed down with bags filled with Christmas gifts.

'Stupid bastard! Watch where you're fucking going!' yelled an obese woman swaddled Michelin-like in layers of padded clothing, as she jerked her glowering young daughter into her side out of harm's way. The child emitted a pained howl, and burst into tears.

'Be quiet! I'll not be having none of that grizzling girl.' She paused from her shouting to take a puff on her fag, a rough stub now nearly burnt down to the filter, 'And look where you're bloody well going while you're at it! What do you think your eyes are for, eh?'

'Do what yer mum tells ya!' added an angry looking dad, as broad and red faced, but not as jolly, as Father Christmas.

'Pick your feet up! Go on! Now, don't you go looking at me like that, or you'll get a slap!' continued the mother. The yowling rage of an underclass mother in full spate penetrated and shattered the cosy ambience of the Range Rover, forcing its way into Lionel's good ear, as he brought the car to a halt in an available bay.

'I see that someone's full of festive spirit,' commented the critic dryly.

'Whisky or gin?' added his wife.

'"Whisky or gin?" Pah! Own-brand value vodka, or super-strength lager no doubt.'

'Welcome to Grimstone Peverell, husband.'

'Indeed. Not quite as I'd imagined it from your sister's descriptions, admittedly.'

'You'll find the architecture quite charming, if not the people.'

'Well, that's some compensation, but I'd not expected to see examples of *that type* here. They seem to be out of their natural habitat.'

'That being?'

'Out-of-town shopping centres; those places where they only have to haul their lazy backsides the short distance from the car to the mall, where their sweating bulks are transported around by escalators and moving pavements.'

'Their physiques would seem to suggest that they would find such an environment perfectly convivial.'

'It would also be highly convivial to me if they were to be in such a place, rather than *here*. I'm sure that they would much prefer the opportunity to indulge their taste for "retail therapy", fuelled by credit card debt, all under one roof, rather than outdoors exposed to the elements. History and architecture are wasted on them.'

'Well, I'm afraid that Grimstone Peverell isn't big enough for a retail park, so, my dear, sensitive husband, the hoi polloi have nowhere else to shop but the town centre, unless, that is, they wish to venture further afield to Dorchester or Weymouth.'

'Hmm. That must be very upsetting for them: no opportunity to drive into some fast-food "restaurant" where they can shovel the deep-fried contents of a cardboard box down their gullets, the food itself, of course, tasting no better than the box in which it is served, and probably less nutritious.'

'Talking of which, did you remember to book a table at the Hind Spared?'

'I did. We're booked in for 12:30,' Lionel's eyes twinkled with anticipatory delight, 'and I must say that I'm most looking forward to it. One thing I have to hand to your sister is that she has an unrivalled capacity for ferreting out a good restaurant.'

Frances gave her husband a withering look: 'Monica would doubtless be delighted to learn that her brother-in-law views her in the same light as a *ferret.*'

'Well, she's got a good nose on her, and she'd never dream of recommending a vegetarian establishment to anyone. Besides, being compared to a ferret is a step up from being compared to a weasel, isn't it?'

'They're both snappy and difficult to handle, although ferrets are larger.'

'That's what made me think of Monica; she's a robust old girl, isn't she? Not a bit like a pretty slip of a weasel; too blunt and lacking in cunning.'

'If I were you Lionel, I'd stop right there, as you really aren't redeeming yourself through employing this analogy. It makes me wonder what you compare me to when I'm not around.'

'Hmm, I'd say that you're more of a stoat: elegant and athletic, but with a bit of a bite.'

'Lionel!'

'Sorry dear.'

'Are we going to sit here wittering all day, or are we going to get out and take a look at the town?'

'We're going to appreciate Grimstone Peverell in its full glory my dear, whatever that may prove to be.'

'Well, if you wouldn't mind opening the door?' she said with some impatience.

Lionel gave her a stare which expressed a weary acknowledgement of his customary duty, which had somehow arisen without it ever having been explicitly stipulated, or agreed. Thus it was that Frances sat in near regal posture, awaiting the opening of the door, her faithful servant being there to offer his hand to steady her as she gingerly stepped down onto the icy tarmac below.

'Hold steady now!'

'They should have put down more grit.'

'They've probably run out. After all, when can you last remember weather like this, excepting our winter trips to Austria?'

'It must have been back in '96.'

'Precisely. You know what councils are like for economising, and I can't say that I blame them.'

To Square and Minster

The town square was bustling with market traders, almost all of whom were attired in period costume that possessed a certain degree of authenticity, although all looked cleaner, and smelt far sweeter, than would have been the case a century-and-a-half earlier. Another break with the past could be detected in the fact that none of them bore the bow-legged stamp of rickets, nor the pockmarked complexion gifted by smallpox, and the sound of consumptive coughing was notable by its absence. An atmosphere of joviality reigned, a Dickensian scene of Pickwickian goodwill purged of all trace of nineteenth-century misery, with the smell of roasting chestnuts and freshly-baked pies providing an olfactory link between the past and the present. Motorised traffic had been banished, whereas its equine predecessor had long since ceased to trot and clatter through the square, leaving the air free of both the sickly stench of diesel, and the pungent whiff of freshly deposited manure. The shoppers therefore needed not to look too carefully at where they stepped, the cobbles being clean, but for the occasional discarded cigarette butt, or gobbet of gum.

Stallholders smiled at their prospective customers, bidding them pause to try, or purchase, their wares: confectionary, mulled wine and cider, cheese, bread and cakes of many varieties, and cured meats. Others sold the usual knick-knacks attendant upon such occasions, as well as clothing and second-hand books, but it was the smell of coffee that caused the Smallwoods to halt and seek the restorative warmth of a hot drink. Lionel stared first at the mobile coffee van, adorned anachronistically with Victorian-style lettering, and then at the young man sporting mutton chop whiskers that appeared to have been sprouted especially for the occasion: 'Hampton's Hand Ground

Coffee', declared the sign with proprietorial pride. 'Artisan coffee?' he thought to himself, 'What is *artisan coffee*, other than an overpriced, overhyped concoction derived from a bitter brown bean, ground up and served by an underemployed graduate?'

'Americano? Cappuccino? Latte macchiato? Espresso?' enquired the coffee grinder.

'An espresso please.'

'Sumatran, Columbian, Guatemalan, Cuban or Ethiopian?'

'I don't mind; any one of them will do.'

'In that case, I'll give you a shot of the Ethiopian. It's something special,' grinned the young man, 'Would you like a sprinkle of cinnamon with it?'

'No.'

'Nutmeg?'

'No. The espresso as it comes will be just fine.'

'Right you are squire. Anything for your good lady?'

'She doesn't drink coffee, no matter how it's tarted up. You don't happen to serve tea, do you?'

'Tea? No,' he said, a note of pronounced disdain evident in his voice, 'I don't find that there's much call for it.'

'A pity. Never mind.'

Lionel handed over his money, took the steaming paper cup from beneath the dismissive gaze of the entrepreneurial hipster, and then directed a slightly embarrassed grin at Frances, before the two of them wandered off to explore the market.

'He seemed like a pleasant enough young man, but his attitude when you enquired as to whether he sold tea rather spoilt things,' remarked Frances.

'Yes, my dear. It would seem to be characteristic of a lately emerged tendency amongst young coffee drinkers to look down their noses at those of us who drink tea; a certain snobbery has sprung up amongst them.'

'A quite unfounded one, and one to which, for a change, you are not party.'

'Of course! It is, I fear, but illustrative of the coarseness of the youthful palate when it comes to appreciating the delicacy of a Rose Pouchong or Darjeeling, the smoky savour of Lapsang Souchong, or the robust richness of an Assam.' He here paused to sip his coffee. 'It also strikes me as likely that these young pups are transfixed by the paraphernalia and gadgetry associated with coffee making, which is absent from the brewing of tea, and, moreover, I'll warrant that tea is perceived to be a rather more insular drink than coffee; an outmoded signifier of Englishness, rather than of continental cosmopolitanism.'

'I suspect that what you say on the subject – which is a considerable amount – has much to commend it, and given the nature and content of your observation, I can see why Radley has accused you of trying to "out-Sewell Sewell".'

'Sewell? Humph! He has his moments of insight, perhaps, but Radley was somewhat overstepping the mark by making such a patently absurd comparison, plainly with the intention of riling me.'

'Which she appears to have succeeded in doing, but let's put that aside, as the combination of you ruminating over your professional rivalry with Sewell and Claire Radley's put downs will do little, along with that espresso, to alleviate your blood pressure.'

'Granted. Why should I let Radley spoil our visit? I can assure you that I shall endeavour to put her quite out of my head for the rest of the day.'

'Good! Now, as you will be at the wheel later in the day Lionel, I wouldn't mind a glass of mulled wine; my fingers are red raw with cold.'

'Of course you may, but that's still no reason to stop me from taking a glass or two with my lunch.'

'Do you think that wise? They're cracking down on drink driving again this year you know.'

'"Wise"? What's not wise is foregoing half the pleasure of one's lunch to satisfy the letter of an ill-considered law.'

'If you must then Lionel, but don't look to me for support should we be pulled over by the police.'

They stopped at the next stall, from which wafted the aromatic steam of hot red wine, imbued with the fragrances of cinnamon and nutmeg. Lionel duly purchased a glass for his wife, who cupped it in her chilled hands, bringing life stinging back to her numb fingertips. She raised the sweetened beverage to her lips, and drank. Her head fizzled and buzzed with pleasure, as the alcohol relaxed her veins. Thus fortified, she suggested that they turn their attention to the town's Minster for the hour that remained before lunch.

'Do you know much about it?' asked Lionel.

'Not a great deal, for as you know, the Gothic isn't really my thing, although Ruth was quite insistent that we ought to visit. She says that it contains some particularly fine stained glass, some of it surviving from its mediaeval heyday, although the most impressive piece is the Beke commemorative window – the work of Christopher Whall – despite it only having been installed in 1895.'

'You have a remarkably precise memory for dates Frances – unusual for a woman.'

'I shall try to take that as one of your rare compliments.'

'As you should. You're unlikely to receive another this side of New Year. Now, come on, and let's take a look inside.'

Lionel twisted the thick iron ring of the handle, and eased open the heavy oak door. It possessed a satisfying solidity, its movement smooth, well-oiled and timeless, and as they stepped inside, they felt as if they were leaving the modern world behind them, such was the hush that they found within. The light was dim, the smell vaguely musty. On warmer days, they would have perceived a distinct chill to the air inside the Minster, but such was the weather this particular day, that they felt it to be warm. They nodded and smiled to the top-hatted trimly dressed attendant, who sat in the small gift shop close to the entrance, as they walked into the fullness of the roomy interior, which they found, to their surprise, to be empty of visitors. They moved slowly, somewhat solemnly, up the nave, pausing to look up at the elaborately carved ceiling bosses, espying a green man with foliage spewing from his capacious mouth, and angels bearing escutcheoned shields. In the south transept, they paused to regard the slate commemorative plaque of a tomb set high up on the wall, its death's head motif, crossbones and copperplate lettering betraying its early eighteenth-century origins.

'It would seem that this family took death seriously,' commented Lionel, 'given the expense that this must have occasioned. Then again, all families did back then, didn't they?'

'They did; they seemed to be possessed by a tireless morbidity. And all, of course, to no purpose.'

'Indeed. Whether it assuaged their grief, or served only to accentuate it, can only be guessed at. Still, the legacy of such beliefs is aesthetically agreeable, albeit rather grim.

Now, as Ruth will be wanting to know our opinions regarding that window that she was enthusing about, have you any idea as to where we might find it?'

'No – none at all, other than in the wall of course.'

'Very helpful Frances. Very *helpful*,' he said with an evident note of sarcasm. 'Well, let's see if we can find it then. Seeing as she was so vocal about its exceptional quality, it seems odd that we should not have noticed it. It's so strangely quiet here, isn't it?'

'Absolutely. Very odd, especially when considering the weather, not to mention how beautiful it is. Other than the sales assistant in the gift boutique we've not seen, or heard, another soul.'

Lionel gave a shudder: 'Good God Frances! Did you feel that draft?'

'Draft? No. Where would a draft come from in here?'

'Other than the door, which is shut, I don't know, but I felt the queerest sensation, as if my shoulder blades had been set in ice.'

Here he turned, and with a start found himself facing an old woman neatly attired in what appeared to be late-Victorian mourning apparel. She fixed him with her gaze, hard and unblinking, the very picture of blackness but for her deeply lined and sickly pallid face, that stared at him through a veil of light gauze speckled with flecks of knotted black. Her shoulders appeared to heave upwards as she drew breath, and then rose from the worm-eaten pew with an ease suggestive of being lifted by invisible strings, imparting to the onlookers the impression that her corporeal substance was but slight.

'Is this your first time at the Minster?' she enquired in a voice endowed with enthusiasm, and a confidence born of speaking to countless strangers over the course of many years.

'It is,' he replied, 'my wife's sister, Monica, suggested that we pay a visit.'

'She suggested well. She lives locally?'

'Reasonably.'

'Then I have little doubt that she and I must be acquainted. There are few who frequent this place whom I do not know, by sight, if not by name.'

'Your costume is most remarkable,' commented Frances. 'Where did you have it made? I can see that you have truly taken the spirit of Victorian England to your heart.'

'By a local seamstress, of course. It is no effort on my part, believe me; it could not be otherwise,' she commented matter-of-factly. 'Now, as you are first-time visitors here I can, if it would interest you, tell you something about the history of the Minster?'

Before the Smallwoods could give their assent or otherwise, she had started to speak: 'That tomb that you have been viewing belongs to the Maunders family, significant local landowners who donated much money to the Minster in the latter part of the seventeenth and eighteenth centuries. Their fortunes were spent and the family fallen into destitution by the beginning of the reign of the late George IV. The bones of the prosperous members of that lineage lie beneath our feet in the family crypt. As they form such a relatively insignificant part of the Minster's rich history, perhaps it would be best if I were to start with recounting the history of its foundation, and the most appropriate point where we should place our feet to commence this story is at its heart: beneath the great tower, that stands as a monument to the ingenuity of its Norman rebuilders.'

Lionel, for once, was left speechless, and out of a wish not to offend the old lady, the critic and his wife smiled, and obediently followed her to the suggested starting point, as if they were well-behaved schoolchildren on an educational excursion.

'Grimstone Peverell Minster has a long, prestigious, and fascinating history, although next to nothing of what we see around ourselves today dates from the time of its foundation, other than the shattered remains of 'the Giant', a great standing stone that was the focus of veneration amongst the local Britons until they were conquered by King Caedwalla of Wessex in AD 686. He ordered that it be broken up and incorporated into the foundations of what was to become Grimstone Minster, it not acquiring the Peverell element of its title until the early twelfth century in keeping with the name of the dominant local Norman family. You can see its roughly hewn fragments at the base of the wall supporting the central portion of the nave over there,' she said, pointing with a hand gloved in black kidskin.

'I recall, from my reading of the Anglo-Saxon Chronicle, that Caedwalla employed a great deal of force in his conversion of the pagans in his conquered domains, but I do not remember reading anything about his association with Grimstone Peverell,' remarked Frances.

'Caedwalla was a righteous Christian king,' said the old woman with a sudden rush of passion, 'who put the heathen to flight in the name of our redeeming Lord Jesus Christ. The account of Caedwalla's foundation and endowment of the Minster was handed down through oral tradition, and was inscribed by the monks in the ninth century in the diocesan chronicle. Unfortunately for us, however, that account was lost at the time of the Henrician Reformation, destroyed along with so many other artefacts of the Minster's past.'

Frances flushed a little, taken aback and irritated by their guide's forceful profession of faith. 'Badly bitten by the God bug,' thought Lionel, his voiceless opinion finding vivid expression in his face, 'or, then again, perhaps it's all just some act the old girl puts on?' The stranger continued with her righteous narration, oblivious to the feelings of her godless listeners.

'If you would be so good as to direct your attention to the slab on the floor to your right,' she said with a swish of her arm, 'you will note the presence of a number of darkened indentations in the stone, which, according to legend, have a most interesting provenance. King Cynewulf of Wessex was out hunting with a party of noblemen when they happened upon a hind suckling a fawn and gave chase with their hounds. The fawn was soon brought to ground, causing the mother to look back and let out a plaintive bark, but the fleetness of the hind's feet kept her ahead of them. It was said that she moved so swiftly that her hooves seemed to blaze with light, and happening upon the Minster, she made for its open door. One of the monks – a Brother Ealdwine – saw the panic in the creature's eyes, and once she was inside, slammed shut the door, believing God to have granted her sanctuary.

'The hind slipped and halted there upon that stone, the heat of her hooves burning and scorching those impressions that are so clearly visible even today, and rousing Abbot Godric from his contemplative prayer. Upon his making of the sign of the cross, she became still and bowed her head to the holy man, who took this supplicatory act as a sign that the beast was blessed. Meanwhile, a member of Cynewulf's party was hammering upon the door and demanding admittance to the Minster for the King and his party, but the Abbot would not allow this until Cynewulf himself had sworn that no harm would come to the hind. Once the hounds were leashed, he and his retinue were granted entry, and Godric bid the hind pay due obeisance to the monarch, which it did in meek and gentle fashion, giving a lick to the king's hand, before springing forth to its freedom in the woods from which it had been chased. Since this time, the Minster has taken the figure of the hind spared as its symbol, whose presence you may have divined represented in both stone and glass.'

'A most picturesque story,' commented Frances, 'and thus explaining the name of the restaurant at which we will be dining this lunchtime.'

'I find that most visitors derive much satisfaction from my recounting of this edifying tale,' said the guide with a smile, 'but which restaurant is it to which you refer?'

'The Hind Spared in the town square.'

'It must be new, for it is unknown to me.'

'My sister-in-law says that it opened back in '92,' added Lionel.

'That is most peculiar, for I do not recall such a restaurant as opening in that year,' replied the guide, 'and I'm sure that I should have noticed it in the years since. Now, if you would be so good as to follow me to the crypt, but before we descend into that solemn place, I should like you to examine a unique niche in the north wall which once harboured something of great value.'

She led them on with a slow, awkward gait, silent but for the slight wheeze of her breath, whilst they admired the Romanesque vaulting of the great tower, which brought to mind the cathedrals of Winchester and Durham, before they finally halted below a small recess in the wall. She turned to address them.

'Here we find ourselves beneath what was home to the Minster's most precious relic: King Alfred's fingernail. It was held here in a golden reliquary studded with amethysts, until taken by Thomas Cromwell's commissioners in 1538, bringing an end to its residence of six-and-a-half centuries. The fingernail was torn from Alfred's hand when it snagged upon the baptismal robe of the Dane Guthrum, when he was received into the Church at Aller in 878. It was said to be endowed with the most miraculous curative properties, and would be processed about the Minster during times of pestilence in an effort to ensure the recovery of the afflicted townsfolk.'

'The credulity of the mediaeval mind is quite remarkable,' commented Lionel in a scoffing tone.

'I prefer to think of the people of the time as not being so much credulous, as possessed of great faith and piety,' replied the old woman with a certain tartness. 'Their example serves as a reminder to our unregenerate age, that we should submit ourselves to the understanding of our loving creator, rather than trust in the hubristic claims of science.'

'Priceless! That little speech of yours really was rather good,' added Lionel, 'You have truly managed to capture the mentality of a certain type of backward-thinking – if "thinking" should be the correct word to use – Victorian. I had no idea that it was customary for the locals to don nineteenth-century beliefs as well as attire during the period of the Christmas Fair. You must have spent quite some time researching the beliefs of the time.'

The old woman looked affronted: 'I am sorry, sir, but please forgive me for saying that I do not understand you. As we are in a place of worship, we should conduct ourselves accordingly, and leave the spirit of levity at the door. There is no place here for the voice of the *sceptic*.' She enunciated this last word with all of the opprobrious abhorrence that one would normally reserve for describing the most despicable and loathsome being imaginable.

Lionel darted a worried look at Frances, now entertaining the opinion that he had misjudged the guide's character, mistaking her deeply held beliefs for a mere act. He had no taste for such deluded dogmatism, and was growing agitated and eager to leave the Minster, but his innate politeness prevented him from doing so, for he did not wish to hurt the feelings of the elderly stranger, who plainly meant well.

'We now descend to the crypt. I would beg your forbearance for my slowness, but I find the steps uneven, and neither my sight nor my balance are what they were,' remarked the lady in black, her bony leather-clad fingers grasping at the handrail to steady herself. She positioned herself in the centre of the spacious vault, and stood beneath the beam of the artificial light. Satisfied that she had her visitors' attention once more, she began to speak.

'This ranks amongst my favourite places, owing to the presence of this tomb – the resting place of Mortimer de Peverell, a knight who served under Richard the Lionheart during the Third Crusade; a remarkable monument to a most remarkable man, whose crusading zeal should be hallowed forever in Christian remembrance, just as the memory of the late General Gordon is treasured by all. You will note that he holds in his mailed grip a severed hand, which is symbolic, as I will explain.

'Mortimer served under Richard with distinction, saving his life at the Siege of Acre. It was after breaching the walls of that city that a fearsome brute of a Saracen swordsman, later discovered to be one of Saladin's most able champions, succeeded in cutting through the King's bodyguard with the intent of glorifying his name with the shedding of regal blood. But this man had failed to reckon upon the bravery of Mortimer, who acted swiftly, and interposed himself between the assailant and the monarch. With a swing of his broadsword, he took off the sword hand of the attacker, before despatching him with a thrust of his weapon through a gap in the armour, up and into, the Mahometan's chest. He thereafter kept the hand as a trophy, and returned with it to England. It is said that it lies buried with him.'

'A tale told with great verve and conviction,' commented Lionel with approval, 'I can imagine that such a commentary goes down extremely poorly with some types these days though, as you'll doubtless know. Would you happen to be involved in amateur dramatics by any chance?'

'Indeed, I have noted that in recent years a degree of distaste has been expressed by a growing number of visitors whom have cast aspersions upon the character of the noble Mortimer and his motivations. It is a matter that perplexes me greatly, although a number of them would appear to have come from the colonies, and thus may, I would conjecture, be of a heathen disposition. As for any involvement with the stage sir, I would not engage myself in so frivolous a pastime.'

Although initially disquieted by her apparent religious conviction and fervour, he was now, once again, coming to question his assumptions. Surely she could not subscribe to so fundamentalist an interpretation of Christianity, for if she did, would she not have abandoned the Church of England for some evangelical sect? This consideration suggested that it had to be an act. Rather than being convinced by her disavowal of any connection with the stage, he was coming to quite the opposite conclusion: this act of hers, to which she stuck with an unwavering adherence, was as convincing as any presented by many a pro who trod the boards with critically acclaimed regularity. He found himself pondering whether she might consider taking this performance to London, perhaps under a title such as 'The Widow in Weeds', or some such like; it could, with the right management, be a hit. With this in mind, he could not refrain from allowing a smile to break forth upon his lips, only for it to melt before the stony glare of the woman to whom it had been directed.

'You will note that even here in the crypt, such a devout figure as Mortimer was not able to find sanctuary from the zealous attention of the Puritans, who broke off a fragment of his sculpted sword, as well as his nose.'

'A terrible act of vandalism! Talking of which, how is it that the Minster came to escape dissolution?' asked Frances.

'The Minster's survival is a cause for some celebration, for its fate was at one time quite uncertain, being decided by the most unexpected turn of events. Once it had been stripped of its gold and silver plate, the building and its lands were sold by the Crown in 1538 to Edward Finch for the sum of £248 twelve shillings and sixpence. It had been Finch's intention to level much of the structure, and to build a grand family seat upon the site, but within ten days of the purchase having been concluded, he lay dead. With the family providing no explanation for his death, his sudden demise became a point of conjecture for the townsfolk, amongst whom the consensus soon arose that he had been punished for his impiety, and carried off by the Devil for daring to countenance the destruction of a house of God. This conclusion was seemingly confirmed by his son's decision to desist from the Minster's demolition, and to focus instead upon the remodelling of Grimstone Peverell Manor, funded by the sale of timber and rents from the extensive lands lately acquired.'

'Your knowledge of the Minster's history seems quite encyclopaedic. How did you come to acquire it all?' inquired Lionel.

'I have had a long association with the Minster, as has my family. My paternal grandfather was rector here during the reign of William IV, and it was from him that these stories were passed down.'

'Her grandfather was rector during the reign of William IV?' thought Lionel, looking at her askance, 'That's ridiculous, not to mention quite impossible. Another part of her act, carried out, as the rest, with aplomb.' He kept his thoughts to himself.

'I'm afraid that we're running a little short of time,' interrupted Frances, noting that lunchtime would soon be upon them, 'so we really will need to be going soon. We have booked a table you see.'

'I quite understand,' replied the old lady, 'but there are one or two other points of interest that I should like to show you before you leave. I can assure you that they won't take any more than a few minutes of your time.'

Frances smiled. 'Very well. Lead on,' she conceded.

'The war memorial is quite spectacular, being fashioned from marble, green slate and Portland stone. It was funded by both public subscription, and a significant private donation from a Mr Vincent. Upon its honour roll, you will see the names of the many men who fell at Sebastopol and Inkerman, as well as the many more who died from cold and disease in the Crimea. It was the greatest military loss of life experienced by the town.'

'Since, doubtless, eclipsed by the losses occasioned by the Great War,' commented Lionel, looking in the direction of three long boards affixed to a neighbouring wall, their gilt lettering picking out scores of names spanning the alphabet from Abbot to Young. The guide paid them no attention.

'We have no general memorial to the Great War against Napoleon,' she replied, 'although you may find an inset stone commemorating the fall of Captain Stockman at Waterloo in the Lady Chapel.'

'No, I mean the Great War: World War One,' clarified Lionel pointing to the boards and eliciting a confused look from the guide.

'Oh, yes. You must bear with me, for I sometimes forget to make reference to some of the newer additions,' she answered, leafing through the pages of the official Minster guidebook: 'Yes, you are quite right – that is the memorial to the First World War.'

Frances had now reached a peak of anxiety regarding the possibility of missing their booking at the Hind Spared: 'I'm so sorry, but you really must excuse us, as we must leave now: our booking is at half twelve.'

'It is such a shame that you must hurry so, for there is more to which I would like to draw to your attention, and—'

'Well, thank you very much for your time,' interrupted Lionel. 'It's been most interesting; very informative. We'll be sure to recommend the Minster to friends as a place to visit. Goodbye, and a happy Christmas to you!'

He promptly turned, took Frances by the arm and marched her towards the door.

'I didn't' wish to be so abrupt with her, but I feared that we'd never manage to extricate ourselves otherwise. Besides, given the length of her lecture, I'm quite sure that she would have been pleading with us for some sort of donation if we'd given her the opportunity to ask.'

'A "donation"? I can't recall you ever having made one.'

'I have – on rare occasions, admittedly – given money to those causes of which I approve, but as for the Church – well, you know fully well my views on that institution.'

'Really? Those occasions seem to have passed me by, doubtless the mark of some reckless youthful indiscretion on your part. As for the Church, everyone who knows Lionel Smallwood, or who has even heard of him, knows his opinion of religion, for it would be impossible for them not to.'

'In this respect, you wouldn't guess that Ruth was our daughter, would you? What with her pronounced religiosity, and weakness for High Church ceremonial.'

'Well, as the adage goes – God moves in mysterious ways. Oh, dash!'

'What is it?'

'Despite all of the time we've spent here we didn't even get to see the Beke Window.'

'Yes, you're right. It had escaped my mind during our period of *captivity*. Would you wish to chance returning after lunch to see if we can find it? We'll have to look sharp if we do though, lest our unbidden guide makes a reappearance.'

'I think that we ought to, otherwise Ruth will be dreadfully disappointed with us.'

The Hind Spared

A briskness entered their stride as the two of them walked out into the square, which was soon tempered by the necessity of maintaining their balance on the icy cobbles and by the crush of the crowd. Frances's attention was distracted once more by the steam and aromas issuing from the mulled wine stalls, as well as the greasy odour of the eco-friendly burger van which proudly displayed the sign: 'fuelled by chip fat', like, no doubt, a number of the shoppers.

'Are you having second thoughts about the restaurant? Hankering after a burger instead, by any chance?' ribbed Lionel.

'A burger?' she said, a pronounced note of disdain in her voice, 'I should hardly think that it qualifies as food, and have not the faintest inkling as to why anyone would wish to consume such an item.'

'And from what I have seen, read and heard, the affixation of the word "beef" to such burgers is, in general, almost without justifiable foundation, and one would certainly not wish to partake of one which had been rarely cooked.'

'Well, the rarer the better, as in never, wouldn't you say?'

'Hah! Why, of course! Did Monica make reference to any specialities that the Hind Spared might offer?'

'She said little with respect to its culinary range other than "Lionel would most certainly appreciate its menu", which I take to mean that it caters for the carnivorously inclined amongst us.'

'Hmm, most encouraging. We shall see, we shall see!'

With such an utterance did he take a manly hold of the handle of the door to the Hind Spared, and give it a firm twist.

'After you my dear,' he said, ushering his wife into Grimstone Peverell's most exclusive dining establishment.

'Thank you. Your manners are, as ever, quite impeccable, Lionel.'

He smiled, as a waitress, neat and pert, her hair gathered up in a protuberant blonde ponytail that sprouted from the crown of her head like a luxuriant over-fertilised spider plant, stared at him blankly with large grey eyes and asked: 'You have reservation?'

'Yes. Smallwood – Lionel and Frances Smallwood. We've reserved a table for two at 12:30.'

'Smallwood. Yes – I know this name. Come with me, please.'

'Thank you,' replied Lionel, following the young woman as she weaved her way between the chairs and tables of the other diners.

'This your table, I think. Sit here and I take your coats.'

'Thank you,' he said, handing over his long overcoat before Frances followed suit.

'I get menu, you sit please,' continued the waitress flatly, as she bobbed off to the coatrack.

'Polite, isn't she?' commented Frances.

'"Polite"? A little curt, I'd say, as well as being somewhat prone to omitting the indefinite article and the present tense of the verb "to be".'

'Such linguistic transgressions normally both count as cardinal sins with you, judging from your previous reviews.'

The return of the waitress cut short their discussion.

'Here – menu. Please take.'

'Thank you,' replied Lionel as she took her leave, unsmiling and impassive.

'Polish?' suggested Frances.

'Could be Russian, considering her manners, but certainly a Slavic speaker, which enables me to absolve her, to a certain extent, from committing the aforementioned "cardinal sins".'

'And the fact that she's pretty, presumably?'

'I can't say that I noticed.'

'Really Lionel, there's no use in trying to hide that glint of yours; I saw it. I should know, as I saw it myself once, but that was many years ago.'

'You're doing it again Frances.'

'Doing what?'

'Going all Mills and Boon on me with that maudlin tone of yours. Anyone would think that I had forsaken you given the way that you're carrying on.'

'You're a strange old fish; for all your protestations to the contrary and apparent crustiness, I swear that I just caught a twinkle of the old Lionel in those eyes of yours, or did my eyes deceive me?'

'Maybe, or then again, it could have been the angle of the lights. "Fish"? "Crustiness"? You make me sound as if I were some sort of crustacean: a Cromer crab or such like. And let's have a little less of the *old* Lionel, if you don't mind.'

'That's my Lionel! Just as unromantic as he ever was.'

'Well, that's how you like it, isn't it?'

'Did you ever offer me any choice in the matter?'

'Hmm. No. No, I don't suppose that I did.'

Something unexpected here caught Frances's attention, causing an abrupt alteration in her expression, her eyebrows creasing in puzzlement: 'How strange. Look behind you.'

'Behind me?'

'At the wall. Look at the wall.'

He turned to behold a blown-up sepia photograph of a dour-faced woman in Victorian dress, the name 'Agnes Beke' printed beneath in a distinctive period font.

'Seems familiar, doesn't she?' continued Frances.

'She most certainly does. She bears the most remarkable resemblance to the woman to whom we've just been speaking in the Minster. In fact, I'm convinced that the two are one and the same. Judging by her pose, grim expression and period costume, she seems to have been swallowed up by all things Victorian; a real enthusiast. Irrespective of what she said, I'm quite convinced that she walks the boards with some regularity.'

'Yes, it's her, I'm quite sure of it too, but someone has done an exceptional job in ageing the original photograph from which this print was taken, even going so far as to put creases into it, and fading out certain areas.'

'Computers, Frances, computers. They're the root of an incredible amount of fakery these days, and I've little doubt that some cyber-wizard has been at work in this case. Ah! Here comes the waitress again. We'd better take a look at the menu.'

'You ready to order?'

'Not just yet.'

'Perhaps you like drink while you decide?'

'Yes, yes, a good idea: a bottle of the Châteauneuf du Pape '95, please.'

'Okay. I bring.'

'Wait a moment would you, but you wouldn't happen to know who this is, would you?' enquired Frances, pointing at the picture.

'I am sorry, but I do not understand.'

'The woman in the picture – do you know who she is?'

The waitress screwed up her eyes, then looked at Frances as if she were stupid: 'Of course I know: Agnes Beke. Look!' she said, pointing to the printed name.

'Yes, but do you know her?'

'No, of course not. She is dead. I get your wine,' she said, somewhat tersely.

'How peculiar,' remarked Lionel.

'Quite.'

'Perhaps our guide is a descendant of this Agnes Beke? Dare we ask her should she be around when we return to the Minster?'

'Not her herself, perhaps, but how about one of the kiosk attendants?'

'Agreed. Far less risky. We wouldn't wish to be ensnared by her again, would we?'

'Absolutely not. I can already see fear in your eyes Lionel.'

'"Fear"?'

'Yes. Fear of having to make a donation.'

'Very droll my dear. Look, let's order otherwise we might be struggling for time. It's odd that our mysterious guide said that she'd never heard of this place, owing to its prominent position overlooking the square. It'd be worth her colleagues mentioning this picture to her, so that she can drop in and take a look at it for herself.'

The waitress returned with their wine, her expression swiftly changing to an impatient scowl upon learning that the couple had still not made their selections. She hovered over them, an unwelcome glowering presence that refused to leave until they had placed their orders. Still, the menu, much to Lionel's gratification, did indeed cater to his carnivorous palate, and in quite an extensive fashion too, although the absence of 'grouse terrine' displeased him. After much consideration, he plumped for an entrée of spatchcocked partridge in pear purée, followed by a main of rabbit in mustard sauce with seasonal vegetables. Frances selected the same seasonal starter, but opted for duck confit for her main, briefly excusing herself from the table before the arrival of the latter, bidding her husband not to wait on ceremony, and to continue with the next course, if he so wished, which he did.

'Delicious!' he thought to himself. 'Not what I was expecting at all from so small a provincial establishment. The rabbit itself is cooked to succulent perfection, and the roux of the sauce of an agreeably thick and creamy consistency, its flavour piquant yet subtle, bringing to mind Adrien's creations at de Montfort's. The presentation is somewhat crude and rustic, as befitting such a humble meat once beloved – of necessity – of the peasantry. Its singularity and originality is marked out by a trail of soft black pearls, the like of which I have neither seen, nor tasted, before. Their flavour is somewhat earthy with a hint of grassiness, with a – Jesus! Good God! – it's rabbit shit! I've just eaten rabbit shit!' His inner reflections were, much to his embarrassment and horror, no longer mere thoughts, but public exclamations. It was at this point that Frances returned to view a scene of consternation and mirth at the neighbouring table.

'Lionel! Whatever are you saying?'

'I'm sorry Frances, but good God! What have I eaten? Shit. I've just eaten *shit*. I'm feeling quite queasy at the very thought of it.'

'What? Are you sure that you ate what you thought you did?'

'Quite sure.'

'If you are "quite sure" of this fact, then I fail to see how you came to be foolish enough to eat it.'

'I hardly suspected that it would be what it was, given that it was served up as part of the meal. Who'd have suspected that anyone would dare to serve up such *choice* morsels of execrable excrement?'

'Well, what *did* you think they were?'

'I thought that they might be caramelised pearls of something or the other, not rabbit droppings.'

'This is beyond belief Lionel, it really is. You're making this up.'

'I'm not. I swear it!'

'Then what are you going to do? Are you going to complain?'

'"Complain"? How could I possibly *complain*?'

'You seem to be doing a very good job of complaining at the moment, if you don't mind me saying so. Yes – complain you jolly well should. Who wouldn't complain about having animal excrement served up in their lunch?'

'Anyone who'd not realised what they'd done until they'd eaten it all up, that's who. Can you imagine how stupid I'd look if this got out? I'd be a laughing stock. I can see it now: bon viveur and renowned critic, Lionel Smallwood, a man known for his peerless taste in matters gastronomic, has recently discovered a hitherto neglected dish for the discerning palate: rabbit droppings in cream and mustard sauce. No Frances, it simply won't do: I'm not going to complain.'

'Don't be ridiculous Lionel! How would anybody get to know about it?'

'These things have a way of getting out, particularly these days with the internet and all of its attendant evils.'

'Especially, presumably, when the aggrieved customer in question offhandedly lets drop his name in a restaurant full of strangers?'

'I'm such a damned fool at times!'

'I'm saying nothing, but as I'm hungry I'm going to sit here and eat this. So, what are you going to do?'

'I don't think I can face anything else. I've lost my appetite.'

'So, you really aren't going to complain?'

'No.'

'Have it your way then.'

The duck confit was, as Frances termed it, 'sublime', and mercifully free of unpleasant surprises. Whilst she ate, Lionel retreated to the gents where he found the taps to be of that irksome variety which one has to press down firmly, that invariably unleash a high-pressure torrent such as that favoured in firefighting, but wholly unsuitable for the maintenance of personal hygiene. Despite his best efforts, he thus found himself repeatedly drenched. His face, hair, front and hands were sodden with water, whereas despite numerous rinses his mouth still felt soiled. For a moment, he contemplated the idea of making himself sick in the toilet cubicle, but thought better of it, lest another customer catch him at it. After five minutes or so, he returned to the table, feeling little better, his mood considerably worsened.

'What *have* you been doing Lionel? Your jacket cuffs are soaked, and you've a wet stain all down your trousers which really doesn't look very becoming.'

'It's obvious what I've been doing, isn't it? I've been trying to cleanse myself.'

'"Cleanse" yourself?'

'Yes – from the ill effects of those *earthy dark pearls*.'

'Your means of doing so would appear to be highly unorthodox, for you led me to believe that you had swallowed them, rather than plastered them down your front. Did you succeed?'

'Your sarcasm is as misplaced as it is unwelcome Frances. It's difficult to say what, if any, success I have achieved, but my stomach is feeling distinctly unsettled.'

'Then if that's the case, why don't you complain?'

'No, no, no – we've been through why not already. Now, you just *stay there* and finish your main course whilst I settle up, and if you don't mind, I'd like to stop off at a chemist before returning to the Minster.'

'Of course I don't mind, but are you sure that you're feeling up to it? You did say that you felt as if your shoulders had been encased in ice this morning.'

'I'll be fine. I just need something to calm my stomach, which means, unfortunately, no more wine.'

'That's not like you at all. You really are feeling off colour, aren't you?'

Dyspeptic Relief

Lionel and the waitress exchanged black looks and few words as he paid the bill, his sense of dissatisfaction and resentment so self-evident in his expression and manner, as not to require verbalisation. There was, on this occasion, to be no tip. Frances, meanwhile, finished her meal, and drained the wine from her glass with well-practised, albeit unanticipated, speed, and rose for Lionel to help her into her coat. As they met the cold air that seemed to have grown colder still during their lunchtime sojourn at the Hind Spared, his stomach rose in rebellion but was beaten back into submission with some effort and discomfort. A chill sweat broke upon his temples and in the small of his back.

'We must find a chemist as soon as possible. I think that I spotted one on our way here from the carpark.'

'Oh yes – the shop rather effectively decked out as a Victorian druggist. It must have cost them a fortune to have all of that paintwork done especially for the Christmas fair.'

'Yes, they do seem to have gone to inordinate efforts to fit in with the Victorian theme. It must have been costly. Perhaps they had the boards painted some years ago, and reuse them each December?'

'That would seem to make sense, yes, but they even seem to have gone to some length with the lighting, which for all the world looks like gaslight.'

'Highly unlikely. As you well know, energy-efficient lightbulbs are equally capable of achieving a dim glow that would have been perfectly familiar to our Victorian forebears.'

'Of course. After all, what other explanation could there be?'

Their progress through the choke of people in the square was slow; the cobblestones beneath their feet now sheening wet from the snow, melted by the coarse rock salt cast upon its surface. The crowd thinned as they mounted the pavement into Trinity Lane, flanked by mounds of slush, and strewn with briny puddles, as they splashed through the water.

'Execrable weather,' remarked Lionel.

'You say so so frequently that I wonder when it isn't,' commented Frances.

As they drew towards the chemist, they looked up at the prominent black signboard upon which was emblazoned in large white Victorian lettering 'Rowland's Druggists'. In the already fading light of this tired December afternoon, a distinctive yellow cast from the lamps within could be discerned upon the ground without, luring them to seek the warmth of the glow inside, but as they were about to enter, a figure clad in black emerged from the door, and turned to face them. They recognised her in an instant: the guide from the Minster.

'Good afternoon,' she said. 'What an unexpected pleasure this is, for I really didn't expect to see you again. I hope that you enjoyed your lunch. What brings you here?'

'It's my husband – Lionel,' replied Frances, 'he has an upset stomach.'

'An upset stomach? Oh dear, oh dear, I must own to be most sorry to hear that, but serendipity would have it that I have just the thing for such a disorder here about my person. Look!' she said with a sly smile, drawing a six-sided glass bottle from her wicker basket. 'I was taking it home for my husband, but his need of it is not great at this moment. I think you will find that it will put a stop to your pain once and for all, as it is a most efficacious remedy for such troubles. It is best taken mixed with food, but as you have already eaten, it could be taken if followed by a little water. Taking it without food is not a problem in itself; it's just that it has something of a strong flavour of garlic. Not one which many people would find agreeable, I'm afraid.'

'Oh, that's not a problem at all,' interjected Lionel, 'as I happen to be rather keen on garlic, just ask Frances. But we really cannot impose on you so and deprive you of your husband's medicine.'

'No, no my good man – believe me, it would please me if you were to take it.'

'Really? Very well then, that is most thoughtful of you. How much do I owe you?'

'Oh, nothing really: look upon it as a gift.'

'Nonsense! How much was it? I can't take this without giving payment.'

Very well: it was three shillings.'

'Oh, now that's very droll! Very good, very good! Did I not say earlier that you walk the boards? Do you have an agent? I know someone who'd be able to make good use of this act of yours. Now, as for this bottle, it must have cost at least eight pounds, surely?'

'Eight pounds! No sir – three shillings. And as I said previously, I possess no interest whatsoever in the unsavoury world of the stage.'

'Well, here's ten, and no arguments please. Keep the change!'

'If you insist,' she said with some reluctance, handing him the bottle and bidding him and his wife a good afternoon.

'It's beautiful!' remarked Frances. 'Such a rich green colour, and those flutes are so pretty. Look – one side smooth, the next fluted.'

'Not what you'd typically expect from Boots, that's for sure.'

'No. I think it worth keeping once it's empty.'

'Still, it strikes me that some of the locals may be taking things a little too far with this Victorian business if they're repackaging medicines without instructions; someone could do themselves some harm if it weren't something as harmless as Milk of Magnesia.'

'Milk of Magnesia? Are you sure that's what it is? After all, she didn't state that it was, although she did say that it tastes of garlic, and from what I can remember, it normally tastes of mint.'

'What else could an over-the-counter liquid remedy for stomach pains be? Perhaps the Victorians added garlic flavouring rather than mint?'

'Don't be absurd Lionel. You know as well as I how averse the English have been to garlic until recent years, so I really cannot imagine that our nineteenth-century forebears would have been adding garlic flavouring to Milk of Magnesia.'

'Well, I'll concede that it is an odd choice, but I may as well take a draft now and be done with it.'

'Shouldn't you find some water first? What's the dosage?'

'Water with Milk of Magnesia? Now who's being ridiculous? As for the dosage, I'm sure a good gulp should do the trick.'

He removed the rubber stopper, raised the bottle, and poured a quantity into his mouth.

'Ugh!'

'So, you're not keen on the garlic flavouring, I take it?'

'Oh, God – that's strong!'

'How are you feeling?'

'A bit heady, to be honest. Jesus – the strength of this stuff! Here – take a smell of it.'

'I'd sooner not.'

'As you please. Jesus!'

'How's your stomach?'

'None the better, or, at least, not yet.'

'Then perhaps you should take no more until later this evening once we're back home, if you should still feel under the weather. You'd not wish to rush home for this review of Radley's if you were unable to fulfil your duty now, would you?'

'Radley! Claire ruddy Radley again. My stomach is jumping somersaults at the very mention of the woman.'

'Don't be so melodramatic. Now, come on: let's get back to the Minster, as time is marching on. Oh dash!'

'What's wrong?'

'We forgot to ask the guide her name, and whether she possesses any connection with Agnes Beke.'

'Oh yes; so we did. Incredible what havoc an upset stomach can wreak upon your memory you know.'

'We can ask at the Minster. Come on! Let's get going.'

With that, he slipped the bottle into his jacket pocket, and she chivvied him off back towards the square.

The Beke Window and Matters 'Luciferian'

They found the Minster busier than when they had left it, with half a dozen people or so milling about here and there. Much to their relief there was no sign of their erstwhile guide. This time they stopped at the gift kiosk, with a view to enquiring as to the identity of their anonymous guide, as well as the whereabouts of the Beke Window. There they found an elderly lady and a slightly younger gentleman, perhaps in his mid-sixties, seated in silence, the former reading, whilst the latter peered through leaden, drowsy eyes at a stock inventory. Frances walked up, and placed her handbag on the counter, diverting his attention from the dull task at hand.

'I hope that you don't mind me interrupting you, but we were wondering if you could answer a couple of questions for us.'

'Not at all, not at all – this can wait until later. How might I be able to oblige you madam?' he said with a note of mock gravity as he doffed his top hat.

'Well, my husband and I called into the Minster this morning upon the recommendation of both my sister and our daughter, but we didn't quite have time to see everything that we would have liked to. There was one particular window that my daughter said should not be missed – the Beke Window . . .'

'Oh, the Beke Window, yes, yes, I'm not surprised; it's quite a spectacular work. I can show you that, no problem. And there was something else, was there?'

'Yes. It's concerning one of your guides whom we met; she was most helpful, and had embraced the spirit of the Victorian fair quite wholeheartedly, and was dressed in one of the most authentic looking period costumes that I've ever seen.'

'One of our guides, you say?'

'Yes – one of your guides.'

'What time did you say it was again?'

'Oh, it must have been coming up to eleven when we arrived, but we had to rush off for lunch a little after midday.'

'Interesting, interesting, but it couldn't have been one of our guides.'

'Really? She seemed to be highly knowledgeable and informative.'

'No, definitely not one of our guides, definitely not, as our volunteers only work in the afternoons.' Here, he stopped, and turned to address his companion: 'We didn't have any of the volunteers in here this morning did we Nellie? Nobody training? This lady says that one of our guides showed them around.'

'No, there was nobody in this morning Harold. Nobody at all. Jennifer was to come at 1pm, but she called in to say that she has an upset tummy. All sorts of nasty bugs doing the rounds at the moment.'

'Oh dear, oh dear, that is sad Nellie. I hadn't realised.'

'Probably eaten something at the Hind Spared,' thought Lionel.

'Well, it seems that a member of the public must have taken the role of guide upon themselves,' continued the man behind the counter.

'Oh that is a pity, as we were wondering if you would be able to tell us her name, as whilst we were dining at the Hind Spared we saw her spitting image in one of the old photographs there, and wondered whether it might be one of her ancestors.'

'Yes, yes, that is a pity, isn't it? A real pity, yes.'

'I'm quite convinced that she must have been, for she was even wearing the same costume.'

'Really, really? Well, that is surprising, yes, quite surprising.'

His manner of speaking – a seemingly disinterested nasal whine peppered with unnecessary repetitions – had begun to grate on Lionel's nerves.

'She was in black mourning dress, and wore a matching veil flecked with knots. Her name was Agnes Beke.'

Upon mention of this name, Harold let his pen drop. It rolled to the edge of the counter, before falling and clattering onto the flagstones beneath. 'Agnes Beke?' His expression, hitherto relaxed and nonchalant, was now focused and alert, his voice, more forceful. The name appeared to have jolted him from his mental slumber.

'Yes.'

'You say that this woman resembled Agnes *Beke*?'

'Absolutely. If I had not been informed that the woman in the photograph was long since departed, I would have been convinced that the two women were one and the same.'

'It is quite impossible, of course, and I've no idea as to the identity of the woman that you met here this morning, but as for Agnes Beke, she was a curious and contentious character, who bequeathed to the Minster something both beautiful, and yet unsettling. If you should have the time, I would be happy to relate the story to you, although it might take a few minutes. Would you want me to do that?'

Lionel put aside his irritation with Harold's whine, so piqued was his curiosity: 'Thank you; we would be most obliged if you did.'

'Wonderful! Wonderful! Well, Agnes Beke was a local lady with a strong connection to the Minster; a woman of faith and good standing amongst the local community, who lived without the least stain upon her character. Her maiden name was Lamb, but in 1850 she married her sweetheart – Giles Beke – under this very roof. The two of them were greatly attached to each other, and the following year she gave birth to their only daughter, Cordelia. Shortly thereafter, they moved to London, where, much to their mutual grief, Cordelia was to fall victim to cholera at the age of three. The experience marked them deeply, leading them to return to Grimstone Peverell to escape the insanitary conditions that they had encountered in the capital.

'Agnes never recovered from this loss, which led to a deepening of her Christian faith as she sought solace in scripture and good works, and became a regular worshipper here. However, for her husband Giles, his reaction to the death of their daughter was to be quite different, and was to lead to a rift between the couple, that grew ever deeper with the passing of the years. His faith wavered, with his scepticism being compounded by his reading of Darwin's *On the Origin of Species* during the early 1860s. At this point, Agnes was horrified by his revelation that he had become an agnostic. She viewed this as a dereliction of his spiritual duty towards their lost daughter, and asked him if he cared nothing for her soul. By this point, as you can imagine, little love remained between them, but the law being as it was in those days, divorce was out of the question.

'Giles Beke soon acquired a reputation for being a freethinker, and as such was shunned by many of the more prominent townsfolk, who looked with a great deal of sympathy upon Agnes's plight, wedded, as she was, to a godless and unloving husband. His radical sympathies manifested themselves further in his involvement with the fledgling activities of the National Secular Society, and campaigning on behalf of Charles Bradlaugh's right to affirm his loyalty to the Crown, rather than to swear an oath, in the House of Commons.

'By this point, he had become an out and out atheist, and made himself known as such. Agnes pleaded with him to return to the warm bosom of Christian belief, but he bitterly scoffed at the very suggestion, and when she remarked that they should make a will, given their advancing years, he made it clear that not a penny of their substantial fortune would be left to the Church. She now denounced her husband's attitudes and activities as 'Luciferian', which elicited from him little more than a burst of sardonic laughter. He, however, was not to laugh for long, for shortly afterwards he fell ill and died, his estate passing to his widow. This was in 1889.

'Thereafter, she was ever seen dressed in mourning, and laughter, which never had come to her lips with ease, never came to her again. She would frequent the Minster with great regularity, and when she herself died in 1894, the entirety of her estate, with the exception of a few personal effects, papers and items of furniture which passed to her younger brother Edward, was bequeathed to Grimstone Peverell Minster. In her will, she made it clear that the Minster was to dispose of the funds thereby acquired howsoever it wished, although there were two specific stipulations. The first of these, was that a commemorative window should be installed, and the second that a sum of money be set aside for an endowed scholarship to pay for local children with the intelligence, but not the necessary means, to study medicine. Thus it was that the Beke Window came into being, and the Beke Trust, which possesses a long list of grateful beneficiaries, was founded.'

'A most moving and remarkable tale. The loss of their daughter must have weighed heavily upon them. Would you be able to show us the window?' asked Frances.

'Yes, a dreadful loss, quite dreadful. But, of course! Please, come this way,' he replied, leading them out into the nave, and thence onwards to the easternmost end of the building commenting, 'And as for the tale, there is more, but I shall leave its telling until after we have viewed this magnificent window.'

They stopped, and looked up at the large expanse of coloured glass.

'Here it is: the Beke window. Commissioned in 1894 shortly after the death of Agnes Beke; designed, created and installed by the renowned maker of stained glass – Christopher Whall, in 1895.'

'Its luminosity is quite remarkable, even on so cold and dull a day as this. I can now appreciate why my daughter was so insistent that we should see it,' remarked Frances. The guide smiled.

'As for Whall, the trustees were lucky to secure his services, for this was not a part of the country that he normally frequented. He happened to be in the county at the time, working on a window for the new Holy Trinity Church in Bothenhampton, and what you see here drew not only on Whall's highly accomplished and regarded skills, but also employed a new type of glass that had just then been introduced. This was, somewhat paradoxically, described as "Early English glass".'

'It must have cost a fortune,' commented Lionel.

'It did, although please don't ask how much, as the figure eludes me at present. I have a poor head for figures. Not the best for someone working with stock, I suppose.' He laughed, nervously.

Frances was curious: 'You made mention that you had more to say with respect to the Beke story. I'm curious: would you be able to tell us?'

'Oh, of course, of course – not a problem at all; I can be such a scatterbrain at times, I really can – yes! A total scatterbrain!' He laughed a little, then resumed: 'Well, the

Beke bequest, which paid for both this window and the funding of the Beke Trust, was much celebrated at the time, and the diocese went so far as to consider erecting a memorial to their benefactor. The idea, however, was eventually rejected, with both clergy and the great and the good of the borough concluding that the window and the Beke Trust were, in and of themselves, quite sufficient memorials to the lady's Christian character. She had led a life with neither stain nor blemish, or so it would seem, for a revelation that emerged in the local press some five years after the completion of the window in 1896 was to cast a pall over the reputation of Agnes Beke that has never since been dispelled.'

'"A pall"? What kind of pall? Did she prove to be a hypocrite, like so many who overly loudly profess their faith?' asked Lionel.

'Some people might wish to put it that way, but I would rather prefer to present the unembellished facts as they were reported at the time. As you may remember, I made mention that a certain number of personal effects from the Beke household were left to Agnes's surviving brother – Edward Lamb. Now, although a considerable amount of paperwork fell into his keeping, his grief at his sister's death was such that he could not bring himself to look into it until some years later. It was thus not until one day early in November 1901 that he came across a sealed envelope that had been addressed to him, quite clearly, in Agnes's hand. For some reason, he had overlooked it all these years. Upon its opening, he was to fall into a state of shock, for it divulged something of which neither he, nor anyone else, had possessed the least suspicion: Agnes had written a confession.

'In this letter, she admitted to poisoning her husband, whom she referred to as having become a "Luciferian". She had been enjoined, so she believed, to do away with him by the Archangel Gabriel, in the wake of their argument over his will, and his steadfast refusal to leave any fraction of his fortune to the Church. The diocese initially attempted to keep this hushed up, but the due process of the law could not be impeded, and thus the local press got hold of the story, with the *Blackmore Vale Gazette* providing extensive coverage and commentary. Nonetheless, despite a subsequent inquiry, it was decided that the monies bequeathed to the Minster should remain with it.'

'Remarkable!' commented Lionel.

'Yes, it was a great scandal at the time, and served as a source of considerable embarrassment for the Minster. Her brother was dogged by a sense of shame for the rest of his life.'

'But what about descendants? Does the family still reside in the area?'

'The Bekes had only the one daughter, and Agnes's brother – Edward – was a lifelong bachelor. The lines of both Bekes and Lambs came to an end with the individuals we discussed, so no – there are no descendants.'

'Are you certain of this? The woman whom we spoke to this morning bore the most striking resemblance to Agnes,' continued Frances.

'Absolutely certain, absolutely. You must have encountered one of our more enthusiastic Victorian re-enactors who, taken with the macabre reputation of the lady under discussion, has done their best to emulate her appearance.'

With his narration completed, Harold Bentley excused himself with some haste and awkwardness, explaining that he should return to the kiosk to complete his stocktaking.

Frances looked at Lionel in disbelief, unsettled by the story, and unconvinced by the assertion that neither the Bekes nor the Lambs had left any local offspring. Divining this sense of unease in his wife's features, in a sceptical tone of voice that she found familiar he commented: 'I have a feeling that I know what you're thinking Frances, but this is no time to be running to fanciful conjecture with respect to the identity of this mysterious woman. She must be a local eccentric, and nothing more.'

'But, don't you think that, that . . .?'

'Think what? What else would you have me think? Do you have any better, more plausible explanation?'

'No, no. I don't suppose that I do. How are you feeling?'

'Not overly well, it must be said. Are you ready to leave?'

'Yes.'

'Good, as it would be helpful if we could get past Southampton before the rush hour sets in.'

* * *

As the medicine had failed to settle his grumbling digestive system, Lionel called at the public conveniences on the way back to the car. He remained inside for some time, exiting still clutching his stomach, but not as soaked as on the previous occasion.

'Are you sure that you're all right to drive?'

'Of course I am. It's just a slight stomach cramp,' he replied, wincing.

'That medicine really doesn't seem to have done you much good.'

'No, it doesn't, does it? I keep getting this blasted garlic-flavoured reflux.'

'Well, I'd be quite happy to drive, if—'

'I'm fine,' he said tersely, 'absolutely fine. And besides, I'd rather not risk you scraping the car on any of the other vehicles here.'

'You never have had much confidence in my driving,' she said, a note of resignation in her voice.

'Neither have you,' he replied.

They said little as they left Grimstone Peverell, with the only voice being that of a presenter that issued from the radio as they sped along the A31 through the leafless expanse of the New Forest. It was invisible but for a few bare limbs dusted with snow that stood stark in the fast fading light, soon to be blotted out by the fresh flakes that began to fall, thick and fast. Frances sent Ruth a text, expressing her admiration for the beauty of the Beke Window, and saying how much she looked forward to discussing it with her when they next met. From there it was but a short distance to the freedom of the motorway, but as Lionel put his foot down, he was seized by a searing pain in his bowels that caused him to scream out. His eyes clenched shut in reaction to the spasm that gripped and tore at his insides, which promptly evacuated their liquefied contents into his trousers, soaking into the seat, and slopping into the footwell. Frances shrieked and grabbed the wheel in an attempt to straighten the vehicle, but to no effect. It lost its traction in the slush, swerved violently to the left and careered across the carriageway into the path of a lorry. The latter's brakes could do little to slow its progress as it slammed into the Range Rover, and sent it hurtling into a clump of trees on the embankment. Fate, it seemed, had intervened to preserve Lionel Smallwood from having to endure *The Scurrillion* or anything like it ever again, but it was rather an exacting price to pay to avoid two hours of displeasure in the trendy London venue that went by the name of the Hoxton Observatory.

Radley's Farewell

Claire Radley rose from laying a wreath on the Smallwoods' grave, having been invited to the funeral by their daughter, Ruth. She was there in a professional capacity to show a mark of respect to a colleague on behalf of his paper, as evidenced by her expression, which was befittingly grim and solemn, yet betrayed little trace of sadness. She had found someone else to review *The Scurrillion*; a pity, really, for she would have liked to have raised Lionel's ire one last time, before dismissing him for being too out of touch, which is to say, 'too White, too male, and too English.' It was the one socially acceptable racism that could be indulged in, and in this, she indulged freely and enthusiastically, her attitude having caused Lionel to remark, in somewhat poor taste, that Radley's motto might best be summed up as 'diversity *macht frei*'.

Despite her parents' pronounced irreligiosity, Ruth had insisted upon a High Church service, and the church had been packed with family, friends and colleagues from the theatre and the arts, and had ensured that proceedings had been conducted in a manner sympathetic to her own and to her mother's refined aesthetic sensibilities. As they had died intestate, the familial estate passed in its entirety to her, their only child, and she had firm ideas as to how it could be best put to use.

Ruth had found some comfort in the fact that her mother had communicated how much she had appreciated the genius displayed in the Beke Window just before she died, and thus it seemed fitting that at least part of her substantial inheritance should be used to further augment the Minster's ornamentation. It was with a sense of both honour and delight, that she therefore received confirmation from the diocese that they were willing to accept her gift of a new commemorative window in memory of Frances and Lionel Smallwood. They were, moreover, honoured in their own turn to have such a skilled authority on mediaeval and Victorian stained glass as Ruth Smallwood personally design, craft, and oversee the installation of the new window.

The glass of the Smallwood Memorial Window would replace a number of transparent panes that had been inserted after the destruction of the greater part of the original stained glass in the 1640s. Ruth would have liked to set about this work with immediate effect, but her busy schedule of restoration at Hinton St Cuthbert Manor meant that it had to be delayed until it was completed, so it was not until 2014 that she finally devoted herself to the execution of the task.

From April to December she was absorbed in devising and creating this token of her love for her parent's memory, refining and perfecting the design until it fulfilled the highest standards of her craft. Working closely with the rector – the Reverend Lois Elmsley – she ensured that the new window was ready for its official unveiling on the date of the fifth anniversary of her parents' death: 21 December 2014. Coinciding, as it did, with the Christmas Fair, the Minster was filled with locals and visitors, many in Victorian costume, as well as reporters from the local press and regional television. As the organ breathed its last in line with the closing line of 'Rock of Ages', the Reverend Elmsley ascended the steps of the pulpit and delivered the following dedicatory eulogy.

'It is in both joy and sadness that we gather here to commemorate the lives of Frances and Lionel Smallwood, whose daughter, Ruth, has so generously, and lovingly, chosen to mark their passing with the gift of this window, that she herself has designed and crafted. In the play of its colour and light, that will hold the regard of generations to come, the living and eternal message of our Saviour and Lord Jesus Christ, will be brought to life in a vibrant luminosity, that will serve to remind all who look upon it, that we shall enjoy resurrection and the life eternal. We thank the Lord for the lives of Frances and Lionel, and for the gift that they brought into this world in the form of their daughter Ruth, whom I now call upon to unveil this latest ornament to the Minster.'

The congregation stood hushed as Ruth rose to her feet, walked towards the smiling reverend and shook her hands, before being directed to a cord that had been attached to some makeshift curtains. The two paused to turn and face the assembled photographers and camera crews from the local press and television, before Ruth pulled open the drapes to reveal the window, whose rich colours shone with a luminous intensity, lit by the rays of the midwinter sun. A spontaneous applause swelled through the crowd, as tears of joy welled up in the eyes of one of the elderly onlookers, trickling down her cheeks, and moistening her veil.

With this, the dedicatory service was brought to an end, and the congregation began to disperse. One of their number, however, possessed no desire to leave the building, and instead made her way with some eagerness towards the east end of the Minster, and there patiently waited for Ruth to finish speaking to the reporters. At the moment the artist set eyes upon this figure, elegantly dressed in the pristine black apparel of Victorian mourning, the latter lifted the diaphanous veil draped across her aged face, and with a look of great sorrow said: 'I knew your parents, and mourn their loss.'

'You knew them?' said Ruth, taken aback by the stranger's declaration.

'Perhaps I am overstating it a little to say that I *knew* them, but we were acquainted, and I spoke to your mother at some length on the morning that she died.'

The young woman breathed in sharply, her eyes moistening as she involuntarily glanced to the floor, before raising her head to meet the old woman's gaze: 'How did you come to know them?'

'I was here the morning that they came to visit this blessed spot, told them of its history, and showed them some of its treasures.'

'My mother texted me, on the . . .' Here the young woman's voice broke, as she choked back the memory of that final message to which she had had no time to reply. Her body heaved, and she broke into a sob.

'Do not worry child: they are at peace now.'

Ruth's eyes reddened as tears trickled down her cheeks, dappling her white jumper with darkened spots.

'All flesh is grass, and although the losses of our loved ones are hard to bear, we must submit to the Lord's will, and endure our loss with grace. I sympathise with you, child. Believe me when I say that it is such a pleasure to meet you, a daughter who has expressed her love and devotion in honouring her father and her mother through this wonderful work.'

'Thank you,' she said, wiping away her tears with a handkerchief.

'The time allotted to us all is short, and thus it behoves us to make timely arrangements for our departure, for we may be called at any moment.'

'Life is short, indeed, but—'

'I can see that you are a young woman of faith, and that you plainly value the work of the Church. Although I realise that what I am about to say may run the risk of appearing insensitive, I will say it anyway: marking the words that I have spoken regarding our mortality, would you consider making a bequest to the Minster in your will? The Beke Trust, for example, is always in need of funds to further its good works.'

Ruth was somewhat taken off guard by the directness of this question, and with a hesitant note in her voice replied: 'I've never thought about it – making a will that is, but what you say makes a lot of sense. My parents were not to know what was to befall them five years ago today, and they died intestate.'

'None of us knows when our hour will come.'

'No, indeed not. I think that I shall make a will – just in case.'

The old woman smiled, and the suggestion of a satisfied twinkle stole into her dark eyes: 'Then I should be glad if you would do me the honour of coming here this time next year, so that I can show you around this building, one last time, and point out where your parents and I last spoke. Will you come?'

'I shall. But tell me – what is your name?'

'My name?' She creased her eyes in puzzlement, seemingly bewildered as to who she was, turned her back on the visitor, lowered her veil, and took her leave in a series of slow, and halting, steps. The building was cold, but a certain warmth seemed to come with her leaving, and as she headed into some silent recess of the Minster, her form appeared to grow less distinct as it faded from view, as if merging into the fabric of the walls themselves.

Ruth looked on, beset by a sudden ringing in her ears, not of bells, but of tinnitus. She needed to get them syringed; she had been digging wax out of them for weeks, just like her father used to. She would ask her aunt – Monica – if she could stay in the guestroom next December. Yes, she would be sure to return; it was out of the question that she should disappoint the expectations of her new acquaintance, and she was so looking forward to hearing what she had to say.

3:05 am

Events come in threes

'I've a meeting with the senior partners this afternoon.'

'What about?'

He raised his right eyebrow as he usually did when he felt pleased with what he was about to say, complementing this with a smile that served only to underscore his sense of self-satisfaction. He didn't, however, volunteer an answer, for he wished to pique his wife's interest still further.

'I know that look, Mark Hillier. Something tells me that the cat thinks it's got the cream. Well, go on then, tell me. You can't leave me in suspense now!'

He laughed. 'No. Later.'

'Mark! Stop it! Stop teasing me!'

Philippa Hillier swung around behind her husband and draped her arms around his neck, then playfully flexed and tightened her fingers about it. She bent over and whispered in his ear.

'If you don't tell me what it's about, I swear I'll strangle you, you handsome devil.'

'Strangle me? I wouldn't do that if I were you, as I'm rather fond of breathing. Moreover, I happen to know a very good solicitor who would bang you to rights. Besides, who'd sort out the car if you were to knock me off?'

'You're such a spoilsport.'

'I know.'

'So, what's it about then? This meeting of yours? Does it have anything to do with this "very good solicitor" that you know?'

'Of course.'

'And who might that be?'

'You know him pretty well.'

'Do I now?'

'You certainly do.'

'And might this certain solicitor be in line for some sort of recognition for his being so very good?'

'Quite so, Watson. Quite so.'

'And what form does Holmes expect this recognition to take?'

'I do believe that he may be offered the opportunity to become a partner.'

Philippa beamed, and tousled his hair with her hands.

'In that case, I think you'd better change your tie,' she said

'Why?'

'You've dribbled egg yolk down it.'

'Damn!'

She laughed.

'Still, at least it's not as bad as what you'll be covered in later today,' he commented.

'Are you seriously telling me that you wouldn't relish the prospect of shoving your arm up a cow's behind?'

'I've suddenly lost all appetite for my toast. Look, I've got to go. We can discuss your exploration of the bovine anatomy later.'

'Change your tie!'

'Ah, yes. Almost forgot.'

'Oh, and before I *forget*, feel here.' Philippa placed his hand upon her stomach.

'What do you want me to say? You're getting fat?'

'No!'

'You've lost weight?'

'No!'

'Well, what then?'

'Can't you guess?'

'No. It's gone eight, and I really must be going. Mutley will be snarled up by now.'

'Just a minute Mark. Look at me. I want you to remember this moment.'

'Can't it wait?'

'No Mark,' she paused. 'We're going to be three.'

'So, we're adopting the royal "we" now, are *we*? Is a child entering or leaving toddlerhood at three? It's never been clear to me.'

'Must you always be so obtuse Mark? I'm pregnant.'

'Ah!' His face flushed red with embarrassment. He felt such an idiot. Still, this was unexpected but good news, and his smile could not be suppressed. He lent forward to embrace her.

* * *

Mark's mood was buoyant, despite the heavy traffic on the morning commute from Horrabridge to Plymouth. Already it was humid and sticky, and beads of sweat had begun to trickle down from his armpits, soaking his shirt.

'Damn!' he thought, 'I've forgotten to use deodorant. I'll be humming by this afternoon.'

He felt cross with himself for having made such an oversight. He wanted nothing to disrupt the smooth flow of his meeting with Watkins and Peters, least of all negligence in matters of personal grooming and hygiene. His future depended upon it.

When he returned home that evening, the heat of the day hung heavy about the village, and Philippa gave a warm reception to the news that the meeting had been a success. Their future was now secure. He was to be made a full partner of what would henceforth become Watkins, Peters and Hillier of Bretonside. With their first child on the way, it meant that they would be able to move out of their cramped and rather characterless semi at 12 Creber Court, and seek out a rural dwelling more in keeping with Philippa's bucolic tastes. Raised on the family farm near Stow-on-the-Wold, she had never taken to urban life whilst studying towards her degree at Bristol. Veterinary science was a long course – five years in all – and although she found it engrossing, she was glad to leave the city behind. Her first job brought her to Horrabridge, which is where she met her husband, but even this village was deemed excessively 'urban' for her liking. It was her dream to live somewhere solid, built of stone back in a time when written records of such things were not kept. She wanted to feel that her family and her home were a natural part of the landscape, embedded within, and growing out of it. This – their concrete-panelled semi – most decidedly was not.

They retired to bed early, but the heat and humidity of that late evening in June 1998 afforded them little sleep. The windows of the upper storey had been left wide open in an effort to tempt what little breeze there was inside, but it brought as much torment as it did relief, in the form of mosquitoes that whined about the bedroom until silence announced that they had halted to probe the resting couple for food. There, upon their bodies, they rested, gorging themselves upon their blood until glutted, then flying off to leave reddened, irritable welts in their wake. Sore payment for rendering such a satisfying meal.

The two of them tossed and turned in that state between sleep and wakefulness that brings neither relief nor opportunity for leisure, their sense of time dissolving into an unspecified span of disgruntled discomfort. Philippa, it seemed, was the first to yield to sleep, fitful as it may have been, yet for Mark, sleep would not come. He kept going over the preceding day's conversation regarding his promotion, and speculating as to what this might mean in practical terms, not only for his home life, but also for his working day. Mike Pearce had given him such a look that he could see that not all in the office shared in his delight at his personal advancement. Then again, few could be said to experience delight when looking at Pearce, other than his mother, perhaps.

Mark's throat had grown so dry that it felt as if it was about to split. It could be ignored no longer. He would have to drink, which meant a trip to the kitchen. A pint of water with some ice should do it. He raised himself from his bed, and walked out onto the landing. He felt the thick pile of the carpet between his toes as he trod down the stairs in the darkness, grasping the banister for safety. He opened the kitchen door, but hesitated before flicking on the light, his attention arrested by a dim glow that was emanating from the screen of the portable television that sat on the worktop. He stood there in the darkness, staring at it. It was not something that he had expected. The picture was fuzzy, with neither sound nor colour, and appeared to show a darkened street scene. A figure could be seen, poorly illuminated by the streetlights. It stood a while, loitering, then promptly vanished, only to reappear to wander aimlessly about the empty scene. It was at this point that he recognised the location: the pedestrianised precinct in Plymouth's Armada Way. 'Very odd,' he thought to himself. 'I swear the television was off when we went to bed. What is this rubbish anyway? I've heard of cheap television, but this takes it to a new level. Surely even Channel 5 wouldn't be screening this?'

He moved a little closer to the screen and peered at the shadowy form. He didn't get a good look as it was partially obscured by the foliage of a maturing palm. 'Good fashion sense,' he thought. 'He's wearing a jacket just like mine.' There was a digital time signature at the bottom right of the screen like that displayed on a CCTV monitor: 3:05 am. At that moment, the image fizzled out, contracting to a pinprick in the centre of the screen, leaving him in darkness. He felt his way back to the wall, flicked on the light and walked back to the television; it was switched off at the socket. He blinked, rubbed his eyes, and looked again. His thirst was forgotten as the peculiarity of the situation struck home, and for the first time that hot night, he shuddered. There would be no more sleep for Mark Hillier before sunrise.

Philippa proved to be out of humour at breakfast. She was tired and complained that her eyes felt gritty. He could see that they looked puffy, but thought better of mentioning it. On her right cheek, there was also a large mosquito bite that no amount of makeup could conceal, that stood proud of the surrounding skin like some angry dormant volcano. Her usual conversational self had been banished by hours of ill repose, to be replaced by a sullen doppelganger, silently stuffing Sugar Puffs into its mouth.

'Are you okay?'

'Yes.'

'How did you sleep?'

'Badly.'

'Me too.'

'Really?'

'Yes. Scarcely a wink in fact. I went down to the kitchen to get some water.'

'Hmm.'

He felt awkward. Even if she had been in a good mood, his reticence regarding broaching the subject would have been little different. Should he tell her what had happened? He hesitated, before deciding to adopt a roundabout tack.

'Have you noticed anything odd about the kitchen portable?'

'"Odd"?'

'Yes. Something unusual. Anything, really.'

'No. Why?'

'Well, I think that there may be some kind of electrical fault with it.'

'What makes you say that?'

'Last night, I came down to the kitchen for a glass of water, and when I opened the door, it was on.'

'Why didn't you switch it off before we went to bed?'

'I didn't switch it off, because it wasn't on.'

'Huh? What do you mean? I'm sorry, but I don't understand. Either it's on, or it's off.' A pronounced note of irritation had entered her voice. This was just what he had feared would happen. He knew that he would have to tread gingerly to avoid having his head snapped off. The crocodile was stirring.

'Well, yes, I know. Of course it has to be either on or off, but last night, at least for a short while, it seems that it was neither.'

'I've got a headache Mark, so could do without you setting stupid puzzles for me this morning. What are you digging at?'

'I'm not "digging at" anything. It's just that when I opened the kitchen door during the early hours, the television was on, only it was the most boring programme that you could imagine: no sound, no colour, no plot, just a fuzzy black and white screen showing a man wandering about aimlessly in Armada Way.'

'Isn't that what people always do in Armada Way? They put any old rubbish on the telly nowadays. What was it? Channel 5?'

'No, no, it wasn't Channel 5. Besides, not every channel would want to screen endless reruns of *All Creatures Great and Small*.'

'Well, I like watching it.'

'Now, that's a given, obviously. Anyway – the television. What makes it all the stranger, is that the power wasn't even switched on at the wall.'

'Well how could the television be on then?'

'I don't know. That's what's so puzzling.'

'Well in that case, how did you turn it off?'

'I didn't. It switched itself off.'

She shook her head and frowned with annoyance.

'That's mad. You must have dreamt it. Televisions can't work without electricity, and don't switch themselves on and off.'

'Perhaps you're right,' he conceded in an effort to defuse the situation, fully convinced of the reality of what he had seen.

'I'm going now Mark. I've got a Labrador to put down in Walkhampton.'

'I'll see you later.'

'Better effort with the tie today by the way: no egg yolk.'

'Thanks.'

'Ciao!'

The inimitable Mr Pearce

Watkins and Peters was a small firm of solicitors with a dozen or so employees. Its office was cramped and markedly behind the times, as evidenced by the absence of word processors and the continued use of electronic typewriters. This had not been a cause of concern for Mark when he had been begun working there almost seven years earlier after graduating from Exeter with a 2:2 in Law, but he was now of the opinion that they should welcome the personal computer, before their more tech-savvy competitors swept them aside. He got on well enough with the existing partners, but having been focused upon his career and domestic life, he had made little effort to socialise with the younger members of the team, one of whom – Mike Pearce – irritated him exceedingly. The feeling was mutual.

Pearce was a new arrival, having started work the preceding year, and like himself was an Exeter graduate. Beyond that, the two of them possessed nothing in common, with the former being unusually and outspokenly coarse for an aspirant solicitor. He spent most of his nights drinking, and when his spirits were suitably fortified by this activity, he tried his hand at picking up women, with whom he enjoyed a singular lack of success. At drinking however, he was highly adept, as attested to by his growing gut. He had been out on a spree the preceding evening, and for some reason insisted upon waylaying Mark as he left the office to stretch his legs that lunchtime.

'You're a right one, aren't you?'

'I'm sorry?'

'You're a right one; a real dark horse.'

Pearce's tone was mocking. His bloodshot eyes winced and narrowed from the brightness of the sunlight admitted by a nearby window; a sneer discernible about his lips and nose.

'I'm sorry Mike. I don't know what you're talking about. Now, if you'll excuse me, I need to get out for my lunch.'

'You think you're a cut above the rest of us, don't you? But I've seen you. I've been watching you. Don't you go pretending that you're summat you're not. I know. You're a one you are.' Pearce let out a sarcastic laugh.

'Look, I don't know what it is that you're driving at here Pearce, and I don't know why it is that you have taken such a dislike to me. If you want to get on here, it would behove you to try and be a little more civil, and be mindful of my position.'

'Hah! Hark at that! *Mindful* now is it? Oh, I'll be *mindful* all right, be assured of that. Like I say, I've been watching you, and I wouldn't be so confident of that position you do refer to.'

Mark walked out, fuming at Pearce's insolence, and bewildered as to the substance and meaning of his vague and threatening insinuations. Once he was confirmed as a partner, Pearce would have to go, one way or another, that much was plain.

He took his customary stroll through the Barbican and up onto the Hoe, savouring the fresh sea breeze that blew in from the Sound. As he looked over the water to Drake's Island and Mount Edgcumbe beyond, a myriad jewels of sunlight sparkling upon its dimpled surface, his sense of composure returned. He breathed deep and slow, his thoughts turning to Philippa and their future, but just as he was beginning to relax into this vision of domestic contentment, Pearce's face and voice forced their way into his consciousness, blowing it away. The afternoon proved to be a trial, and there would be no soothing breeze at home that evening to temper the heat and the humidity, or to blow away the cares of the day. It seemed that another poor night's sleep would be in the offing.

* * *

Philippa's working day had not been altogether satisfying. It had begun with despatching a Labrador, and had ended in her trimming away melanomas from the tips of a cat's balding ears. The feline was a particularly ugly beast – a Devon Rex – a veritable animated gargoyle, which had been rendered uglier still by the surgery. In the intervening hours, she had clipped the claws of a parakeet and administered laxatives to a constipated guinea pig called Greg, which had proven to be exceptionally fast working. Neither she nor her husband therefore felt in particularly high spirits that evening, and as they slogged up the stairs for an early night, the two of them held little confidence in getting the rest that they needed. Nonetheless, such was their exhaustion that both were soon unconscious.

It was Mark who awoke first, his body bathed in a pungent sweat, vaguely aware that his waking had been occasioned by a nightmare involving Pearce. He reached out and quickly emptied the glass of now tepid water that he had earlier placed on the bedside table, yet his thirst still raged. He would have to go to the kitchen. He got up and carefully trod his way downstairs in the darkness. Upon opening the kitchen door, he was surprised to see a dim glow once again issuing from the television screen. As on the previous night, the picture was fuzzy, albeit this time slightly sharper, resembling a live relay from a CCTV, the time stamped in the bottom right-hand of the screen as 2:43 am. The same figure was present, but this time seemed to be much more active, albeit less steady on his feet. He swayed a little whilst regarding the plate glass front of one of the department stores, then staggered backwards behind some bushes, before re-emerging with a large stone which he proceeded to lob at the window. The sheet of glass shattered, but did not give way. The man turned to the viewer, his face a blank but for his laughing mouth. Off went the set, plunging the kitchen into darkness.

Mark was both perplexed and unnerved, and for a few moments stood with his heart racing and his mind blank, before turning on the light to examine the television. The power was switched off at the socket (bizarre, yet not unexpected). He placed a hand upon the back of the set, but there was no warmth to indicate that it had been left on; it was no warmer than the air that surrounded it. He was baffled. Had he really seen it? Was his mind playing tricks on him? With the exception of the preceding night he had never previously experienced anything like this. Furthermore, nobody he knew had ever recounted such a phenomenon. Should he speak to Philippa about it? No sooner was the thought entertained than dismissed, given her reaction to his account at breakfast yesterday.

'Better get a drink,' he thought. He walked stiffly to the freezer for ice, dropped a number of cubes into his glass, filled it with water, and then regarded it with curiosity as they melted like miniature icebergs in a tropical sea. The tumbler was drained with a greedy rapidity, then refilled. He retraced his steps to the bedroom, slumped back into bed, and lay there with a jumble of half-formed thoughts and visions wandering as aimlessly through his mind as the figure had staggered about Armada Way. When it came, the dawn chorus put pay to his final hopes of sleep, so when the alarm went, Philippa opened her eyes to behold her husband's face, hag-ridden and devoid of warmth. It somehow did not resemble the face of a man who had just been promoted, and who was about to become a father for the first time; there was no joy in it.

'The heat doesn't agree with you, does it?'

'No,' he replied.

***

It was Mark's turn to be the taciturn one at breakfast, and when he arrived at the office, it dawned on him that he had no recollection of the intervening drive. His attention had been elsewhere, his thoughts preoccupied with the events of the past two nights.

The ensuing morning proved to be more trying than the norm. He couldn't focus, and kept having to ask colleagues to repeat what they had just said. This did not escape notice, and there were mutterings that this perhaps signified that his promotion to the partnership had been poorly thought through. Was he up to the job? It was thus a great relief when lunchtime finally arrived, providing him with the opportunity to leave the stuffy and claustrophobic confines of the office for some fresh air. Mike Pearce, however, wished to speak to him again, so interposed himself between Hillier and the doorway.

'Not very sharp this morning now, are we?'

'I'm sorry?'

'You've not been very sharp, have you? Least not this morning. I might go so far to say that you've been a bit *dozy*.'

'Oh, I see. It's true to say that I'm tired, which is why I need to get out for some fresh air. So, if you don't . . .'

'Now, hang on a minute; Josie's been upset by the errors that you made in the Cooper case. She almost passed on the notes to Mr Watkins, but I spotted them see, and got her to redo them. I did *you* a *favour*.'

'Ah, right. Thanks.'

'Well, I'm glad to see that you're giving me some credit *for a change*. I'd like to see some more of that in future, if you don't mind, *Mr* Hillier.'

Mark stared at Pearce in his full fat-necked, flabby-jowled and piggy-eyed glory, overcome with a visceral loathing for the man. The newcomer seemed to have displayed an ill-defined sense of resentment at his position ever since he had arrived, and this had rankled with Mark. Pearce could sense this antipathy, yet found it gratifying, as was evident in the self-satisfied grin traced out by his thin lips.

'Don't worry, I'll not tell Mr Hopkins. You *can't help it* – you're tired. No surprise that, given what you were up to last night.'

'What?'

'You're a card you are, *Mr* Hillier! Up to all them shenanigans, and yet pretending to be all so proper.' Pearce broke down into laughter.

'I've had enough Pearce. I don't know what you're talking about. Now, if you wouldn't mind getting out of my way.'

Mark squeezed past his younger, fatter colleague, thoughts of the recent strange events momentarily displaced by his sense of indignation at the latter's behaviour. He exited the office at a purposeful pace, teeth and fists involuntarily clenched, his eyes fixed at some indeterminate point in the middle distance, blind to his surroundings. He oozed anger. Fellow pedestrians looked askance, and gave him a wide berth. His feet were carrying him to the Barbican, their choice of destination automatic. It was then that a thought occurred to him: 'Should I take a walk to Armada Way instead? Why not. Yes, yes, I'll go there.' His brain took over from his feet.

He deviated from his normal routine in which he would saunter past the Citadel and onto the Hoe, and instead sought out the crowds of shoppers in the city centre. His pace slowed as he negotiated his way past the pushchairs and pensioners that filled the pavements of Royal Parade, the sunshine beating down on his left cheek, his face flushed, and his armpits sweating beneath his jacket. He undid his top button and loosened his tie in an effort to cool off, but to little avail.

Within a few minutes, he was walking through the pedestrianised precinct of Armada Way, in search of the spot he had seen the preceding night. It was not long until he found what he was looking for: the remains of the department store window, clearly the same one that he had seen smashed from the comfort of his kitchen some ten hours earlier. The glaziers had yet to make good the damage, and a barrier had been put in place to prevent shoppers from getting too close. Beyond this, and the brushing away of the resultant shards and splinters of glass, the scene had been left unchanged since the enigmatic stranger had unleashed his act of vandalism.

Mark's stomach began to churn. He felt confused and a little sick, so sought out a bench. For a few minutes he sat there scanning the surrounding buildings for CCTV cameras, but found none that would have afforded the view of the scene that had appeared on his television screen these past two nights. He had no appetite, so bought nothing for lunch before heading back to work. He should be happy he reasoned, stood as he was upon the brink of two major positive life events, yet instead he was beset with a great sense of personal unease occasioned by a portable television. It was beyond explanation.

That night Mark placed two pint glasses upon his bedside table instead of one, for he had no desire to venture down to the kitchen. Philippa found it odd that he should choose to take two glasses to bed, for wouldn't one of them, at least, get too tepid to drink during the night? He shrugged off the question, claiming that he was too lazy to get up and walk to the kitchen in the small hours, but there was something about his statement that did not ring true. Her suspicion was aroused.

After two nights of broken sleep, he fell swiftly into a slumber, only to be awakened some time later by a clap of thunder. He lay awake as the storm rumbled on for an hour or so, the torrential rain illuminated by the occasional flash, eventually yielding to silence and a cooling of the air conducive to sleep. When the morning came, he awoke feeling refreshed. The heatwave had broken, the serene blue skies replaced by an unbroken blanket of grey cloud, more in keeping with the nature of the moor and the settlements that hugged its fringes. From it drifted down a good thick Dartmoor drizzle, bringing succour to the thirsty moss that mantled the stones of the villagers' walls. Somehow,

Philippa had managed to sleep undisturbed through the turbulence of the night, so the two of them were in a playful mood over breakfast. This restoration of their good humour banished thoughts of the recent unusual events from Mark's mind and as June gave way to July, and then to August, they began to fade from his memory, eventually becoming relegated to the realm of dream.

On the morning of Thursday 13 August, the couple awoke to a fine summer's day. It promised to be hot, and upon that promise, it delivered. The two of them enjoyed a salad that evening, the rocket and tomatoes supplemented with liberal amounts of Parma ham and chorizo, that for some reason brought the person of Pearce to Mark's mind. Philippa refrained from drinking, but he took to the Rioja with a certain amount of relish. They retired to bed early, but neglected to take any water with them despite the warmth and closeness of the air. When he awoke in the early hours, his thirst accentuated by having consumed the best part of a bottle of wine, there was thus only one thing for it: he must go to the kitchen.

The unsteadiness of his feet signalled that the alcohol was still in control, although a feeling akin to being trepanned announced the onset of an incipient hangover, which he was desperate to halt in its tracks through drinking as much water as he could. He tripped from the bottom stair, barging open the kitchen door to find the room illuminated by a low greenish light. There sat the television on the kitchen worktop. It fizzed with static, frantically speckling the glass with multi-coloured dots, the hiss of white noise clearly audible; and then it stopped. He found himself looking upon the familiar scene of Armada Way in Plymouth city centre, but this time, the picture had resolved itself with a greater clarity, and he could see that the figure that wandered within it was plainly the same one that had shown itself to him in

June. It appeared to pause and gaze out at him. It smiled, then turned its back and started to tear at the greenery, ripping at the bushes, and then breaking off the branches of some of the smaller trees, before carrying out a frenzied attack on a litter bin. As this was happening, he noted that the figure was wearing a jacket, shirt, trousers and shoes that resembled his own favoured attire for a night out. He called out.

'Philippa! Philippa! Come down! Now! It's back! It's back! Shit, I can't believe it! Quick, quick!' He was going into meltdown.

She awoke with a start, his shouting sending her into a panic. She called from the bedroom. 'What? What's going on?'

'The television – the man's back!'

Philippa leapt from her bed and rushed downstairs into the kitchen, to find her husband staring at the screen, a figure clearly visible running into the distance, as if alarmed by his yelling. The picture snapped off almost instantly.

'Shit Mark, what are you doing? What the hell is going on?' She flicked on the light. 'What are you playing at?'

'I'm not playing at anything. You saw it. You did, didn't you?'

'That the television was on? Yes, I saw that.'

'Well?'

'Well what?'

'Look! Look at the socket! It's switched off, isn't it?'

She rubbed her eyes, and then shuffled over to take a look.

'So it is. How did you do that?'

'How did I do what?'

'How did you get it to work when the socket's switched off? Have you rigged it up so that it looks as if it's off when it's on?'

'No. Of course I haven't. Why would I do that? More to the point, how would I do that? I'm not a bloody electrician.'

'I don't know. You tell me.'

'Look, I don't know what to make of it. The last time that I walked down the stairs to find it on, that figure smashed one of the windows of a department store on Armada Way. So, during my lunchbreak the next day, I took a walk up there to see if anything had happened. When I got there, what did I find? The self-same window broken, with a cordon put up to keep people at a safe distance. It's as if we're having CCTV beamed into our home.'

'When was this? You never mentioned anything to me. Why not?'

'It was the night after this happened for the first time. Given how snappy and dismissive you were about it, I didn't want to risk mentioning it.'

'Maybe I was, but this is still nonsense Mark.'

'I know, I know. It makes no sense at all, but it's true. Just before you came down, he was tearing at the trees and shrubs in the pedestrian precinct. I'm going to walk up there during my lunch hour today, and I'm willing to wager my job that I will find evidence of the vandalism that I've just seen played out on this television.'

'This is ridiculous Mark. I'm going back to bed. You can believe what you want, but I need some sleep. You should try and get some too.'

'You see what I said about you being snappy and dismissive? Look, he was dressed just like me.'

'I'm too tired for this Mark. I'm going up, whether you are or not. Goodnight.'

Trouble at Toffs

For Mark, the end of the morning could not come soon enough. His colleagues noted that he was agitated and more short-tempered than usual, but attributed his mood to the heat which the office fans did nothing to ease. At 12:30, he drew his dictation to a prompt close, picked up his jacket and headed for the exit. Pearce sat and stared at him as he walked past, his jowls juddering and sheening with sweat beneath his wispy ginger stubble as he shook his head, a knowing smile upon his lips. 'Why's Pearce wearing that insufferable expression?' he thought to himself.

'What's the matter Pearce? Have something to say do you?'

'Oh no, nothing's the matter *Mr* Hillier. *Nothing* at all.' Pearce's eyes and the cast of his mouth were as mocking as the tone of his self-assured whining voice. The urge to plant a fist in his porcine face had never been stronger.

'Good. Good!'

'Enjoy your lunch, *Mr* Hillier.'

Mark Hillier stormed out of the office, bringing an abrupt halt to the secretaries' lunchtime gossip. He headed for Armada Way, eager to confirm or refute his suspicions regarding what he had that past night witnessed. Ten minutes later, he found himself at his desired destination, surveying the mess left by the torn and broken foliage and branches that he had seen ripped and twisted from the trees and bushes. The city planners who had hoped that these would soften the concrete brutalism of post-war Plymouth would surely be disappointed to see that someone had so vigorously objected to their design. 'What does this mean? Why did I see this? How is it possible? Why me?' To these questions, he could muster no answers. He sat down next to the nearby water feature, took his sandwiches from his lunchbox and nibbled at them in a listless daze. His appetite had gone. The rest of the working day was spent in near silence, his uncommunicative mood carrying over to his evening with Philippa, who, bored with his company, left him alone to down a bottle of chilled Chianti before he finally joined her in bed. His assertions regarding what he had seen that lunchtime did nothing to dispel her disbelief; she was nettled that he would not drop this delusional obsession that he seemed to be developing.

The clouds built, but no storms broke the heat of that Friday night, although, as was so often the case, thirst broke Mark's slumber. And so it was that he once more found himself heading to the kitchen in search of refreshment, only to be greeted by the static glow of the television screen. His heart sank at the sight, and he let out a groan. The picture at once resolved itself, this time pin sharp; it was so detailed that it appeared as if he was looking through a window. However, unlike on previous occasions the familiar figure was nowhere to be seen, and it was not Armada Way that he looked upon, but a row of cars parked in Guildhall Square. He stood and looked, waiting for something to happen. A minute passed, but nothing. He was about to go to the tap when he noticed something move next to the furthest car. The lighting was poor, but he could see that it was a figure, which grew larger as it moved towards his point of view, pausing at each car. At the first, he appeared to pour a can of lager over its windscreen. At the next, he bent the aerial with a deft twist of the wrist, before deflating the tyres of its neighbour, and committing sundry acts of petty vandalism on each vehicle until he reached the last in line. This one was closest to what Mark assumed to be the camera that was relaying the scene to him. Here, this unknown player stopped, stared, and the sound of the television crackled into life as he looked out to address the viewer.

'It's a hot night Mark, I'll grant you that. Not comfortable for sleeping now, is it? Still, you'll find it hotter yet mate; you'll find it hotter yet.'

With that, the man turned to the final car, removed a jemmy from beneath his jacket, and raising his arm unleashed a mighty blow that smashed the driver's window. From one of his bulging pockets he drew a rag, and from another, a small can. He dropped the cloth onto the driver's seat, dowsed it with lighter fluid, lit a match and dropped it inside. He backed off smartly to stand at a safe distance, where he paused to regard his handiwork. The flames flickered up, rapidly taking hold of the car's interior, its vinyl seats igniting and starting to melt. Tonight, the lurid yellows and oranges of the flames and black of the toxic smoke were depicted with an uncanny fidelity. So real did it seem, that Mark felt as if he were there with the arsonist. The figure was laughing as he turned once more to his viewer.

'I told you it'd be a hot one Mark. See? I don't tell no lies mate. I don't tell no lies.'

The figure grinned, his features at last clearly resolving themselves, plainly the worse for drink and delighted in the disorder in which he was indulging. Mark winced and let out a shriek. The unknown man responded with a laugh.

'You're a card Mark Hillier! You're a card! What do you think you're up to, eh?'

That voice. That familiar, whining, snide voice. How often he had heard the irritating tones of Mike Pearce, but he had never expected to hear them here in his own kitchen, least of all issuing from a television set. Yet, as for the face . . . Good God! Philippa barged into the kitchen having woken to discover that her husband was absent.

'Mark! What's wrong? What's going on?'
'Look!' He pointed at the set.
'What's this?'

'It's him again! Look! Damn it, he's turned away. He's just set light to that car.'

Philippa looked on in disbelief, catching only a glimpse of the man's features before he turned to run from two police officers who gave chase. She heard their whistles blow, and after another couple of seconds the picture vanished and the television fell silent.

'Put the light on! Put the light on!'

'Okay, okay Mark. Don't panic. Be calm.'

Their eyes smarted as the neon strip buzzed into life.

'See – it's switched off at the wall, but you saw for yourself that it was on.'

'I did, I did.' She looked at her husband in disbelief.

'This is really getting to me. You weren't here when he spoke, were you?'

'He spoke?'

'Yes, he spoke. He spoke to me. He called me by my name. It was Pearce's voice, but it wasn't Pearce.'

'Pearce's? Mike Pearce's?'

'Yes.'

'But that's impossible; it's ludicrous.'

'The whole thing is impossible, so why would he speaking to me be any more outlandish than all the other stuff that's been going on?'

'I don't know Mark. Why is this going on? You tell me.'

'How do I know? I haven't a clue. Do you believe me now?'

'I don't know what to think. I just don't know. Look, let's get rid of the set. I don't like it Mark. It's upsetting you.'

'Thank God you believe me Philippa. I was beginning to doubt my sanity. That thing's got to go. I'll take it to the tip tomorrow.'

'Why not sell it?'

'I don't want to risk giving it to anyone we know. It's got to be disposed of. I don't want it under this roof for one night longer. I'm putting it out now. Open the door for me. I'll not sleep until it's out of this house.'

The television was dumped on the patio to await its fate, allowing the couple to return to bed safe in the knowledge that they would no longer be confronted by the unpredictable imagery that had recently flitted across its screen.

They slept in late, uncharacteristically so, even for a Saturday, but Philippa was awoken by a persistent knocking at the door. Mark slept on, so she pulled on her dressing gown and hurried downstairs into the hall. There she caught sight of two tall dark silhouettes showing through the frosted glass of the front door. She opened it.

'Good morning madam. Constables Merrick and Robertson here. Would you happen to be Mrs Philippa Hillier?'

'Why, yes, I am. Good morning officers. How can I help?'

'I'm sorry to be the bearer of bad news Mrs Hillier, but we're here on a matter concerning your husband.'

'My husband?'

'Yes. You may well be wondering where he is, but we can assure you that he is safe and sound and currently sobering up in one of our cells.'

'What?'

'I know that this often comes as a shock, but . . .'

'I'm sorry for interrupting constable, but there seems to have been some kind of mistake. My husband is here at home. He's in bed.'

Constable Merrick smiled whilst Robertson scowled.

'Now madam, is this, or is this not, your husband?' asked Merrick, handing her a mugshot. Her eyes widened.

'That's amazing! It looks just like him.'

'Your husband works for a firm of solicitors in Bretonside by the name of Watkins and Peters, does he not?'

'He did, but it recently changed its name to Watkins, Peters and Hillier; he's just become a partner.' She smiled.

'Well, that's very nice Mrs Hillier, very nice, but evidently they've not got around to changing that in the Yellow Pages yet. Now, otherwise, is this the firm for which he works?'

'It is.'

'And one of his colleagues is a Mr Mike Pearce?'

'I believe that's the case, yes.'

'We took your husband into custody last night having apprehended him in Plymouth city centre. He had set light to Mr Pearce's Volkswagen Polo, and vandalised a number of other cars parked in the vicinity of the Guildhall. Mr Pearce reports that he and your husband had had a heated argument whilst at Toffs Nightclub, and that Mr Hillier had stormed out having made a number of threats to Mr Pearce, whom he addressed as "an underhand, scheming shit." Can you remember this argument?'

'What? Remember? I wasn't even there. Neither was my husband.'

Constable Merrick looked at Robertson, then back to Philippa and shook his head slowly.

'Come now Mrs Hillier. We have a statement from Mr Pearce that you and your husband were at Toffs Nightclub with him last night. Furthermore, a taxi driver has confirmed that he took a fare from a woman living at this address at 1:15 am this morning. He said that after entering the cab, she had told him she was returning home alone because she had rowed with her husband over his drinking to excess.'

'What? That's ludicrous. What kind of bizarre joke is this?'

'"Joke"? Now, if you don't mind Mrs Hillier . . .'

'Look, this is ridiculous. Just a moment.' She walked to the bottom of the stairs and called up to her husband. 'Mark! Mark! Come downstairs! I need you!' There was no reply. 'Mark! I'm sorry constable, but he's a heavy sleeper. He's slept badly lately. I can prove that what I say is true. He's still in bed. Please, come and see for yourself.'

The two men looked at her with incredulity.

'Please! Something's gone badly wrong here. You've got the wrong man. Please, come in. Follow me upstairs.'

'Madam, wasting police time is not something that I would recommend.'

'It must be that man Pearce. He's behind this. He's been lying to you!'

She ran off upstairs, the two policemen following.

'Mark! Mark! For heaven's sake, wake up!'

She flung open the bedroom door, only to find the bed empty.

'Mark! Where are you? For God's sake Mark, stop playing around and come out. Stop playing around and come out. We've the police here. The police!'

She ran to the bathroom, and to the guest bedroom. Both were empty. He could be found neither upstairs nor downstairs, nor in the garden. There was no trace of him.

'I'm so sorry madam. I've seen this before. We understand. It's the shock. None of us like to face up to things when a man behaves so out of character. We'd like you to accompany us to the station.'

Philippa froze.

'To the station?'

'Yes madam. For identification purposes.'

'Okay, okay, I'll come. I can prove that it's not him. This is so odd; really odd. I just need to put some clothes on.'

'Of course madam. We'll wait here for you.'

'Thank you.'

'Madam!'

'Yes?'

'Is this purse yours?' asked Robertson, picking up a brown leather purse from the telephone table.

'Oh, yes. Thank you constable.'

'And what about this? Recognise it?'

Her mouth dropped.

'It's a ticket for Toffs Nightclub, isn't it madam? Now, let's take a look at the date. Hmm. Friday 14 August.'

Philippa collapsed onto her knees, and broke down into tears.

The Cleft Owl

Quick and shallow gasps

The ruts had set like stone, held in the grip of an early season's frost, their forms picked out by the shadows cast by a reddening sky. Bare were the hedgerows, but for the hips and haws, and quiet was the lane, apart from the wheezing and panting of a young man hastening through the dusk, his breath noisily steaming in vaporous, dragon-like snorts. Stumbling forwards, he slipped, and held out his hands so that he might break his fall. There he sat some moments upon the frozen muck, his head singing with the high-pitched whine of pain, and held up his palms to behold them grazed and torn. A thickening trickle of blood beaded, and dropped onto his jerkin. *For my sins.*

Rising to his feet, he redoubled his pace towards Tooley's Cott. A wisp of woodsmoke, fragrant and lightly sweet, coiled from the stone of the chimney stack into the stillness of the air. A welcome sight: someone was tending the hearth. His pace slackened. He eyed the door, collecting his breath in quick and shallow gasps, as a blackbird from a neighbouring tree trilled its farewell to day.

God grant that 'e should be 'ere, and that it be not too late.

His hand smarted as he rapped on the unforgiving wood. The sweat of his exertions now cooling, his fingers nipped by oncoming winter's bite, he heard the scuff of a chair and the shuffle of feet within. The door eased open; an unwelcoming face, its features sharp and suspicious, looked at, and into him.

'What business have you here? Pray speak!'

He had heard that Tooley could be abrupt, but such displeasure he had not expected.

'Begging your pardon, sir, but we be in sore need of 'elp. Father's taken ill, and 'as grown much worse this past day.'

'Father? And who might you be, boy? Your name, if you will?'

He stared hard into the young man's eyes.

'Meade, sir. John Meade.'

His surname gave him pause. A memory, long buried, stirred.

'Could you find no other to minister to his wants?'

The lad anxiously shook his head. 'No sir. Besides, there be none in Widecombe that do 'ave a reputation such as yours. We've 'eard it said that you do 'ave knowledge that may bring 'un out of 'is low state, which be not of the usual sort.'

'Who told you this?'

'Widow Spencer. She did say that you do 'ave command of certain arts, of which others do know but little. 'Er opinion of you do stand 'igh, and we do reckon on 'er word.'

Tooley paused, weighing the earnestness of the young man's speech.

'And your father has ready coin?'

'That 'e do sir, yes.'

'And you have this with you?'

He shook his head. 'No. But be assured that 'e'll pay should you come.'

The cottager summoned a brief and mirthless smile.

'And does he know how much I would ask of him should I choose to render him my services?'

'Please sir. 'E will pay. Doubt not that 'e will. Will you come?'

'I take it that you wish me to come now?'

'If it so pleases you, sir, then yes.'

'It does not. I shall think upon what you have asked. If I do decide to administer physic, I shall come and seek you out tomorrow.'

The young man's mouth dropped and his eyes widened. 'But—!'

'I shall come in the morning,' interrupted the cottager, raising his hand. 'Where is it that you live?'

'Next to the smithy, sir. In Widecombe.'

'Very well. You look cold, boy. Had you not best be making your way home? The light already casts great shadows about the land. Four miles is a long way to make before nightfall. You'll have to run, and be sharp about it. A good evening to you.'

With that, Tooley abruptly closed the door and retreated inside, leaving a shivering John Meade to thank the Lord for the little light that the moon and the stars would afford on his way home. He took to his heels, and scuttled off back down the lane, taking pains so that he might not slip once more.

He says that he has ready coin, reflected Tooley as he lit a candle from the fire. *Of that, all men find themselves in want. I shall take it, and more, should he have it. As for his malady, then either God or the Devil may decide its course and dispose of him as they will, but that should be no reason for me not to practise my art in return for due payment. Given that neither the Almighty nor Lucifer finds himself in need of his lucre, then it may as well be of service to my pocket, and to my pocket alone.*

A ewe, heavy with lamb

Venus and the first bright stars of night pierced the purple vault of the sky as John Meade reached the family home. His throat parched and burning from the frosted air, his mother poured him small beer which he drank down in greedy gulps, the cold of the cottage as of nothing to the bitter chill outside. His hands were as numb as his thoughts, their digits stinging with returning warmth. Sensation was returning.

'Your father do still lie abed. What did 'e say, John? Will 'e come?'

'Not tonight. On the morrow; in the morning 'e did say.'

Joan Meade's eyes were restless, and deeply creased about with lines made stark by the glow of the fire. She looked to the floor, then to her son, whose hair hung lank with sweat, his hands bloodied and smeared with mud.

'What 'appened, son? Your 'ands?'

'I did slip and fall. 'Twere the ice.'

She fetched a bowl of water, moistened a rag, and wiped them free of dirt and dried blood. He seemed to her a young child once again, as he smarted and winced, his tender cuts weeping red tears that coloured the water a warmer hue. Cries issued from the room upstairs. There was a slam upon the floor as a toppled stool signalled the need for a calming hand. A rushlight was lit, and a dutiful wife ascended the steps by its sputtering light.

'It were the dog, Joan. The dog! Again! The very same one. I did try to fend 'un off; I did try my utmost, but I couldn't stop 'un,' raved her husband, breaking into heaving sobs and clutching at his wife. She bent down to cradle his head as if he were a helpless child.

His eyes were wet with tears, and red from want of rest. Each day for a month had come the same nightmare: he is high on the moors, and a ewe, heavy with lamb, is caught fast in the gorse. She is skittish, and tugs to get out, her fleece snagging in the thorns. He beats the thicket down with his crook and reaches in to pull her out, but she struggles and the tangle grows worse. The shepherd reaches forward, but falls and puts out his arms to protect his face, countless thorns piercing his palms, their tips breaking and lodging beneath the skin. She frees herself and he rises in great pain to stare at his hands, thanking God that he had not to suffer such piercings about his head. The ewe bleats in distress, and he turns to see a great dog standing over them, its coat black, shaggy and gleaming, its teeth bared in a snarl. All he can move are his tongue and lips, whose wild workings bring forth no sound. Such is fear's grip; the beast holds him in its thrall. The sheep takes fright, miscarries, vents much blood and staggers off to die. The hound fades into the mist, and Henry Meade wakes with a griping in the guts, and the sensation of a tightening band about his head.

'Hush! Hush, husband! Master Tooley will come on the morrow.'

'Master Tooley?'

'The wise man. John did speak with 'un today. You do need sleep.'

Henry Meade begged for drink, and was given water. He coughed, cried out once more, and slumped into a night of fitful and restless slumber.

A dancing, smiting orb of light

Robert Tooley rose before daybreak, gathering the stock of his trade: phials of powdered snakestone, thunderbolts and Devil's toenails.

The boy made no mention of what ails his father. How then, should I proceed? 'Twas foolish of him. No matter, I shall make a show of it, for whatever the treatment, the outcome shall be the same. To purge, bleed or clyster, or to administer some other cure? My ephemeris shall guide me, once I have cast his natal chart.

'When should I expect you, master?' asked Sarah, her voice quiet, quavering, uncertain.

'By nightfall.'

'And what would you have me prepare?'

'Stew of mutton, girl, with turnips. Now, be quick and help me with the saddlebags.'

He turned and walked towards Speedwell, placing a halter about her head and a saddle upon her back. She stood, placid and obedient, and let out a snort. There were no flies to bother her this day, for now was not their season. Sarah stood by, straining to hold the bags that she had lugged after her master. He took them from her and draped them over the pony's loins, but gave no thanks. His taking leave of her was a peremptory 'Be about your duties,' accompanied by a stern eye. He looked ahead, and with a cry of 'Hup!' and a kick, the pony moved forward, her hooves picking their way down the frost-hardened track to Ponsworthy, swathed in the chill of an early morning mist.

With the descent the sunlight yielded to a grey drabness that still held fast in the hollow between the hills, where the woodsmoke from the cottages mingled and lingered. A rook passed harsh comment from its bough, but Tooley cared not to respond. *What does a bird know of my business?* A cottager paused to wish him 'Good day,' and he nodded in return. Up the lane and out of the mist he rode, and wended his way to Widecombe.

It was bright as he entered the village. He paused to regard the church in which five-and-forty years earlier as a boy of seven he had witnessed the Devil's work in the house of the Lord. The only miracle he had ever witnessed. God, it seemed, had left off such things, and let loose his fallen angel to wreak what ill he would. He had heard the crash of stone, and seen a dancing, smiting orb of light; a beauteous thing that had seared and scorched in its glancing path. From his pew he had seen such wonders. It was there that he had come to know the smell of brimstone and burning flesh. England, in the guise of a charnel house, would come to know both soon enough thereafter, but who knew then? Not one soul.

A face took form and floated up from the depths of his memory; it was the face of a man silently seated in his pew, his expression serene, and his eyes closed. A friend called out in an effort to wake him, but seeing that he did not move, drew closer, and reaching out to jog him from his slumber, stalled. The hindmost portion of the sleeper's head was no more; the skull had been shattered. His brains lay shat out in the seat behind. Tooley found himself exclaim aloud 'Meade! Robert Meade!' The grandfather of the boy who had called him here. How strange that the boy's expression should have been so full of worry, and that of the dead man have been so at ease.

He left Speedwell at the smithy to be reshod, then retired to the alehouse before setting about his morning's work. It was dim and quiet within, with only the alehouse keeper and two others present: young men, who ought to be about some business rather than indulging their leisure. The pair were savouring Raleigh's stinking herb as they sank their pots, eyeing Tooley as he entered. *Young curs!* he thought as he returned a glare in answer to their impudent appraising looks, fixing them with an unspoken menace that declared he was no man to be crossed. Their attention shifted to a pack of cards, which the taller of the two flexed and shuffled with aimless intent.

'Well, Robert. It be a long while since 'ee did last come this way,' said Edward Baker, whose house this was.

'Aye. A long while indeed. But business spurs me abroad. A tankard of small beer, if you will.'

'Business? Of what manner?' asked Baker as he poured his ale.

'A matter of effecting a cure.'

'A cure?'

'For a most curious malady, the nature of which I as yet remain ignorant. 'Tis for one of the Meade family. Their boy, John, sought me out yesterday, and begged help in curing his father. What know you of this?'

''Tis no secret that things have gone bad for them of late. Henry's not been seen about the village this past month. He's taken to his bed, and, I've 'eard it said, do oft rave of visions.'

'*Visions*? Of what sort? Spirits? Devils?'

'Some matter to do with a dog; nothing more than that.'

'A dog? Is it believed to be madness, or possession?'

'Best ask the parson. Let 'un deal with otherworldly spirits, devils and the like, and leave I out of it to be getting on with what I do know.'

Tooley frowned with displeasure.

'I'd sooner not. Be any other member of his family thus stricken, or any of his neighbours?'

'No. None, although I'll tell 'ee one thing I do know,' he replied, hesitating.

'Well?'

'He did take to his bed after the business with William Huccaby.'

Mention of Huccaby's name caused the young men to prick up their ears and cease in their chatter.

'I'd heard of his most unnatural demise, but I had few dealings with him. I heard it of Mary Bovey. 'Twas by his own hand, was it not?'

'That it were. Opened his veins with a knife.'

'A dark business. The necessary measures, I take it, have been observed?'

'Measures?'

'Regarding his burial.'

'I've had no dealings with any burying, Robert. I couldn't offer 'ee any advice on that, no sooner than I could tell 'ee

205

how to make a cock lay eggs. All I do know is that he were laid in his winding sheet with few there to mourn.'

His quip failed to raise a smile, and Tooley resumed with his questioning.

'Surely you must know if they have made it so that he cannot walk?'

'I can't say that I do catch your meaning. But what I can say is neither I, nor anyone that I've spoken to, did ever see a dead man walk. Huccaby'll not be taking to his heels now.'

'You think not? Well, we shall see about that.' Tooley raised and drained his tankard. 'Brandy.'

'As ever,' replies Edward. 'This were always the spirit that 'ee did most care to conjure.'

A brittle and unconvincing smile curled across Tooley's lips as he took the glass and threw back its contents; an emboldening and fortifying fire that drove out the last vestiges of cold.

'Have 'ee never regretted laying off coopering?'

''Tis not my calling these days, Edward,' he replied, before turning to the young men who sat listening with curious intent, their clay pipes smouldering with dank and acrid fumes. His eyes narrowed, as a smile born of cunning broke forth upon his face. One of the two he knew by sight – Richard Hill – a young shearsman of the parish of dubious character, but the other, he knew not. His companion's station he found difficult to weigh, for there was something about his air suggestive of genteel birth and upbringing, that rendered the man unfit for such low company. He could not help but think that there was something awry.

Hill knew rather more of Tooley than the latter did of Hill, for he was oft spoken of in Widecombe; he took him for a rogue, which is to say that he thought him a kindred spirit.

'Good day to you gentlemen. I should be grateful of your acquaintance. My name is Tooley. Doctor Robert Tooley.'

'*Doctor*, be it? Well, there's a fancy title for 'ee,' replied the younger in a mocking tone. 'And I be Richard Hill of this parish. I do think I've seen 'ee afore?'

'More than likely,' replied the older man through gritted teeth, 'for your face is known to me, despite our not having spoken.'

'And I, sir, am Stephen Damerell,' announced the stranger with an enunciation as clear and polished as his eyes were bold.

'I'm most pleased to make your acquaintance, Master Damerell,' replied Tooley in a voice sonorous and, contrary to his words, devoid of pleasure. 'Unlike Master Hill, I know not your face, and your name, I think, is not familiar to this parish.'

'I am but passing through, sir.'

'Passing through?'

'Upon business. But, finding my progress to be swifter than I had foreseen, I resolved to tarry here for a day or two before proceeding upon my way, for I find this place to my liking.'

'Your tastes must then be modest to take satisfaction from so small a village as this,' observed Tooley.

'The company serves me well enough,' he replied, looking to the shearsman whilst tapping his pack of cards upon the table, 'and, after all, there can be no gaming without company,' he added with a smile.

'Indeed not. I may yet have a game for you to play, Master Damerell, if you are to stay a day or two longer. That is a fine sword that you have there; to keep you safe on the road, no doubt?' said Tooley, eyeing the rapier buckled to his belt.

'The public highway can indeed be a place most dangerous for a man both unwilling and unable to offer his own defence. I, however, find myself quite at ease.'

'I do not doubt it.'

'Now, as for this "game" you mention, pray do enlighten me as to its nature.'

'Later. If it is to be played, you shall know by the morrow.'

'Your words betray little, *doctor*; you hold things close. You may find me here at noon, if you should wish to solicit my engagement in this *game* of yours. What wager is it that you propose?'

'There'll be no wager; no cards. 'Tis not a game of those sorts that we shall play.'

'Then I am not sure that either I, or young Master Hill here, would find it to our liking.'

'If you've a liking for money, then it should please you well enough. Either I, or someone of my appointing, will seek you out and apprise you of its nature. Good day to you,' said Tooley with a cursory nod of the head who then made to depart.

Hill looked to Damerell, the former's mouth agape in dumb puzzlement, his want of wit vexing the latter. The newcomer's patience was beginning to fray, for most of Hill's coin was now his own, and the forbearance that he had shown would soon dissipate with the emptying of the younger man's purse.

'If it were the season of the fly, would you gape so?'

So harsh was his tone that Hill snapped shut his mouth like a startled carp, his thoughts trapped upon his now-caged tongue. He looked askance at his new friend bedecked in his fashionable finery, and now thought him out of place. This change did not escape the coxcomb's attention. He softened, therefore, both in manner and in voice, and with a wheedling mellifluousness sought to coax the last farthing from the countryman's grasp, through first offering another pint of ale to loosen hurt pride's resolve, and then giving another shuffle of the Devil's books to instruct him in the matters of this world.

A sullen shape upon the beaten floor

It was Joan Meade who answered the knock at the door, for her son was out wielding a billhook, pleaching a hedge of hazel and blackthorn at the edge of the moor. She looked up at Tooley and into his eyes, large and looming above a stubble-strewn face. His shadow entered before he was bid inside – a sullen shape upon the beaten floor. He stood tall, dressed in clothes that spoke of a time when sobriety ruled to festivity's detriment; of a time before the return of the King, before the return of Christmas, when Desborough's diktat realised the Protector's will. Yet, for all his looks, he was not one whom the godly would count as one of their own.

'Doctor Tooley, I be glad of your coming.'

'Good morning, Mistress Meade. Your son mentioned your husband's need for physic, but did not elaborate. As to what afflicts him, I remain in darkness.'

'Please, step inside lest the room do lose its warmth. Come over to the fire and take a seat.'

Tooley removed his hat, and stooped as he passed beneath the wooden lintel that lay low over the door. The light was dim and thick with smoke, so weak was the chimney's draw; a good room in which to cure a ham, but not one in which to sit and pass one's leisure. He crouched upon the stool, his back turned to the light of the window, his front to the warmth of the flame.

'My fee for consultation shall be three shillings, but as for treatment, that will require an additional sum.'

He spoke plainly, his tone flat and matter of fact, as cold as the stare with which he regarded the woman before him. 'Are you agreed to this?' She hesitated, then nodded in unenthusiastic assent. Her husband's illness had left him unable to work and the family in want of money. Three shillings in itself would stretch them hard.

'How much more might 'ee be in need of?'

'It may be an additional sum, or sums, depending upon the nature and duration of the treatment.'

The woman gave a feeble nod.

'And now, pray, might you be so good as to enlighten me as to the form of your husband's illness.'

''E's not ventured abroad above a month. 'E's grown weak, for 'e do sleep poorly, and is waked by bad dreams. There be a griping in 'is guts, and 'e do complain of a band about his 'ead that 'e do feel to be tightening, although there be nothing there. 'E do sweat often, and much.'

'And have you or your son been afflicted with such symptoms?'

'No.'

'You have been quite well?'

'We 'ave.'

'And of what humour is your husband?'

''E be a good and kindly man, in the main, but—'

'I enquire of his humour: sanguine, choleric, phlegmatic or melancholic?'

'I know not of such 'umours, for 'tis doctors' talk.'

'Very well, determine this I shall, if you should be able to find the fee: an additional shilling to the three that I have mentioned, for I shall have to cast his natal chart.'

'Begging your pardon, sir?'

'You wish him to be well, I take it?'

'I do.'

'Then I shall have need to draw up such a chart, to learn what influence the planets have upon his humoral composition, and how they may afflict him now. If you can supply me with his date and place of birth, as well as the shilling, I shall take it upon myself to do this tonight.'

'The first two I can supply 'ee with readily enough, for 'e were born on the seventh day of October 1631, here, in this house, but as for the third – the shilling – now that I cannot give without asking permission of my husband.'

'Then you know not the hour of his birth?'

''Is mother told 'ow 'e were born in darkness, but as for the hour, that I know not, for they 'ad no clock.'

'Without knowing the time of his entering this world, his chart will be subject to some degree of imperfection, but not so much as to render its casting an irrelevance. If I might see your husband, I may gauge his condition and let him know of my need of this additional fee.'

She had heard that he was a man possessed of a knowledge and a cunning that may bend the natural order to his will, as well as a pronounced cupidity. That money was his lodestar, she now clearly perceived, for it was not kindness that had brought him hither. However, as this latter observation regarding his character seemed to be true, should it not also hold that his repute as a man of wonders might also be well founded? She eyed him with cautious indecision, caught between her desire to bring her husband to health again, and the need to preserve what little money they had. Her realisation that he had divined what she was thinking sent a pulse of blood throbbing through her head. There was a momentary stab of pain, and her vision shattered into countless speckling shards of light. Her eyes dropped to the darkness of the earthen floor, and her dizzying sickness in an instant passed.

'Well? Might I see your husband; for the sake of his health, you understand?' he asked again, adopting a more emollient tone.

Mistress Meade's head jolted upwards, then down again, before she raised her eyes to meet his gaze, which despite his smile was as sharp and unblinking as that of any hawk. The lid of her right eye twitched, and her hair prickled with sweat beneath her begrimed bonnet, as a trickle of perspiration trailed down a temple, moistening her flushed cheek. She breathed deeply, and said, 'Of course. Follow me,' and gestured him towards a rough-hewn flight of wooden steps.

He followed in the swish of her skirts, which scuffed against the cob-lined wall in her ascent. A spider recoiled to its lair in the rafters.

''E do sleep but little by night, for 'is dreams do torment him so,' she explained.

'Is he awake now?'

''E's not stirred since 'e did last call out a little after daybreak.'

'Called out?'

''Twere the dog.'

'And what dog is this?'

''Twould be better if you were to ask 'im dreckly, for I be not able to make 'ead nor tail of it.'

'What ill work be this?'

Henry Meade lay abed, his body idle but for the sundry twitching motions of limbs and head, his mind fevered and beset with visions. Thus, it seemed to him that he did not lie, but stand, and from some distance off upon the moor, sought with his feet solid purchase upon the soft and yielding ground, and there beheld a scene both familiar and yet unknown. It was a bright autumn day, and within the churchyard grew two fine beeches, great and strong, now nearly bereft of leaf, casting their shadows over the graves below. Without its walls in a neighbouring field stood a solitary oak, old and gnarled, its heart rotten, and its roots clasping themselves about the rocks and boulders of the lower moor, seeking out what little sustaining nutriment could be drawn from the shallow soil. At its sight, bile bubbled up and into his craw, and his mood darkened. A breath of wind announced its presence upon his cheeks, and he found the skies of a sudden overshadowed, for a tempest was about to unleash its lash upon Widecombe.

With a howl came the wind, and with the wind, an overturning. Five-and-forty years were in an instant unwound, for the Devil, it seemed, was once more unbound. He saw the rain, the lightning, and the whirlwind rip its path, tear at the oak, and yet leave it fast. Onwards it span and into the yard, where the beeches, once lofty, majestic, were in an instant downthrown, their roots thrust skywards to grapple with the air. He stood alone in the stillness, for the storm had then flown.

With a soundless scream he ran towards the fallen trees to mourn their loss. Why he felt so he did not know; their forms were new to his eye, though he had lived here all his life. He found himself shedding tears, his sobs making thick his mouth with salt, as he turned to regard the oak through vision blurred, and a mind filled with ireful heat. He stared at the tree with an intense loathing; at its cracked and fallen limbs, and its broken canopy of spindly, sickly growth, like the vestigial hairs sprouting from a balding man's crown. A shaft of sunlight pierced the aperture into its hollowed interior, a glint of gold sheening in a dazzling and alluring glory. Drawn to it, he ran, and with effortless flight found himself stood in an instant before its hollowed trunk. Into this, he plunged his arm, anxious to wrest the treasure from so insecure a store, but instead of touching gold, his hand touched something wet, living and yet dead, and reflexively withdrew. It emerged to a shriek, for he beheld it was rubbed raw, and coated to the elbow with a thick brown slime of a most noisome odour.

'What ill work be this?' he cried, as all went blank and he met the ground with a thud, to awaken with his purse gone, and the hole in the tree closed up as if it had never been.

A sound disturbed him – a seeming shuffle of boots, and the sense of a presence looming over him. He squinted, and discerned a figure clad in black before him: *Old Nick?* he wondered. Then, he heard a voice, at once unfamiliar, and yet in some way known to him: 'Master Meade! Are you awake?' There was a pause, and then came the voice again, 'I say, are you awake man?'

He opened wide his eyes to find himself in bed, his quilt soaked with sweat, and Tooley standing with his wife at its foot.

'Who be it, Joan? Who be this?'

'Do 'ee not recognise him 'Enry?'

'I did think him the Devil 'imself at first, but no, no – I don't know this gentleman's face.'

'It be Doctor Tooley come to minister physic to 'ee. I did send John up to fetch him down. Remember?'

'Doctor Tooley?'

'The *wise man*.'

'Do you not recognise me, Master Meade?' cut in Tooley. 'Your fever must be strong to make me a stranger to you.'

'Master Tooley? *Robert* Tooley? Be that 'ee Robert?'

'It is, Henry; 'tis none other but I.'

'I didn't recognise 'ee. My thoughts do wander so, that I do scarce recognise my own son at times.'

'No matter. We've not spoken since backalong; a long time ago. You may be forgiven. Your good lady tells me that your illness has kept you abed this past month.'

He gave a weak nod. ''Tidn't like I, Robert. But 'tis the dreams I do 'ave. The dreams! Never known the like afore. They do plague I the night long, and whensoever I should sleep other times. No sooner do I shut my eyes, than they do come again.'

'Ill dreams?'

'Terrible dreams; wicked with no sense in 'em,' he said, pushing himself up in his bed.

'Your wife made mention of something regarding their substance, specifically regarding the form of a dog.'

'Ah, yes now: the dog; 'e do come often enough all right. It be enough to make a man wish for the end.'

'How can a mere dream be so terrible?'

''Tis the manner in which it do stand and look at 'ee so, with that great slavering maw. There be such a cruelty in the beast, that the way it do look at I makes I reckon my time be short. It be waiting for I, I be sure of it.'

'What bids you think so?'

'It be the creature's regard, and each time I do see 'un, 'e do get a bit closer; a bit bolder.'

'Do you know this dog? By name? By sight?'

'No. I don't know 'un.'

'Does it take other forms?'

'No. It be always the same – a great black 'ound with a shaggy coat.'

'Have you seen him in your dreams just now?'

'No. What I've just dreamt were worse still.'

'How so?'

Robert Meade grimaced, and looked aside in disgust, before returning his eyes to his visitor and saying, 'It did bring to mind summat that 'appened many years past; when I were a child: the visitation, all them years back, when the Devil wrought his vengeance 'pon the folk in the church that Sunday. 'Ee'll remember it thyself, surely?'

'I do. It was of a nature that could not be forgotten,' replied the visitor with a grave nod, who then recounted the grim scenes that had presented themselves to him just before Tooley had entered his chamber. The cunning man was particularly intrigued by Meade's comment that something in the rotten insides of the oak had caught his eye, and had 'called out' to him, so to speak. By way of clarification, Meade volunteered that 'it weren't in the manner of a cry, least not the kind that a man can 'ear. 'Twere a call that few men can resist: more like a summons, 'ee might say. That there were gold in that trunk, it couldn't be plainer, from the way the sun did set it aglimmer. So, what do I do? Rush over to 'un of course, and reach in for it.'

He got no further in his explanation, for here he paused, and let out a pained groan.

'What's wrong?'

'My guts! They'm set a-griping. Joan, Joan, bring I some water!'

'Course 'Enry! Course I will!'

He doubled up with pain, beset by a pitiful groaning, whilst his wife ran to fetch him a drink. Tooley looked on, now assured that the seriousness of his client's condition would ensure that any money he asked for would be paid.

'My guts! Jesus! Hurry, woman! Hurry!'

'I be coming 'Enry, don't 'ee worry!'

'Aargh! Jesus!'

She lifted the vessel to his lips, which he clasped with a greedy desperation, taking great glugs of liquid until he could drink no more, which he indicated by means of a wave and a shake of his head.

'Enough! I've 'ad enough of it woman. Take it away.'

She stood the flagon by his bedside, and drew back towards the wall, whilst Tooley resumed his questioning.

'Are you well enough to talk?'

'I can talk right enough.'

'When the pain came upon you, you'd just made mention of gold.'

'I did. Yes.'

'What happened after you reached for it?'

'I fell, and then it did disappear. That's when I did wake and see 'ee standing there. What do it all mean?'

'It's plain enough, but it would be best if I were not to tell you now.'

'Not tell I? Why not?'

Although he was not looking at her, Tooley could see from the corner of his eye that Joan Meade was frowning. That she was displeased he did not doubt.

'It would serve neither of us to discuss its meaning presently, for it is by the by. I've heard that not all's been well in the parish these past few weeks?'

'Who told 'ee that?'

'Mary Bovey.'

'What, that old *gossip*?' spat Joan with venomous detestation. It took her caller somewhat aback, for she was otherwise so apparently meek.

'She made mention that William Huccaby died of his own hand, did she not? Is that the truth, or merely *gossip*?' he remarked.

'Truth,' she curtly conceded with a scowl.

'You knew him?'

'What bearing 'as that? Of course we did know him. Who didn't? There b'aint so many of us 'ere who do *keep ourselves apart from our neighbours,*' she snarled, pinning him with her eyes in an unsuspected show of self-assurance. Her husband stared first at this wife, and then at the 'doctor', not quite believing what he had just heard.

This vixen has a temper; who knows what shrewish bites she might mark upon her husband behind these closed doors? reflected Tooley, his demeanour displaying no trace of either displeasure or discomfiture. In a dispassionate tone he added, 'I understand that it was down to a matter of his business going awry, that is to say, piracy.'

'If by this 'ee do mean the loss of a vessel to the Turk, then yes, 'ee might say that it were so,' answered a hoarse voice from the bed.

'It is said that it brought Huccaby to ruin. He was by no means a wealthy man, but this would have brought him low, particularly seeing as he was acting as an agent on behalf of many creditors.'

'There can't be no denying it did strike 'un 'ard. It be reckoned 'e did put all 'is money into it 'n all.'

'What dealings had you with him in this?'

'What do 'ee mean?'

'Investments. Did you entrust any money into his keeping as part of this enterprise?'

Henry paused, before glancing to his wife who shifted uneasily with a sideways look to Tooley, before she gave her husband a nod.

'I did,' he conceded with some reluctance.

'What manner of sum was this?'

'I fail to see what bearing this might have,' retorted the sick man, his bitterness evident.

'It may have some import in this matter, for am I not right in thinking that you took to your bed subsequent to Huccaby's death? Indeed, just after he had taken his life?'

'That may as be, but what do the sum of money 'ave to do with it?'

'Much, perhaps.'

'Why?'

'If it was of a degree to warrant distress or discomfort upon the part of yourself and your family, then I should imagine that there may have been some harshness in your words with him upon learning of the loss. Did you not remonstrate with him, and demand back your money?'

Henry Meade frowned, his great fingers making involuntary work of the bedding, grasping and kneading it like a baker spasmodically working with recalcitrant dough.

'Surely 'twas so,' continued Tooley, 'for I heard that he had many who did demand their money back, oft with menaces, and I doubt not that with you living so hard by that you were not amongst the foremost of their number in making their dissatisfaction known to him. Am I not right in thinking this?'

Despite his sickly pallor, these provoking words brought something of a blush to Henry Meade's cheeks, and he conceded that he had indeed asked for the deceased to return their money, but that it had not been forthcoming. That harsh words had been traded between the two was only natural.

'Well, I did 'ave a choice word or two to say to 'un, I'll not deny,' remarked the sick man. 'We did last speak the afternoon 'e did take his life. I did tell 'un we were in no place to be left short of the money – four pounds the bugger 'ad off us! – but 'e would have none of it; said there weren't no way that 'e could pay it back. Folk as far away as Chagford were after 'un, threatening to ring 'is neck if 'e didn't return their pounds, shillings and pence. 'E did look worried. All over a cargo of baccy. Bloody 'eathen Turks!'

Upon uttering the word 'Turks' he spat upon the floor so as to emphasise his loathsome regard for the heathen.

'And what of Huccaby's spirit? Has it since troubled you?'

The sick man clammed up, and drew the covers up close to his chin, as if seeking to hide from his doctor turned inquisitor.

''Twere two mornings later, and my 'usband's not left the bed since,' said Joan, anxious to fill the silence that her husband had left hanging. Her tone had softened a little since earlier, although an undertow of irritability remained perceptible.

'Do you not find it odd,' said Tooley, looking first to the one, and then to the other, 'that he did murder himself hard upon such heated words between yourselves, and that you did take to your bed so soon thereafter? It is my opinion that his shade wishes to hold you to account, for it believes you to be responsible for his death. Thus it is that his spirit has struck you down, and comes to torment your dreams in the form of a black dog. It is this invisible hound that gnaws at your vitals, and the spirit of the departed man that binds and tightens some unseen rope about your head. You must, therefore, take action to counter his will, for if not, he'll have his vengeance by dragging you down into the next world, for 'tis clear that he has a mind to take you.'

Sweat beaded upon the forehead of the afflicted man, running down to be caught in the coarse, greying hairs that bristled above his sunken eyes, their hollows cushioned beneath by wrinkled bags of skin, and hemmed in by the darkened caverns of his orbits.

"Ee be right, I don't doubt. But, what can 'ee do about it?'

The cunning man stretched and flexed his fingers, as if about to grapple with something physical, rather than theoretical.

'At the inn this morning, I asked of Edward Baker if the correct precautions had been taken with respect to Huccaby's burial. He seemed not to grasp my meaning, and said little other than that the corpse was buried in a winding sheet, and that few were present to witness his committing to the ground. Do you know where this was done?'

'In the churchyard,' replied Joan.

'Are you sure?'

'And where else might a dead man be buried?' she retorted with an evident note of sarcasm.

'You do not know then, it seems. So, 'tis the case that the most important measure against the man's spirit's walking has not been taken.'

'What do 'ee mean?' croaked Henry.

'As a self-murderer, he ought to have been buried at a crossroads, not within the bounds of a churchyard, for only when buried at such a junction will an unquiet and vengeful spirit be prevented from finding those whom it wishes to punish. As matters stand, his ghost may walk abroad and inflict whatsoever damage it has the power to enact.'

"Tis all very well to know such things, but tell us: what might 'ee be able to do about it?'

The visitor paused, and wishing to impart the import of what he was about to say, looked at both parties, and mustered the gravest expression that he was able to contrive, before intoning, 'There are certain things that I can do, but there will be a cost. They must be done quickly too, for as it is, your life, and indeed your soul, remain in peril. Do you understand?'

Upon the mention of 'cost', a fearful look flared up in the eyes of his listeners, alongside a weary recognition that this would have to be borne if they were to be rid of their tormentor.

'And, how much might this "cost" be?' asked the head of the house.

'For what I am to propose, the sum of twenty shillings and a bottle of brandy should suffice, if that should prove agreeable to you.'

'Twenty shilling!' he gasped, as Joan's eyes widened with horror.

'Yes.'

'That much?'

The sick man took once more to kneading his blanket.

'For the services that I will render, it is but a modest amount. From this I will need to pay for the assistance of two young men of stout and strapping build. It is no matter of greed on my part, I assure you. There are simply certain expenses that must be taken into account. I am, however, not an unreasonable man.' He paused here to smile with a cold pleasure, before adding, 'As I realise that you find yourselves in some straits as a consequence of your loss to Huccaby, I will not, of course, expect payment in full at the outset, but will instead consider taking part of it now, and the remainder at some future date that can be agreed between ourselves.'

'And be this besides the three shillings and one 'ee did make mention of when we did speak earlier?' asked Joan, her voice now quavering at the prospect of further expense. *Not so proud and defiant after all*, reflected Tooley.

'No. What I mention is the final sum. With this being a matter involving an unquiet spirit, I shall have no need of casting a horoscope, nor would bleeding, purging nor the administration of a clyster be to any benefit.'

'Why, thank the Lord for small mercies!' rasped the afflicted man.

'Shall we say ten shillings today, a bottle of brandy tomorrow, and the balance by Twelfth Night?'

'What do 'ee say 'Enry?' asked his wife, her face of a sudden so much greyer and gaunt.

'Well,' he began, before dropping his eyes before him, staring at the blanket as if searching there for some answer, or the stipulated sum. 'It be a great deal of money, Robert; *so* great a deal of money. I've not laboured this past four week or more. Our son 'as taken what work 'e can to provide for us, but 'e's little time for anything more. The boy be fair tired witless. Will 'ee not reconsider the fee?'

'Man must eat, and I am but flesh and blood as you are. That is my fee, and if you should not wish to pay it, I will ask no more than my three shillings for this consultation. But, if that should be so, then Huccaby will claim you as surely as the sun will rise tomorrow.'

A hard bargain, and an unenviable choice between near starvation and the risk of a man losing his soul. Between them the Meades had no more than twelve shillings left to their name. It was Joan who decided that Tooley must do his work, and so it was agreed that he would accept ten shillings now, the brandy the following day, and the remainder of the money he would receive by Twelfth Night. Once the first ten pieces of silver were in his purse, he explained what he was to do. He would, he avowed, conjure Huccaby's spirit, a prospect that much alarmed the mistress of the house. In seeking to reassure her he observed, ''Tis plain that Huccaby's spirit already wanders of its own will, so would it not be better to make it my servant, and to place it under my own power until the time that I might bind it for eternity? Once it is under my command, it may not walk of its own volition.'

His words held no comfort for his female listener, whose lack of savour for his proposal was summed up in the words, 'May the good Lord preserve us from so unchristian and unholy an undertaking.'

Henry Meade's condition, however, prompted a more receptive and pragmatic response: 'By what means?'

It was now that Tooley was pleased that he had thought long and hard of what he was to say, for if he spoke his words with conviction, then their money was as good as his.

'There are certain preparations I must undertake, such as the fashioning of charms, in the use of which I shall instruct you. Once you have understood these, and acted upon them, I shall employ two helpers.' Here he paused, and turning to Joan said, 'I spoke earlier with two young men at the inn, whom I wish you to seek out tomorrow at noon.'

'But 'ow will I know them?'

'You know Richard Hill of this parish, no doubt?'

'I do that, yes.'

'Then look for him, and Stephen Damerell, his companion in cups. I doubt not that you will find them there, most likely at cards. Tell them that I have sent you, and ask them to come to your house shortly before nightfall tomorrow. Be sure to let Damerell know to bring his sword, and ask that Hill brings one too. Hill's father fought at Torrington and still possesses that blade of cold steel that served him so well, as he has been apt to let us all know on so many an occasion. Ask that he might fetch it, for tell him that he will have need of it.'

'I'll do it. Richard I do know well enough, but as for swords, why, why—'

'Pray put your mind at rest, for they shall not be employed against any living soul, you have my word upon it.'

His tone was so authoritative and reassuring that her qualms were quite banished.

'Be sure to have that bottle of brandy ready for me, for I shall have as much need of that as they will have need of their weaponry. I will explain all when I return tomorrow.'

'At what hour?'

'Expect me towards sundown.'

'I'll look out for 'ee,' said she, fretting over where to find the money for the brandy.

'Good. Then I shall bid a good day to the both of you.'

Tooley returned to the smithy a satisfied man, and bid the smith fashion a new horseshoe, saying, 'Be sure to place nails into its holes, and beat them securely around so that they be fixed, for no beast shall be shod with this shoe.'

The smith, perplexed, did as he was ordered, after which his customer slipped unnoticed out of the village, to think on the shape of the following day.

A prison of woven withies

Tooley stirred from the sleep of a long November night with a crick in his neck and the knowledge that none of his quack cures could remedy the accumulating aches of age. It was daybreak, and Sarah was already up and about her business. This he knew from the smell of woodsmoke mingled with the aroma of pottage. He had enjoyed a good night's sleep, but a poor one lay ahead of him, for he knew he would not return to his bed until the sun had risen once more.

The spit of an exploding spark caused the young woman to jump, but a greater jolt still she received upon turning to behold her master standing close behind, his eyes fixed upon her with a curious hunger. He saw that she was startled. *Good. She needs must keep her wits about her.* His eyes alighted upon the pottage.

'Bring me spoon and bowl.'

'Yes, master.'

'And water.'

She nodded, and did as ordered. These were the words that passed between them each morning: a ritual in which their bonds as master and servant were displayed and reaffirmed. It pleased her employer to assume airs inappropriate for one so low born – a cooper's son who himself had later left the trade – and yet he had risen no further than to the status of a mere cottager, albeit one who cared not so much to labour, as to make a living by his wits, and others' lack thereof. His title of 'doctor' was but self-conferred.

The pottage was eaten in silence and without savour, as he turned over what needed to be done as he turned the food with his tongue.

'Bring me the cage,' he said upon finishing.

The girl left, and promptly returned to place before him a prison of woven withies, as supple when freshly cut as the girl herself who had fashioned from them this unwanted home.

'Ominous bird! Why stare you so?'

It squawked with a harshness that seemed at one with Tooley's prevailing humour.

'Impudent screecher! You shall have reason to shriek,' says he to the owl. 'Bring me knife and jar. And gloves. Bring me my gloves.'

He drew himself to his feet. He had thought it through.

'Take them outside.'

She opened the door to a morning of low cloud, that here and there touched upon the shattered stone of the surrounding tors. It was warmer: there was a mildness in the air, and the frost had relinquished its hold. The light was grey and flat, but still the owl blinked, its head turning to survey the world of daylight. It raised its wings to half stretch, hindered by the cage, and shrieked afresh.

'Open the cage that I may take the bird.'

She did as bidden.

'Pray take care. Good!'

His hands wrapped themselves about the delicate feathered body as he took a firm grip to ease it through the door of the cage. It bit at his gloves, but the thick leather ensured that the beak drew no blood. He held the bird high, and with a tender and confiding whisper stared into its black eyes and said, 'Look at me and the world beyond. See it! Know that I am your master now.'

He waited a moment, then snapped the bones first of its right wing, and then of its left. The sound of the cracks was masked by a piteous screaming which flew upon the air and down the valley to Ponsworthy, where it caught the ears of an aged hedger, who halted from his labours to ask, 'What murder be this?'

Sarah looked on, her face dressed in the pallor of chalk, as the owl clawed and bit, helpless in its defence, until Tooley broke its neck to bring it peace. It pricked her to think, *Might he serve me so?*

The body lay limp, its beak twitching twice before freezing into a breathless gasp, its lids now fixed half open, half closed. The owl was now deaf to all.

'A creature of the night you were, and to eternal night I entrust you.'

He held it over the jar, picked up the knife, and with its blade made a quick incision. With its heart stilled, the blood oozed slowly from its neck, and when he deemed a sufficient quantity had been gathered, he dropped the body into a canvas bag, placed the lid upon the jar, and returned inside to seal it with wax.

'Bring me the last of the season's sloes, an empty phial, and some water,' he ordered. His servant duly obliged, and as he stood crushing the fruit into a paste, taking care to pick out and discard the stones, he smiled in anticipation of the deception to come. Cajoling the pulp into the glass vessel, he added water, stopped it up, and shook it with vigour. *It will serve; serve well enough to make men think falsehoods true, and women too.*

'If you should speak to anyone but me, say nothing of what I have done today. If you were to do so, there would be consequences. Do you understand?'

'Yes, sir.'

'Good. Then bring me what remains of last night's mutton, and do not stray, for once I have eaten I shall have need of your help with Speedwell.'

A tender discomfort and a gory crown

The knock at the door caused housewife Meade to start, pricking her thumb with her needle. A bead of blood, a deep, sweet berry red, invited her to suck to subdue the sting, and save her lace from stain. She rose to lift the latch, and upon the door's opening, her anticipation was not disappointed: it was the wise man – the *doctor*. His face betrayed neither pleasure nor a lack thereof; he had come for his money, and to make a show of its earning. Speedwell, meanwhile, laboured not, resting upon the green, tethered to a tree at her master's pleasure.

Tooley stood with his saddlebag slung over his shoulder, and having accepted the invitation to step inside, took a seat by the fire, and when offered refreshment, he was sure to ask for brandy. The liquor had been 'purchased' from Edward Baker, with payment being the promise of money from a relative. Tooley took the bottle from her hands, and took a swig to lubricate his tongue, and to prepare his performance.

'Did you speak to Damerell and Hill?' he asked.

'I did. But they did find it strange that I should be seek after 'em.'

''Tis not often, I s'pose, that a woman should call upon men with such an errand. They have agreed to help, I take it?'

'They have, if 'ee should give 'em the money that they do ask for.'

'Good. Did they then ask no questions with respect to their needing to arm themselves?'

'Not Master Damerell, as 'e did inform I that 'e did always carry his sword upon 'im, but Master Hill thought it a little queer, and did ask whether 'ee did have a plan afoot for "bloody murder", but I did chide him for so speaking. I did say that "Dr Tooley will explain all," and that were that, for then 'e did quieten down.'

The caller nodded his head, his eyes twinkling. 'Then we have time in which to do what is needed before their arrival. Is your husband awake?'

''E were when I did last look.'

'Then I have need to see him. I have brought with me two charms that must be kept about his person until I say that they may be laid aside. But first, you must excuse me whilst I make my preparations out of doors. One of these prophylactics may sit ill with him, but that he follow my instructions is of the greatest necessity. It is to preserve him from the risk of a great evil that will issue forth this night.'

'Evil?'

'From Huccaby's tormented spirit. The act of conjuration runs the risk that it might break free before it has been bound by the rite that shall be enacted tonight. It will take evil to repel evil, although what I have done, and will do, is less than what your husband has endured. You, and he, must follow my instructions you understand, otherwise what I attempt will come to nought. Let your husband know that I am here, and see that he is awake for me. I shall be but a short while in readying the charm.'

'I'll do as 'ee ask,' she said, making for the stairs.

Tooley took out the canvas bag that held the body of the bird, and then his knife. He let himself out of the house, and walked the short distance to the green. There, he squatted behind a tree to ensure that no one could see, and cleft the owl from its arse to its neck, wrenching up its breastbone, and ripping out its gizzard and giblets to serve up as dainty treats for the crows. He cursed at the stench and the slime, and returning the carcase to its canvas shroud, sought out the channel from the village well to rinse clean his fingers and palms. He felt that there were eyes upon him, but whose they were he did not know.

Henry Meade had heard out his wife, and refreshed himself with drink before making water in the pot that she had brought for his ease. The hound had not troubled him since he and Tooley had spoken, so his mood had brightened. Having heard the creak of the stairs and the shuffling of feet, it was no black dog that loomed over him as he looked up from his bed, but the form of the cunning man dressed in black, a stained bag of canvas in one hand, a newly-forged horseshoe in the other.

'Good day to you Henry.'

'And to 'ee, Robert,' he replied with a wary eye. 'What do 'ee 'ave in that there bag?'

'You shall see. But we have need to wait some moments.'

'Aargh, well. Be it a charm?'

The visitor nodded, and the sick man rubbed his nose on the back of his hand.

'Joan did tell I that one of 'em might be none too agreeable. Be that right?'

'Perhaps. But before we speak of it, I should like to learn how you have slept since yesterday; what troubles, if any, have come to you in your dreams?'

'Better. No pain in the 'ead neither, but my guts 'as yet to leave off griping. As to dreams, there've been none that I do recall.'

'The hound has not troubled you?'

'No.'

'That, I did not expect. Still, after tonight it should trouble you no more, for Huccaby's spirit shall be laid to rest. However, for this to be so, there are two charms that you must wear about your person until I tell you that you may lay them off. This is the first of them,' he said, producing the horseshoe with a flourish before the Meades' expectant eyes.

'An 'orsehoe?' said Henry in bewilderment.

'Just so.'

'But why do it 'ave nails wrapped about it?'

'To stop spirits from entering its holes, and doing you ill. This you shall wear bound with this cord, next to the skin beneath your right armpit.' Henry's eyes widened, whilst Tooley turned to address his wife: 'Mistress Meade, please be so good as to tie this to that place beneath your husband's shirt.'

She took the charm from his hand, stared first at it, then back at him, as if she were handling some popish relic. 'Please!' he said, gesturing her towards her husband. She followed his instructions, and with a piece of flaxen cord tied it so that it hung where he had specified. Henry smarted at the chill of the metal as it touched his flesh.

'And now,' resumed Tooley, 'I must place something about your head, to protect you from the evil that will be unleashed during the hours of darkness. When I return, you may remove it, but not before. If you do so, your soul will be lost. You understand?'

'My soul, you say? My *soul*?'

'Pray, do not be alarmed, for evil may ward off evil,' continued the cunning man as he loosened the drawstring of the bag, easing out the gore-stained charm. Joan, catching a glimpse of its head, raised a hand to her mouth to stem her cry as she saw the cleft owl emerge.

'Behold – the charm of charms! No malign spirit, Huccaby's or otherwise, would dare lurk at your side whilst this rests about your temples.'

Henry Meade looked on aghast at what was left of the bird, its open beak displaying its tongue in frozen shriek, its feathers darkened with blood about its slit front.

'What? *That*? In God's name, *no!*'

'You *must wear it* as a crown, for if you do not, Huccaby's spirit will seek to take possession of your body, whilst we busy ourselves with the binding of his soul in the churchyard.'

'By Jesus and all the angels! This be a sore undertaking for a sick man.'

'It must be done.'

Tooley stepped closer, his smile for once expressive of genuine mirth. There was a crack of snapping bone as he prised the breastbone forward before positioning the hollowed out corpse of the owl upon the recipient's head, the broken ribs snagging a hold in the bedridden man's greasy hair, scratching and breaking his scalp. It made for a tender discomfort and a gory crown.

'For the love of God, 'ow long? 'Ow long must I wear this, this . . . *thing*?'

'Until we are finished with our business this night. Then, I shall come and take it from where it now rests. Mistress Meade,' he said, turning, 'know you where I might find Huccaby's grave?'

'To the north side of the church. 'Ee'll find it ready enough, for no other 'as been buried there of late. There be no marker, but the upturned soil.'

'Thank you. Then I must wait downstairs for my helpers. You shall both doubtless hear strange noises about the house whilst I am gone. Fear them not, for it will be but Huccaby's spirit, which will be rendered powerless by dint of the charm that I have just placed upon your head. Pray, try to sleep. 'Twould be better if your ears were not to hear what is to come.'

A flourishing of swords

Damerell and Hill arrived, as instructed, shortly after nightfall. That they had been asked to bring swords made them suspicious, and they demanded to know what it was that was wanted of them. When Tooley's intention was explained, Damerell quipped, 'Well, there be nothing easier than to kill a dead man.' Having been told that it would take but an hour of their time, they then set to haggling until settling upon the cunning man's begrudging agreement to pay them a shilling apiece for their efforts. They were sworn to breathe no word of their enterprise, or of what ensued, to any other party.

The night was moonless and starless, the celestial lights hidden beyond and above the unbroken cloud. Only the glow cast by the cunning man's lantern feebly lit their way as they crept along the lane and out of the village, taking care not to trip in the water-filled ruts and potholes. It was deserted and silent, but for the trudge and splash of their steps, the sound of the breeze rattling the sticks of naked hazel in the hedgerow, and, carried from afar, the screech of a still-living owl. *Mourn for your kin if you will, foolish screecher*, thought Tooley.

With the village safely behind them, the three clambered over a gate and into the field. From there, they picked their way from tussock to tussock over the sodden pasture towards the northern wall of the churchyard. Better to gain access by scaling it there, than to risk attracting the prying ears and eyes of the sexton from his cottage by the gate.

The grave was soon found: an unmarked length of soil; a heap of grey clods now breaking down from a month of rain and frost. A fine drizzle drifted upon the air, moistening the men's faces and hair. By the light of the solitary lantern, the three positioned themselves: Damerell at one end of the grave, Hill at the other, and Tooley standing at its side with his back to the church. In his hand, the conjuror held a small calfskin-bound volume from which he recited verbal formulae that he said would lay to rest any unquiet spirit. He paused every now and then to take a swig of brandy, his voice a raised and emphatic whisper, made bold by the liquor's fire. His speech was archaicised to impart a due loftiness to its tone, and by the time of its peroration his hirelings stood soaked to the skin, their arms aching from their constant holding and flourishing of swords. He was determined to have his money's worth of them.

'Unquiet spirit, I call upon thee to quit this parish and this world. Thy time here is done. Thou hast murdered thyself, and shalt murder no other. Leave off thy torment of Henry Meade, and his family. 'Twas not he that was the cause of thy misfortune and death, but thyself, and only thy spirit shalt be held accountable. Thou hast damned thyself by thy self-murder, and to everlasting hell shalt thy soul be entrusted, for no man who doth so badly dispose of a gift by God so freely given, may be adjudged redeemable. Thus, William Huccaby, I call upon thee to leave this world and never return. May the Devil take thee!'

Here he halted, took out the jar from his bag, broke its wax seal and lifted the lid. He moved towards the grave.

'By the blood of this ominous bird, I command thy soul to cease its nocturnal wanderings.'

He stooped three times to dribble the black liquid onto the soil, and withdrew from its stench to the graveside once more. Another swig of brandy, and he resumed.

'Thy body corrupted shalt walk abroad in the land of the living no more. Thou shalt relinquish thy bond with this earthly realm in perpetuity, severed by the steel of these swords, whose points thrust down hereby pierce thy corpse to serve as a reminder of the finality of thy end. Thy body is but food for the worms, and thy soul but a toy for Satan's pleasure.'

Damerell, with a firm hold of the hilt, forced his sword deep into the soil, swiftly followed by Hill, who did so with less panache, snagging its blade and stumbling backwards as he pulled it from the ground.

'Gentlemen, our work is almost done, but we needs make a show of us having fought hard with this restless spirit.

What we are to do might be adjudged by some to constitute deception, but 'tis done only to provide a visible mark of our efforts here this night. I shall mark your cheeks as if bruised in our struggle with Huccaby's shade, through the application of this juice of sloes. Step forward, so that I might daub you.'

Damerell leered in the lamplight as the mixture was applied. Thus made up, they retraced their tracks back through the field. It had grown boggier with the falling rain, the tussocks now less firm beneath their boots. They found the lane still deserted, and Joan Meade a picture of worry when she admitted them to her home.

'Good Lord! What has befallen you two young men? Such bruises! Let I take a cloth and water to 'em.'

'Do not fear Mistress Meade,' said Tooley, 'for they are but the bruises dealt by Huccaby's now departed ghost. As they were administered by his ethereal form, they are not lasting, and will quickly fade. Please, be assured that the two gentlemen do not find themselves in great pain or discomfort. They would, however, perhaps be glad of some small beer, should you have any that they might drink.'

'I be sorry, but we do 'ave none.'

'No matter. Gentlemen, perhaps you should repair to the alehouse for refreshment after such arduous labours as you have undertaken?'

'A most excellent suggestion,' replied Damerell. 'Goodnight madam,' he said, giving a doff of his hat, before turning to exit with a silent Hill in his train.

'There is yet one more thing that must be done this night, before we can be safe in the knowledge that Huccaby's spirit shall trouble you no more,' resumed Tooley once the young men had left. 'We have made sure that his body will never walk again, and sent his spirit hellwards, but the Devil may yet send it back upon some mischievous errand amongst the living. How fares your husband?'

'No better.'

'Is he any worse?'

'No worse.'

'During the time of my absence were you troubled about the house by unusual noises?'

'We did 'ear summat up in the thatch, but by our reckoning it were nothing more than the clawing of mice.'

'Good. And whilst we are speaking of thatch, that touches upon a task that you must fulfil to ensure that Huccaby's ghost will not return. At about twelve of the clock this night, you shall go and fetch seven motes of straw from the dead man's house, and bring them to me. From these I shall fashion a pincase, and this your husband will wear under his other arm next to the skin. Thereafter, his malady shall be cured, and he will walk, and work, freely again.'

'Take straw from the thatch of 'is 'ouse? But 'ow? Would I not be 'eld to account for theft, even though it be but of straws?'

''Tis a simple enough task, once you have gained admission, is it not?'

'But 'ow might I enter his dwelling?'

'Where's your son?'

''E be away at the market in Bovey Tracey, and won't be back 'til the morrow 'pon account of the shortness of the day.'

'A pity. In that case, I advise that you find a ladder and place it against the wall of his cottage so that you might pluck such motes from the eaves. I will lend you my lantern, but it is you that must do it. Be not afraid that the needs of your husband shall go untended, for I shall remain here should he find himself in want of care.'

His words did little to assuage her disquiet, for she relished but little the role of 'thief'. She stood and looked at him as if expecting him to offer to undertake this task himself, but he did not. Guessing her thoughts he added, 'The sooner 'tis done, the better.'

It was therefore with considerable reluctance and hesitancy that she agreed, having said that she knew where a ladder lay in a nearby barn, but added that it was too heavy for her alone to shift. Her plea for assistance went unheeded, for Tooley excused himself on the grounds that he was required 'here' to ensure the barring of Huccaby's spirit. She should instead look to the help of one of the young men, and that she did.

Damerell demurred, but Hill, wishing to maintain good-neighbourliness, agreed to lend his hand. The barn was unlit, and all was still inside. The cows in their slumber took but little notice of the furtive footsteps that padded in the darkness, and the stealthy shadows that shifted in the light of the lamp. The ladder was found and taken from its resting place. Huccaby's cottage lay not far off, and the pair passed unseen to rest it against the wall. Joan climbed up, the darkness an aid to her courage, and took a tug at the thatch. In a matter of moments she had the desired strands of straw, which she placed securely in her pocket. Their care, together with the lateness of the hour, ensured that the village was blind to their business.

The wise man took the straw and set to work. His fingers appeared large and clumsy, but he worked a magic to make them nimble and deft, and plaited from the straws a crude pincase which he returned to the mistress of the house with the words, 'Place this beneath your husband's other arm, and affix it with this twine. He may untie it a week from now, once darkness has fallen, but not before.' He removed the carcase of the owl from the sick man's head, leaving a greasy black sheen of noisome gore upon his grizzled hair.

'Your hair must remain thus anointed for two nights, to fend off Huccaby's spirit should it linger still. After this, you may wash it, if you please,' instructed the ingenious Tooley.

It then being the depth of the night, and he not wishing to subject himself to the dangers of the dark lanes across the moors, he secured himself a lodging with the Meades until the following morning. At daybreak, he made to leave, but as he readied Speedwell upon the green, he heard a woman's voice call him from behind.

'Doctor Tooley! Doctor Tooley, sir!'

He turned to see a young woman, of full figure, but not stout. It was the blacksmith's wife, her shawl pulled close about her to keep out the chill, a curl of chestnut hair peeking out from beneath her bonnet and resting on her ruddy cheek. She struck him as comely; excessively so to be the wife of a village smith, until that is, she opened wide her mouth.

'Yes,' he replied, 'what is it that you want?'

'I be suffering from the toothache.'

'Toothache? Come closer and open your mouth so that I might see inside.'

She did as she is told, opened wide and pointed to a number of molars the colour of bracken as it rots down at the end of the season.

'It be these that be giving I the trouble.'

'Hold still whilst I examine their state,' he ordered, inserting his fingers as if inspecting the teeth of an unknown mare. 'That they should trouble you with pain surprises me not.'

'Well?'

'Hmm?'

'Can 'ee 'elp I?'

'For a fee.'

'How much?'

He paused whilst he mounted his pony before offering his reply of 'Two shillings,' which she liked not at all.

'Two shillings, sir? Would 'ee not take one?'

'Two shillings is my fee, and not a penny less. If you should wish for a cure, come to my cottage tomorrow afternoon with the money, and I shall give you what you need. Otherwise, I will be unable to help you. Good day. Hup!'

He gave his reluctant mount a kick, eliciting from her a disgruntled whinny. She shook her head in irritation and moved forward, carrying her master out of the village to a day of ease at home. His bones ached from having slept but poorly upon the cottage floor, and on his return he bid Sarah confine herself to silent tasks whilst he dozed in his chamber. He spoke nothing of what had passed the night just gone, and she knew better than to ask of his business.

In Widecombe, Henry Meade too still lay abed, unable to sleep, the scratches from the dead bird smarting upon his head, and from the discomfort of a charm secured beneath each armpit. Yet Tooley's efforts, for all their show, had brought no relief, for his sweats grew stronger, soaking the straw of the mattress upon which he lay. Its odour grew increasingly rank, and his thoughts revolved like a waterwheel driven by the runoff from a foetid bog. Ever it returned to the same place, bringing no resolution to his regrets, grinding out the coarse flour of remorse over what had passed between him and his dead neighbour. By the time that the two days were up, and the blood of the stinking bird was washed away, he had taken to vomiting and discharging a bloody flux. His wife feared for him, but with her care, he was nursed back from so frail a condition, weakened and feeling ill-used by the 'doctor'. The two resolved that Tooley should not be paid, for they now adjudged his remedies, and his word, to be false.

To rot in unchristian repose

Sunday had come, and the Reverend John Tickle stepped into the pulpit to preach to his flock. There was an airiness in his gait suggestive of a temperament more suited to that of a dancing master than to a minister of the Church, but it was no merry dance in which he wished to lead his parishioners this day, for someone in his flock had strayed. Whosoever it might have been, must be brought back into the fold, and admonished. He drew up his left hand to brush away the greasy clump of brown hair that adhered to his cheek, attracting the disapproving gaze of his wife, which caused him to flush, before he surveyed the faces that stood in the rows of pews before him. All in the parish were here assembled other than Henry Meade, who sickened still, and the elusive Robert Tooley. The sexton had told Tickle of the discovery of a most unchristian violation, and so it fell to the vicar to bring the malefactor to justice.

'Be seated!' he piped in a voice unsuited in its quavering tone to public speech; it was his misfortune to be the youngest son, and his father's misfortune to have sired him. He coughed in an effort to clear his throat, and to endow his voice with an authority and sense of certainty that he himself lacked.

'Good friends and neighbours; people of Widecombe,' he began.

'It do look like the vicar be warming up for one of 'is speeches,' whispered Mary Carter to her husband.

'May the good Lord and Heaven preserve us,' he mumbled by way of reply. Old Man Sanders had already closed his eyes, and was beginning to nod off, sat where he believed himself to be safely out of sight at the rear of the church.

'A tragedy – a most sinful tragedy – of which we all are most painfully aware – the self-murder of the late William Huccaby – is a crime that even the generosity of our most beneficent Creator may not absolve. As it is said in 1 Corinthians 3:16 and 3:17: "Know ye not *that* ye are the temple of God, and that the Spirit of God dwelleth in you? If any man defile the temple of God, him shall God destroy; for the temple of God is holy, which *temple* ye are."

'In so disposing of the temple of his body, and so vilely abusing the gift of life bestowed upon him by our Lord, William Huccaby has surrendered himself to damnation. He has rendered his soul beyond salvation, as does any man who should follow so wicked and wilful a course as his. The sorrows of this world are as nothing to the sorrows of the next that he shall reap in eternity for his sin. Of this, the Church has no doubt.

'His unworthy mortal remains we have laid in the soil, and there they should remain to rot in unchristian repose. A great sinner he may have been, but it behoves no man to disturb even the fading flesh and bones of the damned, for only evil may ever issue from the despoliation of such a grave. And yet, and yet . . . the sexton has informed me that Huccaby's place of burial has been subject to violation. In the hours of darkness this Wednesday last, unseen and unheard, the despoilers of this man's grave left blood upon its broken soil, and sank narrow shafts into its body. To what purpose this was done, or by whom, we know not, but those who did this deed left their tracks in the long grass to the north of the church. Their route of entry, it seems, was via surmounting the wall with the neighbouring field, for the sexton heard nothing, and their tracks suggest that this was so.

'We may be thankful that the body appears to have been left in its place, but it should serve as a matter of disquiet for all here gathered, to learn that such dark deeds have lately passed. What manner of man, or men, would act so? And with what intent? It is my fear, that some act of devilish conjuration has here been enacted, but pray be assured, that if you be of good Christian faith, that no such act, and no unquiet soul raised thereby, shall find it in its power to trouble you.

'It is my belief, that there sits someone within these walls this morning who knows something of this matter. I leave it to the tender conscience, or consciences, of this person or persons, to come and speak to me, and to atone for this unholy act.'

He paused to scan the faces of the parishioners, to find some hint of guilt or knowledge written in their features. What was it that Widow Spencer knew that made her frown so? *'Tis nothing*, he reflected, *for 'tis but her usual look*. His eyes creased with disdain as he spotted the snoozing figure of Old Man Sanders, but he knew him to be both guiltless and guileless, and as insensible to the Gospel as the mute pillars that had borne witness to more sermons than any parishioner or divine. Was that not an uneasy look that flickered within Joan Meade's eyes? Why did she cast them down so? Was it not as good as declaring some secret shame? Some guilt? Did she not dart her gaze crossways to some other? Was it some co-conspirator? But if so, who? She had no reputation for witchery, but news of her husband's removal from village life had reached Tickle's ears. Seeing no one come forward to confess, he once more broke the silence.

'If you have knowledge of who may have done this, or harbour suspicions as to who this person, or these persons, may be, you may come to me in confidence, for the Lord looks favourably upon those who reveal the perpetrators of injustice.'

Richard Hill swallowed, and his chest tightened as he locked eyes with the sick man's wife. He thought his nostrils caught a whiff of an unwholesome odour of musty decay, and sensed a churning in his bowels. The Reverend Tickle noticed not, continued with the service, and enjoined the congregation to join him in the Lord's Prayer.

There were looks of puzzlement upon the faces of many as they left the church, with gossip breaking out amongst a number of women for whom this was their most favoured pastime. They were glad to have a new subject upon which to discourse, and their speculations proved to be both wide and wild, although Widow Spencer's words attracted an eager hearing, and proved, this time, not to be altogether wide of the mark.

''Twere more than likely the stranger's doing. What business had that young man here? None! Playing at cards and drinking: what manner of carrying on is that? Not a good and godly one, I'm sure you'll agree. And the sword! Did you see it? What a display he did make of it! He no doubt fancies himself a fine young blade, but what use might such a dandy rake as he find for it in a parish such as ours? None! That's what I do say, anyway. Mark my words: that young man's behind this in some ways, which is why he's taken up and left all of a sudden.'

Although liberal with spreading her speculations amongst the womenfolk of the parish, she thought better of speaking to the parson, as for all of his talk of holding the malefactor to account this morning, what would a milksop such as he do to challenge a dissolute young gentleman accoutred with steel? Nothing.

The vicar's plea went unheeded, and as Christmas drew near, labour dawdled and slackened as the darkness of the days and a fierce penetrating cold called a halt to the business of the parish. And then came the snow, that mantled the iron ground in a killing softness, and settled upon the frozen water of the well. Not even Old Man Sanders could remember a cold such as this, and when he died later that season, they had to light three successive fires upon the ground to melt the earth so that they might bury his body. It was a costly and time-consuming business, but as good Christian folk, they were unable to leave him to provide pickings for the fox and the crow.

Tooley had held himself aloof from it all, holed up in his cottage up on the moor, with Sarah his only company. His mood remained as was customary: surly, and sullen. There was little festivity to be had within its walls, with his only cause for rejoicing being the arrival of Twelfth Night, which marked the date of due payment of the balance for his services to the Meades. But when midday came, and none of the family had shown their face, his mood soured further. Though it pained him, on account of the ice and the snow, he concluded that he must venture abroad to collect his debt.

It was an effort to coax Speedwell from her stable, for despite her thick-layered winter coat, the prospect of ice underfoot held little appeal. She came though, eventually, and was harnessed for the ride to Widecombe. Slowly and carefully, she navigated her way through the drifts, great clouds of steam rising from her nostrils as she jerked her head and snorted. As they descended the road into Ponsworthy, a boy jeered at mount and master from a window beneath thatched cottage eaves, causing the pony to start and lose her footing upon the hard ground. She slipped and reared, bringing forth a curse from the rider, who grasped her reins for fear of his life as he stood high in his stirrups. He steadied her with a strong pull to the bit, and darted his angry eyes about the cottages, searching for so pert a boy who would dare yell out to a man such as he. The child, all boldness when hidden from view, was not such a proud cock as would venture to let forth a crow beneath his gaze, for he would surely break his neck for such an impudent display. His voice spent with cursing, Tooley resumed his way, and within the hour found himself at his clients' door.

His knock had been expected, and what was to be said had been long rehearsed. Mistress Meade met her visitor with her son at her side.

'Good afternoon Mistress Meade.'

'Good day to 'ee, Master Tooley,' she replied, her voice betraying that she wished him anything but.

'Might I come in?'

'To what end?'

'Will your home not lose its warmth to the harsh chill outside if you do not shut the door?'

She said nothing, and stared at him with hard and hostile eyes.

'Do you not remember our agreement?'

'I remember all right, but as for any *'arsh chill*, my reckoning be such as that shutting this door will not remove that which do hang yet within this house. Still, that little warmth that the fire do provide, I must preserve, so come inside if you must.'

'Riddles, Mistress Meade, such riddles,' said Tooley in a mocking tone as he entered the room and removed his hat. 'I have come to collect the balance for my services rendered.'

'I do know what 'ee 'ave come for,' she replied, with evident tartness.

'Ten shillings in all, if you please.'

'I do recall that we agreed a fee to cure my 'usband, and to see to it that the ghost of our neighbour be laid to rest.'

'That is so.'

'Then no such fee be owing.'

Tooley sighed, looked briefly to his side, then levelled his gaze with that of the woman, his expression being akin to that of an adult about to explain the obvious to a child.

'How can there be "no such fee owing," when by mutual agreement it was stipulated that this Twelfth Night I would receive the remaining ten shillings?'

'The agreement were that 'ee would cure my 'usband, and yet 'e do still lie abed, worse than the day that 'ee left us. As it be so, we can't see no grounds for 'ee being owed any money, for there's been no cure. By our reckoning, it be 'ee that do owe us, and not t'other way round.'

The listener's lip curled in disgust, and injecting a little venom into his words he said, 'We agreed upon the sum of twenty shillings and a bottle of brandy for me to render my services on your husband's, and family's, behalf. This, I have done, at considerable risk to myself, and to my soul, having conjured the spirit of a self-murderer with which I had to, of necessity, have truck. 'Tis a business that no man would venture to embark upon lightly, and a matter, as you yourself know, that no one else in the parish would have been willing, or able, to undertake. Will you then be so shameless as to deny me my rightful payment, upon the very date that was named by our mutual consent? Do you value your name so low, as to sell its honour for the sum of a mere ten shillings?'

John drew closer to his mother, a resolute and petulant look upon his normally bovine face. The lad was brawny, but he wanted for height when compared to Tooley's lofty stature; he was outmatched in both intellect and strength, for now.

'Well?' resumed their visitor, 'Why the silence? What do you have to say for yourself? Will you pay me, or do you still refuse to do so?'

'I've told 'ee: we'll not be paying.'

He gave a sly smile.

'If you do not, then I shall have you turned out.'

'"Turned out"? By whom, and 'pon what grounds?'

'The law, for the breaking of our contract.'

'Hah! What contract? I don't recall the signing of no contract. And besides, don't 'ee be thinking that running to the magistrate would do 'ee any good: I b'aint so stupid as to think that the law would look kindly 'pon 'ee 'aving dug about a dead man's grave in the depths of the night. Dare do it then! Go on! If 'ee should be so bold, and so stupid 'n all!'

Tooley stood silent, stung by the truth of her words, but his thoughts were quickly gathered, for he knew of another tack that might bring him the money he thought his due.

'You want for civility, Mistress Meade, and your tongue treats me ill, but I shall be indulgent. Look you here: I shall make you an offer. It is as plain to me, as to any man, that the cold has brought work to a near stop these past few weeks, with the consequence being that few have been able to earn ready coin. Doubtless, with your husband still lying ill, you have had want of money to cover those necessities of life that cannot be secured upon credit about the village. My suggestion, therefore, is that I should return for the money upon Lady Day, by which time the frost should long since have passed. What say you to this most charitable suggestion?'

'Thine ears do appear to be stopped up, Master Tooley, for surely 'ee did 'ear what I did say afore? Well, didn't 'ee?'

'Deceitful shrew! Scold! You shall regret this show of ingratitude. My skills may be put to use for ill, as well as to the good. You understand?'

She said nothing.

'I say, madam, *do you understand*?'

He almost barked at her, prompting John to take a lunge at him. With a violent shove he pushed the threatening figure back against the door, cracking his head. He slipped downwards, then regathered his wits and pulled himself to his feet, his mouth frothing with spittle, and eyes wide with rage.

'Whelp! Rancorous snapping cur! You shall have a taste of my whip, and worse!'

He had said too much. John Meade may have wanted for boldness when once before this man had raised his voice to him, but not today. He seized the advantage, lunged forward a second time, and smashed Tooley's head against the door. Grasping his hair, and snarling into his face he said, 'Call me a whelp, will ye? Well, this pup has a fiercer snap than you, ye rotten old dog!' His knee was brought up sharply into the unwanted caller's privy parts, whereupon the unwelcome visitor retched, and crumpled to the floor, a great string of bile drooling from his mouth.

'Get up! Get up! What's wrong? Can't take it, can ya? Soft as a turd! Anyone would think you 'ad need of those old bollocks of yours, the way you be carrying on. From what I've 'eard, you've never 'ad the use of 'em yet. A right old Mary Jane, that's what you be!' He laughed. 'Now – off with ye!'

With his manhood affronted and bruised, Tooley was roughly ejected to vomit, onto the road, his hat cast before him upon the compacted snow. Widow Spencer looked on from her window, her suspicions excited by what she had seen. She resolved to call upon the Meades once this unwholesome wreck of a man, that crouched and spewed before her, had passed upon his way.

It was a painful ride home, with each slip and jolt sorely felt. Speedwell felt the better for it, for her master mustered not the energy to deliver his customary kick. His mind was pricked with schemes of vengeance, none of which seemed to result in satisfaction, or bring an end to his want of money. He resolved to turf these ungrateful Meades out of their home, by one means or another.

'Is there no end to this villain's deceptions?'

The magistrate was at home: the Worshipful Sir William Bastard. His lackey had brought him a petition from two supplicants who sat without, awaiting his judgement. It was not long after luncheon, but he was already at his desk in the library, his astute brown eyes coursing through a list of complaints compiled by the people of Widecombe:

We, the people of Widecombe-in-the-Moor, do call upon the Worshipful Sir William Bastard to bring to justice one Robert Tooley of the said parish, who do falsely style himself 'doctor.' Within this past eighteen months, the said Tooley has deprived the following upstanding folk of the parish of the sums here stated for alleged services hereafter described:

Joanna Rowe: charged two shillings for a bag of moles' feet as a cure for the toothache. With the pain not abating thereafter, she did complain to Tooley, who chided her for her "ignorant stupidity, for who other than a fool would venture to chew upon them rather than wear them as a charm about their neck?"

> *Martin Lyde: paid three shillings and sixpence for the detection and recovery of a lost halter. Tooley did tell him that it was his belief that it had been stolen by an unnamed party residing in Bovey Tracey, but would neither venture to name him, nor to personally secure the halter's recovery. He did tell Lyde to "look to your own memory and suspicions, for if you do, then you shall surely find the culprit." He spoke these words whilst making the pretence of scrying in a pail of muddy water. The money had already been paid, but no amount of sore words thereafter would cause Tooley to give it back.*
>
> *Henry Meade and family: paid ten shillings and gifted a bottle of brandy to quiet the spirit of a dead man, and restore the master of the house to health. Upon their refusal to pay the balance of a further ten shillings with their not having received satisfaction upon this score, Tooley threatened to turn them out of their house.*

Here Bastard broke from his reading, his eagerness for prosecution excited to a great pitch by the allegations of injustice contained therein. He batted aside a fly with his fleshy hand, for the season of such creatures had now arrived.

'Tooley? Robert Tooley? An Irishman, I'll be damned!'

'No, sir. A Devonshire man.'

'Devonshire? Pah! Truly, there is something in the name of this rogue Tooley that is itself suggestive of an Irish provenance, and I'll warrant that he's a papist, dammit, irrespective of any of this scoundrel's protestations to the contrary, and mark my word we'll *make him pay* for this. Is there no end to this villain's deceptions, and to the stupidity of those taken in by him? Are his accusers here?'

'They are, sir.'

'Then show them in, for I wish to learn more of the writhing of this *maggot*. I shall witness him squirm yet, once I have him upon my hook.'

Having lately left off dining and being much afflicted with wind, he belched to release the worst of the excess, before adjusting his light-brown periwig and white neckerchief to gentlemanly effect, and bidding his lackey usher in two visitors of a rank but infrequently seen within his walls. They walked with an awkward waddle, clutching at the brims of their hats, that gratified the Worshipful Lord's sense of propriety; a pair of commoners come to beg favour. He would be magnanimous.

'Edward Foster of Widecombe-in-the-Moor, and John Coucher of Bow, your Worship,' said the servant by way of introduction. His honourable and right worshipful lord nodded in acknowledgement, and the two men placed their right arms across their chests and bowed their heads by way of reply.

'Good afternoon gentlemen,' said Bastard. 'Pray, stand upright and be at your ease.'

'Good afternoon, your Worship. We are most thankful for you giving us this hearing,' said Coucher.

'Being a justice of the peace, it would be negligent of me if I were not to receive you so.'

'Thank you, your Worship.'

'Now, I would wish to hear you make your case, given what I have thus far been able to ascertain of the nature of this rascal Tooley. By the lilt of your accent, which is not of this county, I take it that you must be Master John Coucher of Bow? Am I right in assuming this?'

'You are, your Worship.'

'Good! So, tell me: what is it that brings a man such as yourself all the way from London to so modest a parish as Widecombe, and thence onwards to me?'

'Family connections, your Worship. They are longstanding, although I am but infrequently to be found in Devonshire. As my calling is that of clerk, the villagers asked me to draw up this list of crimes so as to bring it to your attention.'

'I see. That somewhat clarifies matters. And you, Master Foster, pray tell what standing you have in the parish.'

'I be the sexton.'

His Worship nodded. 'Sexton, eh? Well, well! Come now then gentlemen, I would be most grateful if you were to enlighten me a little further as to the nature and character of this 'Doctor' Robert Tooley. Moreover, I would be keen to learn whether there are additional complainants beyond the three mentioned in this list.'

'There are but a handful of people in the parish who would venture to defend his good name, but in the main, I can confirm that he is viewed as being a man of ill repute. Even those who once held some regard for him have of late grown rather cool. Mention of him now arouses much bad feeling, on account of his false claims and promises. As for his title of 'doctor,' it would seem that this is but self-styled, for none know of him as having attended either Oxford or Cambridge, but a number are aware that he once followed in his family trade of coopering in Exeter. Quite when he left off from this, none are sure.'

'So, it would seem that this man's trickery and deceptions range beyond merely making a semblance of conjuration and the preparation of false charms? Venturing into the realm of professional imposture, eh? I should like to know more of his provenance. You say that he practised his family trade in Exeter?'

'That is correct, your Worship.'

'And that is the place of his family's longstanding residence?'

'Being not personally apprised of that fact, I cannot testify to this with any degree of certainty, but it is my belief, and not mine alone, that this is so.'

'Then his family are not Irish?'

'No sir. They are a Devonshire family.'

'And neither he, nor they, harbour papistical tendencies beyond him making a pretence of altering the course of God's will through his ineffectual interference with the natural order?'

'No sir, none.'

Bastard's lips pursed with disbelief at this affirmation.

'Hmm. I see, I see. And you sir, Master Foster, is your opinion at one with that of your friend Master Coucher?'

'It be, your Worship. There b'aint nothing more I can add to my good friend's words, as 'e be a man more used to speaking to folk of quality than I.'

Bastard's thin lips brought themselves into a semblance of a slight grin, before they parted and he added, 'I shall see to it that he is brought to account. And soon, gentlemen, soon, for I cannot forebear such rogues as Tooley to ply their dishonest trade in any locale for which I bear responsibility. Now, I would have you leave and await my calling upon you in Widecombe shortly. Business prevents me from setting forth with immediate effect, but I shall arrive with my men and mastiffs this Thursday. Be sure to be there to guide us to the deceiver's lair. Understood?'

'Understood, your Worship,' replied Coucher, with Foster nodding rather than verbalising his comprehension and agreement.

Upon their leaving, Bastard picked up the petition and once more read it over, this time to the end. He was seized by a fit of involuntary laughter as he acquainted himself with the full facts of the Meades' complaint. 'What manner of a fool would be so deceived as to believe that the carcase of a dead bird placed upon his head would do him any good? Such a want of common sense almost merits its exploitation by any scoundrel wily enough to take advantage of such foolery.'

'Who be the master in this house?'

News of Foster and Coucher's interview with the magistrate was eagerly awaited, and was soon told and retold over many a pint of ale and cider at the village inn, exciting the villagers to a pitch of self-righteous expectation. Joan Meade had just left her cottage to call upon neighbours when John returned to relay this to his father, who had these past few weeks at last been able to take to his feet. Although he had yet to shake off his illness, its severity had slackened.

'When be 'e coming?' he asked of his son.

'They do reckon the magistrate will be 'ere this Thursday.'

'Thursday? Tomorrow? Be 'ee sure of it?'

'Sure as can be, father. That's what they all be saying.'

'The shame of it! Shouldn't 'ave been no need for this. What kind of man might I be taken for, with I not being able to stand up to such a turd as Tooley? 'Tis shameful, that's what it be – shameful I tell 'ee!'

'Calm yourself now! You do know 'ow much mother do worry when you do get worked up so.'

'Damn it, child! Who be the master in this 'ouse? Eh? *Who* be it? Mind who 'ee be talking too, lest I give 'ee an 'iding.'

John fell silent, exasperated by the old man's stubbornness.

'I can't believe I've been so weak as to let that trickster take our money; make fools of us and threaten to turn us out of our own 'ome. I've been nothing better than a weakling. Well, little as my strength 'as returned, I'm going to 'ave it out with 'un man to man before any magistrate do come. I'll make that devil rue what 'e's done, 'ee see that I don't! If it were still light, I'd be off and at 'un tonight, but as it is, early tomorrow it must be.'

'I doubt it not, but you do know that mother'll 'ave none of it, don't you?'

'Course I do! But there b'aint no need of 'er knowing what I'm up to tomorrow, be there?'

'No father. I do s'pose not.'

'Well, 'ee better make sure it do stay that way. Understood?'

'O' course, father. I'll not breathe a word.'

Eyeing her with mock suspicion

The news had also reached Tooley, precipitating a state of agitation the like of which he had not known for many years, for he knew that a man such as Bastard would not venture abroad unless he meant serious business. With him being the prospective object of this business, he was resolved not to be at home when he arrived. He had learnt of it earlier that afternoon in Ponsworthy, whereupon he thought better of making another attempt at turfing the Meades out of their home, and returned instead to his own.

'You're back, master. I didn't expect you so soon,' said Sarah, looking and sounding guilty, even though she was guilty of nothing more than surprise at Tooley's sudden reappearance. He sensed this, and used it to his advantage, eyeing her with mock suspicion, causing her to look away. He had thought over what to say whilst in the saddle, and was of a mind that she would take him at his word.

'Early? Yes. Much earlier than I had expected.'

'I'm sorry, but I've not finished preparing for tonight's—'

'No matter girl. 'Tis of no consequence.'

'"No consequence"?' she repeated in puzzlement, shaking her head.

'I've received a communication of the utmost importance that has implications for your position here.'

'"Implications", sir? For me? Why? What is it that I've done?'

He paused to see what tricks unfounded guilt would play upon her composure, and after savouring her distress for a time, resumed.

'Nothing. You've done nothing girl; at least nothing ill.'

She looked up to him with a weak smile, her eyes smarting with tears.

'Why thank you sir. But, please excuse me for not catching your meaning of the word.'

'Which word?'

'"Implications". What is it that you mean to say?'

'I have just this afternoon received a letter from an old client in Bristol asking me to attend to him with the utmost urgency. His illness is severe, and as he has faith in my cures, he wishes me to administer my own brand of physic. I anticipate that I shall be gone above a month, possibly two, so in this time I shall have no need of your services here. Understand?'

'No need of my services?'

'No. None. Speedwell will, of course, be coming with me, and I have agreed to sell the hens to Peter Sigford in Ponsworthy. He'll collect them tomorrow.'

'So soon?'

'Yes.'

'But, what would you have me do?'

'You may have the five shillings that I owe you this evening. Pack what clothes you have, and be sure to leave for your parents' at daybreak. I shall send for you again when I return.'

She was crestfallen, and said nothing.

'You've no need to cook tonight; we shall manage with bread and cheese. You may pack now, if you wish.'

She nodded, and withdrew to gather up her clothes, uneasy as to how her parents would receive her, and how she might live. Disagreeable as life with Tooley was, whilst she served him she had at least food and shelter. Where she would find these now, she did not know, for her parents had but little love for her.

* * *

At cockcrow, Sarah heard Tooley stir in his bed. He coughed occasionally, a phlegmy tightness audible on his chest. It was often so at this hour, when the sun had yet to fully proclaim the arrival of morning. It was shortly after daybreak when she picked up her bundle and took her leave of the cottage. She did not pause to bid farewell to her master, as he had instructed her not to.

The cool night had left a heavy dew. It was now May, and low cloud scudded about the neighbouring hilltops, blown by a northerly wind. She looked about her and at the still bare hedgerows, bereft of bloom, so harsh and long had been winter's season, and felt a sense of affinity with this state of dormancy. Perhaps, life would burst forth anew for her in the warmth of the town.

It was only six miles or so to Ashburton, so she knew that she would be there well before the morning was out, but she struggled to balance upon her pattens in the mud of the lane, deep, slippery and treacherous. No amount of care could prevent her skirt from acquiring a wet brown trim as it trailed in the muck. She was her own company, for the lane was empty, and nothing disturbed her besides the cawing of the crows and the odd cackle of a magpie, which ignored her load as nothing there sparkled; it was but a drab burden that she carried. The young servant had collected her belongings, but not her thoughts, for she knew not yet what she would say when she once more met her father's gaze, and her mother's tongue.

Tooley was out of his chamber as soon as the latch of the door had dropped. He had to leave soon, but before doing so there were matters to which he had to attend. Before he roused his pony, he would make all appear that nothing departed from the norm. Thus it was that he made up the fire so that it would burn long into the day, and left his best cloak and hat hanging from the peg inside the door. Whenever the magistrate should come a-calling, it must look as if he had ventured abroad for but a short while. He had packed a small chest with money and some of the more important items of his trade, and his saddlebags were filled with clothes. Beyond that, he did not wish to be encumbered.

Despite his earlier words, he headed not for Bristol, but for Tavistock, taking care to avoid Sarah's route, as well as the prying eyes of the people of Ponsworthy. He took the Dartmeet road. The hens would have to look after themselves. Within half an hour, the cottage was still except for the fire that danced about the hearth.

Henry Meade had found a new mettle as he made his way from Widecombe to meet his tormentor. He wished to let him know that with his returning strength his state of supine servility was at an end. His mood was exultant, even if his body was still weak, but when, in time, he saw the smoke rising from the wise man's chimney, his courage wavered. It was, however, but a momentary lapse, for his spirit was soon regained. Then, as he neared the house, he was of a sudden seized with the shudders, for despite his winter clothes, his illness had left him sensible of the least draught, and he felt the sharpness of the wind with a keenness hitherto unknown. *Inside*, he reflected, *I shall 'ave warm words before a warm fire*, then strode up to the door upon which he hammered with his fist.

This uncouth knock brought no answer from within, and he cocked his head and strained to catch any stray sounds that might betray a presence. The odd spark he heard, but nothing more. He knew that Tooley kept a girl, and thus found it odd that there should be no reply. He raised his voice to a scream, and hammered all the harder: 'Open up! Open up I say! Open up, you cheating bastard! Come out and settle up, man to man! Come on! Fucking open up afore I do let myself in!'

He waited for a response. Nothing. The silence unsettled him, and he shifted his weight from foot to foot. Was it that Tooley was too afraid to face him, or that he lurked hiding inside with something heavy at hand with which to deliver a blow? A club? A stick? Perhaps nothing more than his fists. The thought of those hands – large cooper's hands – with fingers as fat and blunt as butchers' sausages, knitting themselves into fists, gave him pause. He placed his ear to the door, and listened. Still nothing, apart from the clucking of the hens behind him, pecking and scratching at the ground for worms. His muscles tensed and he breathed deep. His eyes closed, and upon their opening he barged open the door, with an added kick for good measure.

There was no one there. The logs were burning brightly in the hearth, but no pot simmered above it. There was caution in his step as he mounted the stairs, but with the sound of the first creak, he left off any attempt at stealth, and made a rush for their top. His anger and purpose had propelled him there, but upon finding the cottage empty his muscles slackened, and a limpness seeped into his limbs. He had moved little in months, the inactivity taking a toll on his body, wasting his muscles and making him want for strength. A moment of stillness, of tiredness, led him to realise that if his foe had been at home, he could not have overcome him. *Must've got wind of the magistrate's coming, and done a flit*, he thought.

He descended the stairs to warm himself by the fire. His teeth ground and his nostrils flared as he stared into the flames, rueing the months spent abed since Huccaby's death, the money that Tooley had taken, and his weakness in the face of the latter's threats and menaces. His stomach turned over with hunger. No work had meant no money other than that brought in by his son and his wife, so they had eaten poorly, and his ribs now stood proud beneath his shirt. Every day now seemed cold to him, and spying the absent man's cloak and hat upon the door, he took them for his own, both for warmth, and by way of compensation. His journey home would be slower, but before turning homewards, there was one thing that he felt he must do: revisit the moor.

He retraced his route through Ponsworthy, his head downcast, mulling over Tooley's escape, before taking the road westward up towards Dartmeet. Above the warren lay the rough pastures and the shifting flocks of sheep, the ground strewn with stones and dotted with the rocky remains of long-abandoned huts. He left the road, and stepped onto the ground that was wet and soft. Held by frost for months beneath the winter snows, the late thaw and spring rains had left the moor sodden. And yet, although yielding slightly beneath his feet, there was no bog here. With care, he picked his way from tussock to tussock, and from rock to rock, upon unsteady legs, and held out his arms so that he might better balance. He heard a ewe bleat in distress, and he answered her call. She was caught fast in the gorse.

With a spasm of fear

The Right Worshipful Sir William Bastard and his party had been apprised of the fact that Tooley had absconded. They knew this to be so, for they had it from a Ponsworthy man who had seen him 'walking in a manner most despondent' up the Dartmeet road some half an hour earlier. He had thought it 'most peculiar, that 'e were walking, for 'e do usually ride.' This news that they were close to bringing their quarry to heel found a most welcome reception upon the part of the magistrate.

'We'll have this wretch, soon enough, dammit!' exclaimed Bastard as he looked to Coucher, the latter surprised at his lordship's excitable zeal.

'Rendell! Holne!'

'Yes, sir!' cried Rendell.

'You two hasten ahead with Phobos and Deimos. You've heard his description – black cloak, tall hat – so when you get a sight of this Tooley, unmuzzle the hounds and let them slip. Understood?'

'Course, sir. But what should we do with 'un?'

'He'll doubtless cry out for mercy, worm that he is, but let him have none of it. Let the hounds have their sport with him 'til I do say otherwise.'

'Right you are sir,' he replied before turning to the dogs with a peremptory 'Get on wi' it you buggers! C'mon now!'

The dogs were barking, straining at the leash as if the scent of blood were already in their nostrils. All sensed that there would be soon enough. Great muscular beasts, their pelts a shaggy black, their teeth as sharp as their bites were firm, they were their master's pride and joy. Whether hunting for the fox, baiting a bull or a cornered man, they never failed to excite his approbatory cries. The locals looked on with a combination of fear, wide-eyed envy and admiration. The master's men too were filled with the spirit of the hunt, and they dashed up the road with an eager haste.

'Phobos, ye bastard! Hang back!' Rendell gave the dog a mighty jerk. It surged forward, undeterred.

All now was action. The time for thinking was over, for that of doing was here. The tors ahead stood as flanking sentinels about the road, but they passed no comment, content to remain mute. They would relay no word of warning to Henry Meade, weakened and innocent though he may have been. A shepherd both by trade, and by nature, he had found the distressed ewe, and was pulling her from the gorse, but in doing so lost his balance. He placed his hands before him to save his face as he fell. The pain, when it came, was great, but his sight was saved for the vision to come: the forms of two black hounds bounding up the slope, which he heard before he turned to witness their coming.

The ewe was too slow, too cumbrous, to evade paw, claw and maw, which fastened about her and brought her to ground, and to lamb. A bloody business. Too early, despite the late season, the twins were brought to a premature and sudden birth. With a spasm of fear, she evacuated her unborn, stillborn and smeared with blood and amniotic fluid, a sickly stench arising from the afterbirth. Phobos let her drop to make a meal of her discharge, whilst she staggered off, blood issuing from neck and behind.

'Lord preserve me!' yelled Henry Meade, or so he meant to, for the words lodged in his throat, transformed into nothing more than a near inaudible rasp of terror.

Deimos had come. His hulking form had halted over him. Atop the rocks of Yar Tor he stood, snarling, a great string of slaver hanging from his jaw. It was no wisht hound that Henry beheld, no supernatural demon, but a creature of flesh and blood, and all the worse for that. All had been just as in his dream, but . . .

Rendell and Holne could see that the dogs were now about their work. Their business afoot, and tired from their uphill dash, they were content to slacken their pace, for 'Tooley' could not escape them, and his lordship had not yet arrived from his tarrying in Ponsworthy, where he had been keen to learn more of the character of his quarry.

Deimos drove forward from his haunches into the unnatural element of the air, to land upon the enfrailed frame of Henry Meade, who sank, winded, to the ground. His breath was gone before the teeth wrapped about his neck.

The men were too late to stop the dog as it tore at the silent shepherd, a savage psychopomp to escort him to the new pastures of the Elysian Fields. Although the Worshipful Lord was yet to join them, their Christian charity, insofar as they possessed any spark of this sentiment, bid them take a hold of the mastiff before the victim should yield up his soul. They had come to take him, not to bury him.

'Christ shit himself! Grab a hold of 'un Holne!'

'Why don't 'ee? I'll be buggered if I do want to get near 'un!'

'Get on man! You've got 'is bloody muzzle. B'aint my business to be interfering, as I do 'ave Phobos to deal with. Do it! Grab the bugger!'

Deimos all the while made a bloody work of the man's face, and by the time that Holne took a grip of his collar to haul him off, it was nothing more than a noseless pulp, a streaking spurt of jelly from a burst eye lying beneath a matted mass of hair, resting atop a stringless puppet.

''E be dead!'

'So much the better, Holne. 'E were a bad 'un by all accounts.'

Few wept for 'Tooley' about the parish when it was announced that he had met his end, and many were eager to answer the call to help bury his corpse in an unmarked grave at a moorland crossroads. The dead would not be allowed to rise to torment the living again; they should not repeat *that* mistake.

'Who'd have thought 'e'd grown so thin?' marvelled one of his gravediggers. 'Specially after growing so fat on the money of honest folk.'

''Tis odd, Michael, very odd,' answered another, as he shovelled another spadeful of earth into the hole. 'Must've been the Devil that wasted 'un for 'is sins.'

'P'raps. Anyway, the bugger won't be walking nowhere now, will 'e?'

Michael let out a peel of sardonic laughter. 'No, 'e bloody well won't, will 'e? This old bastard's walking days be over!'

* * *

Tooley sat at his leisure in a Tavistock tavern, a tankard of ale in one hand, a pipe of tobacco in the other. He had taken a room for the night. Tomorrow, he would head north, and then east. Word would come, in time, that he had been seen in Exeter, but that couldn't be so, as everyone *knew* that his body lay beneath the dark sod of the moor.

As for Henry Meade, his presence was missed. Search parties were sent out, but no trace of the man could be found; their efforts yielded nothing. Weeks, and then months passed, and after a certain time longer had elapsed, a service of remembrance was held in his name, for all knew that he would not have left his family of his own volition. There must have been some other agency at play in his disappearance, or so ran common conjecture. Whether human, or of some other realm, there was no consensus, but most would have it that some evil had stirred to abduct him from his station in life. Some had come to hold the opinion that Huccaby's ghost had finally claimed him, whereas others still, and these were the greater in number, held the conviction that Tooley had raised the Devil to make swift Meade's mortal dispatch, before he himself had met his end on Yar Tor.

Further Publications

If you enjoyed this book, please consider leaving a review on Amazon to let other readers know what you thought, even if it should be no more than a line or two. You can keep abreast of the author's publications by clicking H.E. Bulstrode's 'follow' button on Amazon. At the time of writing, the following paperbacks were also available exclusively from Amazon.

A Ghost Story Omnibus Volume Two

A volume for readers who appreciate ghost stories with a twist, where the past looms large, and the old gods lurk in unexpected places. Within you will find nine supernatural tales, spanning the ages from the ninth century to the present day. Some are of a darkly humorous and satirical nature, and others of a rather more sinister, and disturbing, hue. The characters whom you will encounter include bumptious academics, a crass gold-digger, a wistful ex-diplomat, an ambitious Victorian surveyor, a rapacious Norman lord, a garrulous Yorkshirewoman who likes to lend an unwelcome 'helping hand', and families looking to get away from it all, and wishing that they hadn't.

Uncanny Tales

Prepare to meet four spirits: a mediaeval animalistic heretic; a personification of Death that has journeyed far from its Breton homeland; a Celtic goddess thirsting for vengeance, and a mysterious sickle-wielding hedger. Some are guardians of their place and of their values, caring not for contemporary social mores or those who cleave to them. Others wreak a vengeance upon the living to make them atone for perceived injustices, unleashing chaos in the personal lives and relationships of their chosen victims. This volume contains: *The Ghost of Scarside Beck*, *At Fall of Night*, *Epona* and *The Rude Woman of Cerne*.

Upon Barden Moor: An Occult Mystery
Tweed, feathers and blood mix with Westminster skulduggery and the disappearance of a village schoolmaster in this tale of grouse-shooting Edwardian aristocrats with a taste for occult dabbling on the Yorkshire moors. Some forty or so years later, George Haddon leaves an enigmatic note, and as the mystery unfolds the reader is transported back to the events of one stifling afternoon upon Barden Moor. This is the moment with which his fate has become inextricably intertwined. It's climax has been described as 'a shocker of occult terror and death with near cinematic strength'.

Old Crotchet's Return
A high-spirited romp of a ghost story set in 1920s England. George Simpkins is in a state, and it's not just because of the gin. His wife remains missing, his son a curious and callous enigma, and, most worryingly of all, his spouse's erstwhile schoolmate, the witheringly waspish Cynthia, has plans afoot for his future. An invitation to a festive break in the country brings London society into collision with half-cracked Somerset locals steeped in cider and superstition, as well as a far from festively inclined spirit. Welcome to the world of Hinton St Cuthbert, the parish with a past that refuses to remain at rest.

Bulstrode Online
Website & Mailing List: http://hebulstrode.com
Blog: http://www.hebulstrode.co.uk
Facebook: https://www.facebook.com/H.E.Bulstrode